For so many years I lived in constant terror of myself. Doubt had married my fear and moved into my mind, where it built castles and ruled kingdoms and reigned over me, bowing my will to its whispers until I was little more than an acquiescing peon, too terrified to disobey, too terrified to disagree.

I had been shackled, a prisoner in my own mind.

But finally, finally, I have learned to break free.

I *am* upset for our losses. I'm horrified. But I'm also anxious and restless. Sonya and Sara are still alive, living at the mercy of Anderson. They still need our help. So I don't know how to be sad when all I feel is an unrelenting determination to do something.

I am no longer afraid of fear, and I will not let it rule me.

Fear will learn to fear me.

BOOKS BY TAHEREH MAFI

Shatter Me: Series One

BOOK 1: *Shatter Me*

BOOK 2: *Unravel Me*

BOOK 3: *Ignite Me*

BOOK 4: *Restore Me*

BOOK 5: *Defy Me*

BOOK 6: *Imagine Me*

Shatter Me: Series One Novellas

BOOK 1.5: *Destroy Me*

BOOK 2.5: *Fracture Me*

BOOK 4.5: *Shadow Me*

BOOK 5.5: *Reveal Me*

BOOK 6.5: *Believe Me*

Shatter Me: Series One Novella Collections

Unite Me

Find Me

Shatter Me: Series Two

BOOK 1: *Watch Me*

BOOK 2: *Release Me*

The Woven Kingdom Series

BOOK 1: *This Woven Kingdom*

BOOK 2: *These Infinite Threads*

BOOK 3: *All This Twisted Glory*

BOOK 4: *Every Spiral of Fate*

An Emotion of Great Delight

A Very Large Expanse of Sea

IGNITE ME

SHATTER ME: SERIES ONE
BOOK THREE

TAHEREH MAFI

STORYTIDE
An Imprint of HarperCollins*Publishers*

Dear Reader:

The strikethroughs in the Shatter Me books are intentional. The writing in this series is occasionally as erratic as its main character, and serves as a visual representation of the chaos in Juliette's mind. The repetition, the hyperbolic language, the obsession with numbers—these are not errors on the page. As our heroine grows and evolves, so too does the prose, and as she finds her voice, the strikethroughs disappear, the language softens, the repetition dissolves, and the numerals ease into written words. This is, ultimately, a story of change. Thank you so much for reading.

For my readers. For your love and support. This one's for you.

HarperCollins Children's Books, a division of HarperCollins Publishers, 195 Broadway, New York, NY 10007 | HarperCollins Publishers, Macken House, 39/40 Mayor Street Upper, Dublin 1, D01 C9W8, Ireland

Storytide is an imprint of HarperCollins Publishers.

Ignite Me

harpercollins.com

Library of Congress Control Number: 2013951749
ISBN 978-0-06-349767-2

Typography by Ray Shappell
26 27 28 29 30 RTLO 10 9 8 7 6 5 4 3 2 1

SPECIAL EDITION, 2026

ONE

I am an hourglass.

My seventeen years have collapsed and buried me from the inside out. My legs feel full of sand and stapled together, my mind overflowing with grains of indecision, choices unmade and impatient as time runs out of my body. The small hand of a clock taps me at one and two, three and four, whispering hello, get up, stand up, it's time to

wake up

wake up

"Wake up," he whispers.

A sharp intake of breath and I'm awake but not up, surprised but not scared, somehow staring into the very desperately green eyes that seem to know too much, too well. Aaron Warner Anderson is bent over me, his worried eyes inspecting me, his hand caught in the air like he might've been about to touch me.

He jerks back.

He stares, unblinking, chest rising and falling.

"Good morning," I assume. I'm unsure of my voice, of the hour and this day, of these words leaving my lips and this body that contains me.

I notice he's wearing a white button-down, half untucked

into his curiously unrumpled black slacks. His shirtsleeves are folded, pushed up past his elbows.

His smile looks like it hurts.

I pull myself into a seated position and Warner shifts to accommodate me. I have to close my eyes to steady the sudden dizziness, but I force myself to remain still until the feeling passes.

I'm tired and weak from hunger, but other than a few general aches, I seem to be fine. I'm alive. I'm breathing and blinking and feeling human and I know exactly why.

I meet his eyes. "You saved my life."

I was shot in the chest.

Warner's father put a bullet in my body and I can still feel the echoes of it. If I focus, I can relive the exact moment it happened; the pain: so intense, so excruciating; I'll never be able to forget it.

I suck in a startled breath.

I'm finally aware of the familiar foreignness of this room and I'm quickly seized by a panic that screams I did not wake up where I fell asleep. My heart is racing and I'm inching away from him, hitting my back against the headboard, clutching at these sheets, trying not to stare at the chandelier I remember all too well—

"It's okay—" Warner is saying. "It's all right—"

"What am I doing here?" Panic, panic; terror clouds my consciousness. "Why did you bring me here again—?"

"Juliette, please, I'm not going to hurt you—"

"Then why did you bring me here?" My voice is starting

to break and I'm struggling to keep it steady. "Why bring me back to this *hellhole*—"

"I had to hide you." He exhales, looks up at the wall.

"What? Why?"

"No one knows you're alive." He turns to look at me. "I had to get back to base. I needed to pretend everything was back to normal and I was running out of time."

I force myself to lock away the fear.

I study his face and analyze his patient, earnest tone. I remember him last night—it must've been last night—I remember his face, remember him lying next to me in the dark. He was tender and kind and gentle and he saved me, saved my life. Probably carried me into bed. Tucked me in beside him. It must've been him.

But when I glance down at my body I realize I'm wearing clean clothes, no blood or holes or anything anywhere and I wonder who washed me, wonder who changed me, and worry that might've been Warner, too.

"Did you . . ." I hesitate, touching the hem of the shirt I'm wearing. "Did—I mean—my clothes—"

He smiles. He stares until I'm blushing and I decide I hate him a little and then he shakes his head. Looks into his palms. "No," he says. "The girls took care of that. I just carried you to bed."

"The girls," I whisper, dazed.

The girls.

Sonya and Sara. They were there too, the healer twins, they helped Warner. They helped him save me because he's the only one who can touch me now, the only person in the world who'd have been able to transfer their healing power safely into my body.

My thoughts are on fire.

Where are the girls what happened to the girls and where is Anderson and the war and oh God what's happened to Adam and Kenji and Castle and I have to get up I have to get up I have to get up and get out of bed and get going

but

I try to move and Warner catches me. I'm off-balance, unsteady; I still feel as though my legs are anchored to this bed and I'm suddenly unable to breathe, seeing spots and feeling faint. Need up. Need out.

Can't.

"Warner." My eyes are frantic on his face. "What happened? What's happening with the battle—?"

"Please," he says, gripping my shoulders. "You need to start slowly; you should eat something—"

"Tell me—"

"Don't you want to eat first? Or shower?"

"No," I hear myself say. "I have to know now."

One moment. Two and three.

Warner takes a deep breath. A million more. Right hand over left, spinning the jade ring on his pinkie finger over and over and over and over "It's over," he says.

"What?"

I say the word but my lips make no sound. I'm numb, somehow. Blinking and seeing nothing.

"It's over," he says again.

"No."

I exhale the word, exhale the impossibility.

He nods. He's disagreeing with me.

"No."

"Juliette."

"No," I say. "No. No. Don't be stupid," I say to him. "Don't be ridiculous," I say to him. *"Don't lie to me goddamn you,"* but now my voice is high and broken and shaking and "No," I gasp, "no, no, *no—*"

I actually stand up this time. My eyes are filling fast with tears and I blink and blink but the world is a mess and I want to laugh because all I can think is how horrible and beautiful it is, that our eyes blur the truth when we can't bear to see it.

The ground is hard.

I know this to be an actual fact because it's suddenly pressed against my face and Warner is trying to touch me but I think I scream and slap his hands away because I already know the answer. I must already know the answer because I can feel the revulsion bubbling up and unsettling my insides but I ask anyway. I'm horizontal and somehow still tipping over and the holes in my head are tearing open and I'm staring at a spot on the carpet not ten feet away and I'm not sure I'm even alive but I have to hear him say it.

"Why?" I ask.

It's just a word, stupid and simple.

"Why is the battle over?" I ask. I'm not breathing

anymore, not really speaking at all; just expelling letters through my lips.

Warner is not looking at me.

He's looking at the wall and at the floor and at the bedsheets and at the way his knuckles look when he clenches his fists but no not at me he won't look at me and his next words are so, so soft.

"Because they're dead, love. They're all dead."

TWO

My body locks.

My bones, my blood, my brain freeze in place, seizing in some kind of sudden, uncontrollable paralysis that spreads through me so quickly I can't seem to breathe. I'm wheezing in deep, strained inhalations, and the walls won't stop swaying in front of me.

Warner pulls me into his arms.

"Let go of me," I scream, but, oh, only in my imagination because my lips are finished working and my heart has just expired and my mind has gone to hell for the day and my eyes my eyes I think they're bleeding. Warner is whispering words of comfort I can't hear and his arms are wrapped entirely around me, trying to keep me together through sheer physical force but it's no use.

I feel nothing.

Warner is shushing me, rocking me back and forth, and it's only then that I realize I'm making the most excruciating, earsplitting sound, agony ripping through me. I want to speak, to protest, to accuse Warner, to blame him, to call him a liar, but I can say nothing, can form nothing but sounds so pitiful I'm almost ashamed of myself. I break free of his arms, gasping and doubling over, clutching my stomach.

"Adam." I choke on his name.

"Juliette, please—"

"Kenji." I'm hyperventilating into the carpet now.

"Please, love, let me help you—"

"What about James?" I hear myself say. "He was left at Omega Point—he wasn't a-allowed to c-come—"

"It's all been destroyed," Warner says slowly, quietly. "Everything. They tortured some of your members into giving away the exact location of Omega Point. Then they bombed the entire thing."

"Oh, *God*." I cover my mouth with one hand and stare, unblinking, at the ceiling.

"I'm so sorry," he says. "You have no idea how sorry I am."

"Liar," I whisper, venom in my voice. I'm angry and mean and I can't be bothered to care. "You're not sorry at all."

I glance at Warner just long enough to see the hurt flash in and out of his eyes. He clears his throat.

"I am sorry," he says again, quiet but firm. He picks up his jacket from where it was hanging on a nearby rack; shrugs it on without a word.

"Where are you going?" I ask, guilty in an instant.

"You need time to process this and you clearly have no use for my company. I will attend to a few tasks until you're ready to talk."

"Please tell me you're wrong." My voice breaks. My breath catches. "Tell me there's a chance you could be wrong—"

Warner stares at me for what feels like a long time. "If

there were even the slightest chance I could spare you this pain," he finally says, "I would've taken it. You must know I wouldn't have said it if it weren't absolutely true."

And it's *this*—his sincerity—that finally snaps me in half.

Because the truth is so unbearable I wish he'd spare me a lie.

I don't remember when Warner left.

I don't remember how he left or what he said. All I know is that I've been lying here curled up on the floor long enough. Long enough for the tears to turn to salt, long enough for my throat to dry up and my lips to chap and my head to pound as hard as my heart.

I sit up slowly, feel my brain twist somewhere in my skull. I manage to climb onto the bed and sit there, still numb but less so, and pull my knees to my chest.

Life without Adam.

Life without Kenji, without James and Castle and Sonya and Sara and Brendan and Winston and all of Omega Point. My friends, all destroyed with the flick of a switch.

Life without Adam.

I hold on tight, pray the pain will pass.

It doesn't.

Adam is gone.

My first love. My first friend. My only friend when I had none and now he's gone and I don't know how I feel. Strange, mostly. Delirious, too. I feel empty and broken and cheated and guilty and angry and desperately, desperately sad.

We'd been growing apart since escaping to Omega Point, but that was my fault. He wanted more from me, but I wanted him to live a long life. I wanted to protect him from the pain I would cause him. I tried to forget him, to move on without him, to prepare myself for a future separate and apart from him.

I thought staying away would keep him alive.

Stupid girl.

The tears are fresh and falling fast now, traveling quietly down my cheeks and into my open, gasping mouth. My shoulders won't stop shaking and my fists keep clenching and my body is cramping and my knees are knocking and old habits are crawling out of my skin and I'm counting cracks and colors and sounds and shudders and rocking back and forth and back and forth and back and forth and I have to let him go I have to let him go I have to I have to

I close my eyes

and *breathe*.

Harsh, hard, rasping breaths.

In.

Out.

Count them.

I've been here before, I tell myself. I've been lonelier than this, more hopeless than this, more desperate than this. I've been here before and I survived. I can get through this.

But never have I been so thoroughly robbed. Love and possibility, friendships and futures: gone. I have to start over now; face the world alone again. I have to make one final choice: give up or go on.

So I get to my feet.

My head is spinning, thoughts knocking into one another, but I swallow back the tears. I clench my fists and try not to scream and I tuck my friends in my heart and

revenge

I think

has never looked so sweet.

THREE

Hang tight

Hold on

Look up

Stay strong

Hang on

Hold tight

Look strong

Stay up

One day I might break

One day I might

b r e a k

free

Warner can't hide his surprise when he walks back into the room.

I look up, close the notebook in my hands. "I'm taking this back," I say to him.

He blinks at me. "You're feeling better."

I nod over my shoulder. "My notebook was just sitting here, on the bedside table."

"Yes," he says slowly. Carefully.

"I'm taking it back."

"I understand." He's still standing by the door, still frozen in place, still staring. "Are you"—he shakes his head—"I'm sorry, are you going somewhere?"

It's only then that I realize I'm already halfway to the door. "I need to get out of here."

Warner says nothing. He takes a few careful steps into the room, slips off his jacket, drapes it over a chair. He pulls three guns out of the holster strapped to his back and takes his time placing them on the table where my notebook used to be. When he finally looks up he has a slight smile on his face.

Hands in his pockets. His smile a little bigger. "Where are you going, love?"

"I have some things I need to take care of."

"Is that right?" He leans one shoulder against the wall, crosses his arms against his chest. He can't stop smiling.

"Yes." I'm getting irritated now.

Warner waits. Stares. Nods once, as if to say, *Go on.*

"Your father—"

"Is not here."

"Oh."

I try to hide my shock, but now I don't know why I was so certain Anderson would still be here. This complicates things.

"You really thought you could just walk out of this room," Warner says to me, "knock on my father's door, and do away with him?"

Yes. "No."

"Liar, liar, pants on fire," Warner says softly.

I glare at him.

"My father is gone," Warner says. "He's gone back to the capital, and he's taken Sonya and Sara with him."

I gasp, horrified. "No."

Warner isn't smiling anymore.

"Are they . . . alive?" I ask.

"I don't know." A simple shrug. "I imagine they must be, as they're of no use to my father in any other condition."

"They're *alive*?" My heart picks up so quickly I might be having a heart attack. "I have to get them back—I have to find them, I—"

"You what?" Warner is looking at me closely. "How will you get to my father? How will you fight him?"

"I don't know!" I'm pacing across the room now. "But I have to find them. They might be my only friends left in this world and—"

I stop.

I spin around suddenly, heart in my throat.

"What if there are others?" I whisper, too afraid to hope.

I meet Warner across the room.

"What if there are other survivors?" I ask, louder now. "What if they're hiding somewhere?"

"That seems unlikely."

"But there's a chance, isn't there?" I'm desperate. "If there's even the slightest chance—"

Warner sighs. Runs a hand through the hair at the back of his head. "If you'd seen the devastation the way that I did, you wouldn't be saying such things. Hope will break your heart all over again."

My knees have begun to buckle.

I cling to the bed frame, breathing fast, hands shaking. I don't know anything anymore. I don't actually know what's happened to Omega Point. I don't know where the capital is or how I'd get there. I don't know if I'd even be able to get to Sonya and Sara in time. But I can't shake this sudden, stupid hope that more of my friends have somehow survived.

Because they're stronger than this—smarter.

"They've been planning for war for such a long time," I hear myself say. "They must have had some kind of a backup plan. A place to hide—"

"Juliette—"

"Dammit, Warner! I have to try. You have to let me look."

"This is unhealthy." He won't meet my eyes. "It's dangerous for you to think there's a chance anyone might still be alive."

I stare at his strong, steady profile.

He studies his hands.

"Please," I whisper.

He sighs.

"I have to head to the compounds in the next day or so, just to better oversee the process of rebuilding the area." He tenses as he speaks. "We lost many civilians," he says. "Too many. The remaining citizens are understandably traumatized and subdued, as was my father's intention. They've been stripped of any last hope they might've had for rebellion."

A tight breath.

"And now everything must be quickly put back in order," he says. "The bodies are being cleared out and incinerated. The damaged housing units are being replaced. Civilians are being forced to go back to work, orphans are being moved, and the remaining children are required to attend their sector schools.

"The Reestablishment," he says, "does not allow time for people to grieve."

There's a heavy silence between us.

"While I'm overseeing the compounds," Warner says, "I can find a way to take you back to Omega Point. I can show you what's happened. And then, once you have proof, you will have to make your choice."

"What choice?"

"You have to decide your next move. You can stay with me," he says, hesitating, "or, if you prefer, I can arrange for you to live undetected, somewhere on unregulated grounds. But it will be a solitary existence," he says quietly. "You can never be discovered."

"Oh."

A pause.

"Yes," he says.

Another pause.

"*Or,*" I say to him, "I leave, find your father, kill him, and deal with the consequences on my own."

Warner fights a smile and fails.

He glances down and laughs just a little before looking me right in the eye. He shakes his head.

"What's so funny?"

"My dear girl."

"What?"

"I have been waiting for this moment for a long time now."

"What do you mean?"

"You're finally ready," he says. "You're finally ready to fight."

Shock courses through me. "Of course I am."

In an instant I'm bombarded by memories of the battlefield, the terror of being shot to death. I have not forgotten my friends or my renewed conviction, my determination to do things differently. To make a difference. To really fight this time, with no hesitation. No matter what happens—and no matter what I discover—there's no turning back for me anymore. There are no other alternatives.

I have not forgotten. "I forge forward or die."

Warner laughs out loud. He looks like he might cry.

"I *am* going to kill your father," I say to him, "and I'm going to destroy The Reestablishment."

He's still smiling.

"I *will*."

"I know," he says.

"Then why are you laughing at me?"

"I'm not," he says softly. "I'm only wondering," he says, "if you would like my help."

FOUR

"What?" I blink fast, disbelieving.

"I've always told you," Warner says to me, "that we would make an excellent team. I've always said that I've been waiting for you to be ready—for you to recognize your anger, your own strength. I've been waiting since the day I met you."

"But you wanted to use me for The Reestablishment—you wanted me to torture innocent people—"

"Not true."

"What? What are you talking about? You told me *yourself*—"

"I lied." He shrugs.

My mouth has fallen open.

"There are three things you should know about me, love." He steps forward. "The first," he says, "is that I hate my father more than you might ever be capable of understanding." He clears his throat. "Second, is that I am an unapologetically selfish person, who, in almost every situation, makes decisions based entirely on self-interest. And third." A pause as he looks down. Laughs a little. "I never had any intention of using you as a weapon."

Words have failed me.

I sit down.

Numb.

"That was an elaborate scheme I designed entirely for my father's benefit," Warner says. "I had to convince him it would be a good idea to invest in someone like you, that we might utilize you for military gain. And to be quite, quite honest, I'm still not sure how I managed it. The idea is ludicrous. To spend all that time, money, and energy on reforming a supposedly psychotic girl just for the sake of torture?" He shakes his head. "I knew from the beginning it would be a fruitless endeavor; a complete waste of time. There are far more effective methods of extracting information from the unwilling."

"Then why—why did you want me?"

His eyes are jarring in their sincerity. "I wanted to study you."

"What?" I gasp.

He turns his back to me. "Did you know," he says, so quietly I have to strain to hear him, "that my mother lives in that house?" He looks to the closed door. "The one my father brought you to? The one where he shot you? She was in her room. Just down the hall from where he was keeping you."

When I don't respond, Warner turns to face me.

"Yes," I whisper. "Your father mentioned something about her."

"Oh?" Alarm flits in and out of his features. He quickly masks the emotion. "And what," he says, making an effort to sound calm, "did he say about her?"

"That she's sick," I tell him, hating myself for the tremor

that goes through his body. "That he stores her there because she doesn't do well in the compounds."

Warner leans back against the wall, looking as if he requires the support. He takes a hard breath. "Yes," he finally says. "It's true. She's sick. She became ill very suddenly." His eyes are focused on a distant point in another world. "When I was a child, she seemed perfectly fine," he says, turning and turning the jade ring around his finger. "But then one day she just . . . fell apart. For years I fought my father to seek treatment, to find a cure, but he never cared. I was on my own to find help for her, and no matter who I contacted, no doctor was able to treat her. No one," he says, hardly breathing now, "knew what was wrong with her. She exists in a constant state of agony," he says, "and I've always been too selfish to let her die."

He looks up.

"And then I heard about you. I'd heard stories about you, rumors," he says. "And it gave me hope for the very first time. I wanted access to you; I wanted to study you. I wanted to know and understand you firsthand. Because in all my research, you were the only person I'd ever heard of who might be able to offer me answers about my mother's condition. I was desperate," he says. "I was willing to try anything."

"What do you mean?" I ask. "How could someone like me be able to help you with your mother?"

His eyes find mine again, bright with anguish. "Because, love. You cannot touch anyone. And she," he says, "she cannot be touched."

FIVE

I've lost the ability to speak.

"I finally understand her pain," Warner says. "I finally understand what it must be like for her. Because of you. Because I saw what it did to you—what it does to you—to carry that kind of burden, to exist with that much power and to live among those who do not understand."

He tilts his head back against the wall, presses the heels of his hands to his eyes.

"She, much like you," he says, "must feel as though there is a monster inside of her. But unlike you, her only victim is herself. She cannot live in her own skin. She cannot be touched by anyone; not even by her own hands. Not to brush a hair from her forehead or to clench her fists. She's afraid to speak, to move her legs, to stretch her arms, even to shift to a more comfortable position, simply because the sensation of her skin brushing against itself causes her an excruciating amount of pain."

He drops his hands.

"It seems," he says, fighting to keep his voice steady, "that something in the heat of human contact triggers this terrible, destructive power within her, and because she is both the originator and the recipient of the pain, she's somehow incapable of killing herself. Instead, she exists as a prisoner in her own bones, unable to escape this self-inflicted torture."

My eyes are stinging hard. I blink fast.

For so many years I thought my life was difficult; I thought I understood what it meant to suffer. But this. This is something I can't even begin to comprehend. I never stopped to consider that someone else might have it worse than I do.

It makes me feel ashamed for ever having felt sorry for myself.

"For a long time," Warner continues, "I thought she was just . . . sick. I thought she'd developed some kind of illness that was attacking her immune system, something that made her skin sensitive and painful. I assumed that, with the proper treatment, she would eventually heal. I kept hoping," he says, "until I finally realized that years had gone by and nothing had changed. The constant agony began to destroy her mental stability; she eventually gave up on life. She let the pain take over. She refused to get out of bed or to eat regularly; she stopped caring about basic hygiene. And my father's solution was to drug her.

"He keeps her locked in that house with no one but a nurse to keep her company. She's now addicted to morphine and has completely lost her mind. She doesn't even know me anymore. Doesn't recognize me. And the few times I've ever tried to get her off the drugs," he says, speaking quietly now, "she's tried to kill me." He's silent for a second, looking as if he's forgotten I'm still in the room. "My childhood was almost bearable sometimes," he says, "if only because of her. And instead of caring for her, my father turned her into something unrecognizable."

He looks up, laughing.

"I always thought I could fix it," he says. "I thought if I could only find the root of it—I thought I could do something, I thought I could—" He stops. Drags a hand across his face. "I don't know," he whispers. Turns away. "But I never had any intention of using you against your will. The idea has never appealed to me. I only had to maintain the pretense. My father, you see, does not approve of my interest in my mother's well-being."

He smiles a strange, twisted sort of smile. Looks toward the door. Laughs.

"He never wanted to help her. She is a burden he is disgusted by. He thinks that by keeping her alive he's doing her a great kindness for which I should be grateful. He thinks this should be enough for me, to be able to watch my mother turn into a feral creature so utterly consumed by her own agony she's completely vacated her mind." He runs a shaky hand through his hair, grips the back of his neck.

"But it wasn't," he says quietly. "It wasn't enough. I became obsessed with trying to help her. To bring her back to life. And I wanted to feel it," he says to me, looking directly into my eyes. "I wanted to know what it would be like to endure a pain like that. I wanted to know what she must experience every day.

"I was never afraid of your touch," he says. "In fact, I

welcomed it. I was so sure you would eventually strike out at me, that you would try to defend yourself against me; and I was looking forward to that moment. But you never did." He shakes his head. "Everything I'd read in your files told me you were an unrestrained, vicious creature. I was expecting you to be an animal, someone who would try to kill me and my men at every opportunity—someone who needed to be closely watched. But you disappointed me by being too human, too lovely. So unbearably naive. You wouldn't fight back."

His eyes are unfocused, remembering.

"You didn't react against my threats. You wouldn't respond to the things that mattered. You acted like an insolent child," he says. "You didn't like your clothes. You wouldn't eat your fancy food." He laughs out loud and rolls his eyes and I've suddenly forgotten my sympathy.

I'm tempted to throw something at him.

"You were so hurt," he says, "that I'd asked you to wear a *dress*." He looks at me then, eyes sparkling with amusement. "Here I was, prepared to defend my life against an uncontrollable monster who could kill," he says, "kill a man with her *bare hands*—" He bites back another laugh. "And you threw tantrums over clean clothes and hot meals. Oh," he says, shaking his head at the ceiling, "you were ridiculous. You were completely ridiculous and it was the most entertainment I'd ever had. I can't tell you how much I enjoyed it. I loved making you mad," he says to me, his eyes wicked. "I *love* making you mad."

I'm gripping one of his pillows so tightly I'm afraid I might tear it. I glare at him.

He laughs at me.

"I was so distracted," he says, smiling. "Always wanting to spend time with you. Pretending to plan things for your supposed future with The Reestablishment. You were harmless and beautiful and you always *yelled* at me," he says, grinning widely now. "God, you would yell at me over the most inconsequential things," he says, remembering. "But you never laid a hand on me. Not once, not even to save your own life."

His smile fades.

"It worried me. It scared me to think you were so ready to sacrifice yourself before using your abilities to defend yourself." A breath. "So I changed tactics. I tried to bully you into touching me."

I flinch, remembering that day in the blue room too well. When he taunted me and manipulated me and I came so close to hurting him. He'd finally managed to find exactly the right things to say to hurt me enough to want to hurt him back.

I nearly did.

He cocks his head. Exhales a deep, defeated breath. "But that didn't work either. And I quickly began to lose sight of my original purpose. I became so invested in you that I'd forgotten why I'd brought you on base to begin with. I was frustrated that you wouldn't give in, that you refused to lash out even when I knew you wanted to. But every time I was ready to give up, you would have these moments," he says, shaking his head. "You had these incredible moments when you'd finally show glimpses of raw, unbridled strength. It was incredible." He stops. Leans back against the wall. "But then you'd always retreat. Like you were ashamed. Like you didn't want to recognize those feelings in yourself.

"So I changed tactics again. I tried something else. Something that I knew—with certainty—would push you past your breaking point. And I must say, it really was everything I hoped it would be." He smiles. "You looked truly alive for the very first time."

My hands are suddenly ice cold.

"The torture room," I gasp.

SIX

"I suppose you could call it that." Warner shrugs. "We call it a simulation chamber."

"You made me torture that child," I say to him, the anger and the rage of that day rising up inside of me. How could I forget what he did? What he made me do? The horrible memories he forced me to relive all for the sake of his entertainment. "I will never forgive you for that," I snap, acid in my voice. "I will never forgive you for what you did to that little boy. For what you made me do to him!"

Warner frowns. "I'm sorry—what?"

"You would sacrifice a *child*!" My voice is shaking now. "For your stupid games! How could you do something so despicable?" I throw my pillow at him. "You sick, heartless, *monster*!"

Warner catches the pillow as it hits his chest, staring at me like he's never seen me before. But then a kind of understanding settles into place for him, and the pillow slips from his hands. Falls to the floor. "Oh," he says, so slowly. He's squeezing his eyes shut, trying to suppress his amusement. "Oh, you're going to kill me," he says, laughing openly now. "I don't think I can handle this—"

"What are you talking about? What's wrong with you?" I demand.

He's still smiling as he says, "Tell me, love. Tell me exactly what happened that day."

I clench my fists, offended by his flippancy and shaking with renewed anger. "You gave me stupid, skimpy clothes to wear! And then you took me down to the lower levels of Sector 45 and locked me in a dirty room. I remember it perfectly," I tell him, fighting to remain calm. "It had disgusting yellow walls. Old green carpet. A huge two-way mirror."

Warner raises his eyebrows. Gestures for me to continue.

"Then . . . you hit some kind of a switch," I say, forcing myself to keep talking. I don't know why I'm beginning to doubt myself. "And these huge, metal spikes started coming out of the ground. And then"—I hesitate, steeling myself—"a toddler walked in. He was blindfolded. And you said he was your replacement. You said that if I didn't save him, you wouldn't either."

Warner is looking at me closely now. Studying my eyes. "Are you sure I said that?"

"Yes."

"Yes?" He cocks his head. "Yes, you saw me say that with your own eyes?"

"N-no," I say quickly, feeling defensive, "but there were loudspeakers—I could hear your voice—"

He takes a deep breath. "Right; of course."

"I *did*," I tell him.

"So after you heard me say that, what happened?"

I swallow hard. "I had to save the boy. He was going to die. He couldn't see where he was going and he was going to be impaled by those spikes. I had to pull him into my arms and try to find a way to hold on to him without killing him."

A beat of silence.

"And did you succeed?" Warner asks me.

"Yes," I whisper, unable to understand why he's asking me this when he saw it all happen for himself. "But the boy went limp," I say. "He was temporarily paralyzed in my arms. And then you hit another switch and the spikes disappeared, and I let him down and he—he started crying again and bumped into my bare legs. And he started screaming. And I . . . I got so mad at you . . ."

"That you broke through concrete," Warner says, a faint smile touching his lips. "You broke through a concrete wall just to try and choke me to death."

"You deserved it," I hear myself say. "You deserved worse."

"Well," he sighs. "If I did, in fact, do what you say I did, it certainly sounds like I deserved it."

"What do you mean, *if* you did? I *know* you did—"

"Is that right?"

"Of course it's right!"

"Then tell me, love, what happened to the boy?"

"What?" I freeze; icicles creep up my arms.

"What happened," he says, "to that little boy? You say that you set him on the ground. But then you proceeded to break through a concrete wall fitted with a thick, six-foot-wide mirror, with no apparent regard for the toddler you claim was wandering around the room. Don't you think the poor child would've been injured in such a wild, reckless display? My soldiers certainly were. You broke down a wall of *concrete,* love. You crushed an enormous piece of glass. You did not stop to ascertain where the blocks or the shattered bits had fallen or who they might've injured in the process." He stops. Stares. "Did you?"

"No," I gasp, blood draining from my body.

"So what happened after you walked away?" he asks. "Or do you not remember that part? You turned around and left, just after destroying the room, injuring my men, and tossing me to the floor. You turned around," he says, "and walked right out."

I'm numb now, remembering. It's true. I did. I didn't think. I just knew I needed to get out of there as fast as possible. I needed to get away, to clear my head.

"So what happened to the boy?" Warner insists. "Where was he when you were leaving? Did you see him?" A lift of his eyebrows. "And what about the spikes?" he says. "Did you bother to look closely at the ground to see where they might've come from? Or how they might've punctured a carpeted floor without causing any damage? Did you feel the surface under your feet to be shredded or uneven?"

I'm breathing hard now, struggling to stay calm. I can't tear myself away from his gaze.

"Juliette, love," he says softly. "There were no speakers in that room. That room is entirely soundproof, equipped with nothing but sensors and cameras. It is a simulation chamber."

"No," I breathe, refusing to believe. Not wanting to accept that I was wrong, that Warner isn't the monster I thought he was. He can't change things now. Can't confuse me like this. This isn't the way it's supposed to work. "That's not possible—"

"I am guilty," he says, "of forcing you to undergo such a cruel simulation. I accept the fault for that, and I've already apologized for my actions. I only meant to push you into finally reacting, and I knew that sort of re-creation would quickly trigger something inside of you. But good God, love"—he shakes his head—"you must have an absurdly low opinion of me if you think I would steal someone's child just to watch you torture it."

"It wasn't real?" I don't recognize my own raspy, panicked voice. "It wasn't *real*?"

He offers me a sympathetic smile. "I designed the basic elements of the simulation, but the beauty of the program is that it will evolve and adapt as it processes a soldier's most visceral responses. We use it to train soldiers who must overcome specific fears or prepare for a particularly sensitive mission. We can re-create almost any environment," he says. "Even soldiers who know what they're getting into will forget that they're performing in a simulation." He averts his eyes. "I knew it would be terrifying for you, and I did it anyway. And for hurting you, I feel true regret. But no," he says quietly, meeting my eyes again. "None of it was real. You imagined my voice in that room. You imagined the pain, the sounds, the smells. All of it was in your mind."

"I don't want to believe you," I say to him, my voice scarcely a whisper.

He tries to smile. "Why do you think I gave you those clothes?" he asks. "The material of that outfit was lined with a chemical designed to react to the sensors in that room. And the less you're wearing, the more easily the cameras can track the heat in your body, your movements." He shakes his head. "I never had a chance to explain what you'd experienced. I wanted to follow you immediately, but I thought I should give you time to collect yourself. It was a stupid decision, on my end." His jaw tenses. "I waited, and I shouldn't have. Because when I found you, it was too late. You were ready to jump out a window just to get away from me."

"For good reason," I snap.

He holds up his hands in surrender.

"You are a *terrible* person!" I explode, throwing the rest of the pillows at his face, angry and horrified and humiliated all at once. "Why would you put me through something like that when you *know* what I've been through, you stupid, arrogant—"

"Juliette, please," he says, stepping forward, dodging a pillow to reach for my arms. "I *am* sorry for hurting you, but I really think it was worth—"

"Don't touch me!" I jerk away, glaring, clutching the foot of his bed like it might be a weapon. "I should shoot you all over again for doing that to me! I should—I should—"

"What?" He laughs. "You're going to throw another pillow at me?"

I shove him, hard, and when he doesn't budge, I start throwing punches. I'm hitting his chest, his arms, his stomach, and his legs, anywhere I can reach, wishing more than ever that he weren't able to absorb my power, that I could actually crush all the bones in his body and make him writhe in pain beneath my hands. "You . . . selfish . . . *monster*!" I keep throwing poorly aimed fists in his direction, not realizing how much the effort exhausts me, not realizing how quickly the anger dissolves into pain. Suddenly all I want to do is cry. My body is shaking in both relief and terror, finally unshackled from the fear that I'd caused another innocent child some kind of irreparable damage, and simultaneously horrified that Warner would ever force such a terrible thing on me. To *help* me.

"I'm so sorry," he says, stepping closer. "I really, truly am. I didn't know you then. Not like I do now. I'd never do that to you now."

"You don't know me," I mumble, wiping away tears. "You think you know me just because you've read my journal—you stupid, prying, privacy-stealing *asshole*—"

"Oh, right—about that—" He smiles, one quick hand plucking the journal out of my pocket as he moves toward the door. "I'm afraid I wasn't finished reading this."

"Hey!" I protest, swiping at him as he walks away. "You said you'd give that back to me!"

"I said no such thing," he says, subdued, dropping the journal into his own pants pocket. "Now please wait here a moment. I'm going to get you something to eat."

I'm still shouting as he closes the door behind him.

SEVEN

I fall backward onto the bed and make an angry noise deep inside my throat. Chuck a pillow at the wall.

I need to do something. I need to start moving.

I need to finish forming a plan.

I've been on the defense and on the run for so long now that my mind has often been occupied by elaborate and hopeless daydreams about overthrowing The Reestablishment. I spent most of my 264 days in that cell fantasizing about exactly this kind of impossible moment: the day I'd be able to spit in the face of those who'd oppressed me and everyone else just beyond my window. And though I dreamed up a million different scenarios in which I would stand up and defend myself, I never actually thought I'd have a chance to make it happen. I never thought I'd have the power, the opportunity, or the courage.

But now?

Everyone is gone.

I might be the only one left.

At Omega Point I was happy to let Castle lead. I didn't know much about anything, and I was still too scared to act. Castle was already in charge and already had a plan, so I trusted that he knew best; that they knew better.

A mistake.

I've always known, deep down, who should be leading this resistance. I've felt it quietly for some time now, always too scared to bring the words to my lips. Someone who's got nothing left to lose and everything to gain. Someone no longer afraid of anyone.

Not Castle. Not Kenji. Not Adam. Not even Warner.

It should be me.

I look closely at my outfit for the first time and realize I must be wearing more of Warner's old clothes. I'm drowning in a faded orange T-shirt and a pair of gray sweatpants that almost falls off my hips every time I stand up straight. I take a moment to regain my equilibrium, testing my full weight on the thick, plush carpet under my bare feet. I roll the waistband of the pants a few times, just until they sit snugly at my hip bone, and then I ball up the extra material of the T-shirt and knot it at the back. I'm vaguely aware that I must look ridiculous, but fitting the clothes to my frame gives me some modicum of control and I cling to it. It makes me feel a little more awake, a little more in command of my situation. All I need now is a rubber band. My hair is too heavy; it's begun to feel like it's suffocating me, and I'm desperate to get it off my neck. I'm desperate to take a shower, actually.

I spin around at the sound of the door.

I'm caught in the middle of a thought, holding my hair up with both hands in a makeshift ponytail, and suddenly acutely aware of the fact that I'm not wearing any underwear.

Warner is holding a tray.

He's staring at me, unblinking. His gaze sweeps across my face, down my neck, my arms. Stops at my waist. I follow his eyes only to realize that my movements have lifted my shirt and exposed my stomach. And I suddenly understand why he's staring.

The memory of his kisses along my torso; his hands exploring my back, my bare legs, the backs of my thighs, his fingers hooking around the elastic band of my underwear—

Oh

I drop my hands and my hair at the same time, the brown waves falling hard and fast around my shoulders, my back, hitting my waist. My face is on fire.

Warner is suddenly transfixed by a spot directly above my head.

"I should probably cut my hair," I say to no one in particular, not understanding why I've even said it. I don't want to cut my hair. I want to lock myself in the toilet.

He doesn't respond. He carries the tray closer to the bed and it's not until I spot the glasses of water and the plates of food that I realize exactly how hungry I am. I can't remember the last time I ate anything; I've been surviving off the energy recharge I received when my wound was healed.

"Have a seat," he says, not meeting my eyes. He nods to the floor before folding himself onto the carpet. I sit down across from him. He pushes the tray in front of me.

"Thank you," I say, my eyes focused on the meal. "This looks delicious."

There's tossed salad and fragrant, colorful rice. Diced, seasoned potatoes and a small helping of steamed vegetables. A little cup of chocolate pudding. A bowl of fresh-cut fruit. Two glasses of water.

It's a meal I would've scoffed at when I first arrived.

If I knew then what I know now, I would've taken advantage of every opportunity Warner had given me. I would've eaten the food and taken the clothes. I would've built up my strength and paid closer attention when he showed me around base. I would've been looking for escape routes and excuses to tour the compounds. And then I would've bolted. I would've found a way to survive on my own. And I never would've dragged Adam down with me. I never would've gotten myself and so many others into this mess.

If only I had eaten the stupid food.

I was a scared, broken girl, fighting back the only way I knew how. It's no wonder I failed. I wasn't in my right mind. I was weak and terrified and blind to the idea of possibility. I had no experience with stealth or manipulation. I hardly knew how to interact with people—could barely understand the words in my own head.

It shocks me to think how much I've changed in these past months. I feel like a completely different person. Sharper, somehow. Hardened, absolutely. And for the first time in my life, willing to admit that I'm angry.

It's liberating.

I look up suddenly, feeling the weight of Warner's gaze. He's staring at me like he's intrigued, fascinated. "What are you thinking about?" he asks.

I stab a piece of potato with my fork. "I'm thinking I was an idiot for ever turning down a plate of hot food."

He raises an eyebrow at me. "I can't say I disagree."

I shoot him a dirty look.

"You were so broken when you got here," he says, taking a deep breath. "I was so confused. I kept waiting for you to go insane, to jump on the table at dinner and start taking swipes at my soldiers. I was sure you were going to try and kill everyone, and instead, you were stubborn and pouty, refusing to change out of your filthy clothes and complaining about eating your vegetables."

I go pink.

"At first," he says, laughing, "I thought you were plotting something. I thought you were pretending to be complacent just to distract me from some greater goal. I thought your anger over such petty things was a ruse," he says, his eyes mocking me. "I figured it had to be."

I cross my arms. "The extravagance was disgusting. So much money is wasted on the army while other people are starving to death."

Warner waves a hand, shaking his head. "That's not the point. The point," he says, "is that I hadn't provided you with any of those things for some calculated, underhanded reason. It wasn't some kind of a test." He laughs. "I wasn't trying to challenge you and your scruples. I thought I was doing you a favor. You'd come from this disgusting, miserable hole in the ground. I wanted you to have a real mattress. To be able to shower in peace. To have beautiful, fresh clothes. And you needed to eat," he says. "You'd been starved half to death."

I stiffen, slightly mollified. "Maybe," I say. "But you were crazy. You were a controlling maniac. You wouldn't even let me talk to the other soldiers."

"Because they are animals," he snaps, his voice unexpectedly sharp.

I look up, startled, to meet his angry, flashing green eyes.

"You, who have spent the majority of your life locked away," he says, "have not had the opportunity to understand just how beautiful you are, or what kind of effect that can have on a person. I was worried for your safety," he says. "You were timid and weak and living on a military base full of lonely, fully armed, thickheaded soldiers three times your size. I didn't want them harassing you. I made a spectacle out of your display with Jenkins because I wanted them to have proof of your abilities. I needed them to see that you were a formidable opponent—one they'd do well to stay away from. I was trying to protect you."

I can't look away from the intensity in his eyes.

"How little you must think of me." He shakes his head in shock. "I had no idea you hated me so much. That everything I tried to do to help you had come under such harsh scrutiny."

"How can you be surprised? What choice did I have but to expect the worst from you? You were arrogant and crass and you treated me like a piece of property—"

"Because I had to!" He cuts me off, unrepentant. "My every move—every word—is monitored when I am not confined to my own quarters. My entire life depends on maintaining a certain type of personality."

"What about that soldier you shot in the forehead? Seamus Fletcher?" I challenge him, angry again. Now that I've let it enter my life, I'm realizing anger comes a little too naturally to me. "Was that all a part of your plan, too? No wait, don't tell me"—I hold up a hand—"that was just a simulation, right?"

Warner goes rigid.

He sits back; his jaw twitches. He looks at me with a mixture of sadness and rage in his eyes. "No," he finally says, deathly soft. "That was not a simulation."

"So you have no problem with that?" I ask him. "You have no regrets over killing a man for stealing a little extra food? For trying to survive, just like you?"

Warner bites down on his bottom lip for half a second. Clasps his hands in his lap. "Wow," he says. "How quickly you jump to his defense."

"He was an innocent man," I tell him. "He didn't deserve to die. Not for that. Not like that."

"Seamus Fletcher," Warner says calmly, staring into his open palms, "was a drunken bastard who was beating his wife and children. He hadn't fed them in two weeks. He'd punched his nine-year-old daughter in the mouth, breaking her two front teeth and fracturing her jaw. He beat his pregnant wife so hard she lost the child. He had two other children, too," he says. "A seven-year-old boy and a five-year-old girl." A pause. "He broke both their arms."

My food is forgotten.

"I monitor the lives of our citizens very carefully," Warner says. "I like to know who they are and how they're thriving. I probably shouldn't care," he says, "but I do."

I'm thinking I'm never going to open my mouth ever again.

"I have never claimed to live by any set of principles," Warner says to me. "I've never claimed to be right, or good, or even justified in my actions. The simple truth is that I do not care. I have been forced to do terrible things in my life, love, and I am seeking neither your forgiveness nor your approval. Because I do not have the luxury of philosophizing over scruples when I'm forced to act on basic instinct every day."

He meets my eyes.

"Judge me," he says, "all you like. But I have no tolerance," he says sharply, "for a man who beats his wife. No tolerance," he says, "for a man who beats his children." He's breathing hard now. "Seamus Fletcher was murdering his family," he says to me. "And you can call it whatever the hell you want to call it, but I will never regret killing a man who would bash his wife's face into a wall. I will never regret killing a man who would punch his nine-year-old daughter in the mouth. I am not sorry," he says. "And I will not apologize. Because a child is better off with no father, and a wife is better off with no husband, than one like that." I watch the hard movement in his throat. "I would know."

"I'm sorry—Warner, I—"

He holds up a hand to stop me. He steadies himself, his eyes focused on the plates of untouched food. "I've said it before, love, and I'm sorry I have to say it again, but you do not understand the choices I have to make. You don't know what I've seen and what I'm forced to witness every single day." He hesitates. "And I wouldn't want you to. But do not presume to understand my actions," he says, finally meeting my eyes. "Because if you do, I can assure you you'll only be met with disappointment. And if you insist on continuing to make assumptions about my character, I'll advise you only this: assume you will always be wrong."

He hauls himself up with a casual elegance that startles me. Smooths out his slacks. Pushes his sleeves up again. "I've had your armoire moved into my closet," he says. "There are things for you to change into, if you'd like that. The bed and bathroom are yours. I have work to do," he says. "I'll be sleeping in my office tonight."

And with that, he opens the adjoining door to his office, and locks himself inside.

EIGHT

My food is cold.

I poke at the potatoes and force myself to finish the meal even though I've lost my appetite. I can't help but wonder if I've finally pushed Warner too far.

I thought the revelations had come to a close for today, but I was wrong again. It makes me wonder just how much is left, and how much more I'll learn about Warner in the coming days. Months.

And I'm scared.

Because the more I discover about him, the fewer excuses I have to push him away. He's unraveling before me, becoming something entirely different; terrifying me in a way I never could've expected.

And all I can think is *not now.*

Not here. Not when so much is uncertain. If only my emotions would understand the importance of excellent timing.

I never realized Warner was unaware of how deeply I'd detested him. I suppose now I can better understand how he saw himself, how he'd never viewed his actions as guilty or criminal. Maybe he thought I would've given him the benefit of the doubt. That I would've been able to read him as easily as he's been able to read me.

But I couldn't. I didn't. And now I can't help but wonder if I've managed to disappoint him, somehow.

Why I even care.

I clamber to my feet with a sigh, hating my own uncertainty. Because while I might not be able to deny my physical attraction to him, I still can't shake my initial impressions of his character. It's not easy for me to switch so suddenly, to recognize him as anything but some kind of manipulative monster.

I need time to adjust to the idea of Warner as a normal person.

But I'm tired of thinking. And right now, all I want to do is shower.

I drag myself toward the open door of the bathroom before I remember what Warner said about my clothes. That he'd moved my armoire into his closet. I look around, searching for another door and finding none but the locked entry to his office. I'm half tempted to knock and ask him directly but decide against it. Instead, I study the walls more closely, wondering why Warner wouldn't have given me instructions if his closet was hard to find. But then I see it.

A switch.

It's more of a button, actually, but it sits flush with the wall. It would be almost impossible to spot if you weren't actively searching for it.

I press the button.

A panel in the wall slides out of place. And as I step across the threshold, the room illuminates on its own.

This closet is bigger than his entire bedroom.

The walls and ceiling are tiled with slabs of white stone that gleam under the fluorescent recessed lighting; the floors are covered with thick Oriental rugs. There's a small suede couch the color of light-green jade stationed in the very center of the room, but it's an odd sort of couch: it doesn't have a back. It looks like an oversized ottoman. And strangest of all: there's not a single mirror in here. I spin around, my eyes searching, certain I must've overlooked such an obvious staple, and I'm so caught up in the details of the space that I almost miss the clothes.

The *clothes*.

They're everywhere, on display as if they were works of art. Glossy, dark wood units are built into the walls, shelves lined with rows and rows of shoes. All the other closet space is dedicated to hanging racks, each wall housing different categories of clothing.

Everything is color coordinated.

He owns more coats, more shoes, more pants and shirts than I've ever seen in my life. Ties and bow ties, belts, scarves, gloves, and cuff links. Beautiful, rich fabrics: silk blends and starched cotton, soft wool and cashmere. Dress shoes and buttery leather boots buffed and polished to perfection. A peacoat in a dark, burnt shade of orange; a trench coat in a deep navy blue. A winter toggle coat in a stunning shade of plum. I dare to run my fingers along the different materials, wondering how many of these pieces he's actually worn.

I'm amazed.

It's always been apparent that Warner takes pride in his appearance; his outfits are impeccable; his clothes fit him like they were cut for his body. But now I finally understand why he took such care with my wardrobe.

He wasn't trying to patronize me.

He was enjoying himself.

Aaron Warner Anderson, chief commander and regent of Sector 45, son of the supreme commander of The Reestablishment.

He has a soft spot for fashion.

After my initial shock wears off, I'm able to easily locate my old armoire. It's been placed unceremoniously in a corner of the room, and I'm almost sorry for it. It stands out awkwardly against the rest of the space.

I quickly shuffle through the drawers, grateful for the first time to have clean things to change into. Warner anticipated all of my needs before I arrived on base. The armoire is full of dresses and shirts and pants, but it's also been stocked with socks, bras, and underwear. And even though I know this should make me feel awkward, somehow it doesn't. The underwear is simple and understated. Cotton basics that are exactly average and perfectly functional. He bought these things before he knew me, and knowing that they weren't purchased with any level of intimacy makes me feel less self-conscious about it all.

I grab a small T-shirt, a pair of cotton pajama bottoms, and all of my brand-new underthings, and slip out of the room. The lights immediately switch off as soon as I'm back in the bedroom, and I hit the button to close the panel.

I look around his bedroom with new eyes, reacclimating to this smaller, standard sort of space. Warner's bedroom looks almost identical to the one I occupied while on base, and I always wondered why. There are no personal effects anywhere; no pictures, no odd knickknacks.

But suddenly it all makes sense.

His bedroom doesn't mean anything to him. It's little more than a place to sleep. But his closet—that was his style, his design. It's probably the only space he cares about in this room.

It makes me wonder what the inside of his office looks like, and my eyes dart to his door before I remember how he's locked himself inside.

I stifle a sigh and head toward the bathroom, planning to shower, change, and fall asleep immediately. This day felt more like a few years, and I'm ready to be done with it. Hopefully tomorrow we'll be able to head back to Omega Point and finally make some progress.

But no matter what happens next, and no matter what we discover, I'm determined to find my way to Anderson, even if I have to go alone.

NINE

I can't scream.

My lungs won't expand. My breaths keep coming in short gasps. My chest feels too tight and my throat is closing up and I'm trying to shout and I can't, I can't stop wheezing, thrashing my arms and trying desperately to breathe but the effort is futile. No one can hear me. No one will ever know that I'm dying, that there's a hole in my chest filling with blood and pain and such unbearable agony and there's so much of it, so much blood, hot and pooling around me and I can't, I can't, I can't *breathe—*

"Juliette—*Juliette,* love, wake up—*wake up—*"

I jerk up so quickly I double over. I'm heaving in deep, harsh, gasping breaths, so overcome, so relieved to be able to get oxygen into my lungs that I can't speak, can't do anything but try to inhale as much as possible. My whole body is shaking, my skin is clammy, going from hot to cold too quickly. I can't steady myself, can't stop the silent tears, can't shake the nightmare, can't shake the memory.

I can't stop gasping for air.

Warner's hands cup my face. The warmth of his skin helps calm me somehow, and I finally feel my heart rate begin to slow. "Look at me," he says.

I force myself to meet his eyes, shaking as I catch my breath.

"It's okay," he whispers, still holding my cheeks. "It was just a bad dream. Try closing your mouth," he says, "and breathing through your nose." He nods. "There you go. Easy. You're okay." His voice is so soft, so melodic, so inexplicably tender.

I can't look away from his eyes. I'm afraid to blink, afraid to be pulled back into my nightmare.

"I won't let go until you're ready," he tells me. "Don't worry. Take your time."

I close my eyes. I feel my heart slow to a normal beat. My muscles begin to unclench, my hands steady their tremble. And even though I'm not actively crying, I can't stop the tears from streaming down my face. But then something in my body breaks, crumples from the inside, and I'm suddenly so exhausted I can no longer hold myself up.

Somehow, Warner seems to understand.

He helps me sit back on the bed, pulls the blankets up around my shoulders. I'm shivering, wiping away the last of my tears. Warner runs a hand over my hair. "It's okay," he says softly. "You're okay."

"Aren't y-you going to sleep, too?" I stammer, wondering what time it is. I notice he's still fully dressed.

"I . . . yes," he says. Even in this dim light I can see the surprise in his eyes. "Eventually. I don't often go to bed this early."

"Oh." I blink, breathing a little easier now. "What time is it?"

"Two o'clock in the morning."

It's my turn to be surprised. "Don't we have to be up in a few hours?"

"Yes." The ghost of a smile touches his lips. "But I'm almost never able to fall asleep when I should. I can't seem to turn my mind off," he says, grinning at me for only a moment longer before he turns to leave.

"Stay."

The word escapes my lips even before I've had a chance to think it through. I'm not sure why I've said it. Maybe because it's late and I'm still shaking, and maybe having him close might scare my nightmares away. Or maybe it's because I'm weak and grieving and need a friend right now. I'm not sure. But there's something about the darkness, the stillness of this hour, I think, that creates a language of its own. There's a strange kind of freedom in the dark; a terrifying vulnerability we allow ourselves at exactly the wrong moment, tricked by the darkness into thinking it will keep our secrets. We forget that the blackness is not a blanket; we forget that the sun will soon rise. But in the moment, at least, we feel brave enough to say things we'd never say in the light.

Except for Warner, who doesn't say a word.

For a split second he actually looks alarmed. He's staring at me in silent terror, too stunned to speak, and I'm about to take it all back and hide under the covers when he catches my arm.

I still.

He tugs me forward until I'm nestled against his chest. His arms fall around me carefully, as if he's telling me I can pull away, that he'll understand, that it's my choice. But I feel so safe, so warm, so devastatingly content that I can't seem to come up with a single reason why I shouldn't enjoy this moment. I press closer, hiding my face in the soft folds of his shirt, and his arms wrap more tightly around me, his chest rising and falling. My hands come up to rest against his stomach, the hard muscles tensed under my touch. My left hand slips around his ribs, up his back, and Warner freezes, his heart racing under my ear. My eyes fall closed just as I feel him try to inhale.

"Oh God," he gasps. He jerks back, breaks away. "I can't do this. I won't survive it."

"What?"

He's already on his feet and I can only make out enough of his silhouette to see that he's shaking. "I can't keep doing this—"

"Warner—"

"I thought I could walk away the last time," he says. "I thought I could let you go and hate you for it but I can't. Because you make it so damn difficult," he says. "Because you don't play fair. You go and do something like get yourself shot," he says, "and you *ruin* me in the process."

I try to remain perfectly still.

I try not to make a sound.

But my mind won't stop racing and my heart won't stop

pounding and with just a few words he's managed to dismantle my most concentrated efforts to forget what I did to him.

I don't know what to do.

My eyes finally adjust to the darkness and I blink, only to find him looking into my eyes like he can see into my soul.

I'm not ready for this. Not yet. Not yet. Not like this. But a rush of feelings, images of his hands, his arms, his lips are charging through my mind and I try but can't push the thoughts away, can't ignore the scent of his skin and the insane familiarity of his body. I can almost hear his heart thrumming in his chest, can see the tense movement in his jaw, can feel the power quietly contained within him.

And suddenly his face changes. Worries.

"What's wrong?" he asks. "Are you scared?"

I startle, breathing faster, grateful he can only sense the general direction of my feelings and not more than that. For a moment I actually want to say no. No, I'm not scared.

I'm petrified.

Because being this close to you is doing things to me. Strange things and irrational things and things that flutter against my chest and braid my bones together. I want a pocketful of punctuation marks to end the thoughts he's forced into my head.

But I don't say any of those things.

Instead, I ask a question I already know the answer to.

"Why would I be scared?"

"You're shaking," he says.

"Oh."

The two letters and their small, startled sound run right out of my mouth to seek refuge in a place far from here. I keep wishing I had the strength to look away from him in moments like this. I keep wishing my cheeks wouldn't so easily enflame. I keep wasting my wishes on stupid things, I think.

"No, I'm not scared," I finally say. But I really need him to step away from me. I really need him to do me that favor. "I'm just surprised."

He's silent, then, his eyes imploring me for an explanation. He's become both familiar and foreign to me in such a short period of time; exactly and nothing like I thought he'd be.

"You allow the world to think you're a heartless murderer," I tell him. "And you're not."

He laughs, once; his eyebrows lift in surprise. "No," he says. "I'm afraid I'm just the regular kind of murderer."

"But why—why would you pretend to be so ruthless?" I ask. "Why do you allow people to treat you that way?"

He sighs. Pushes his rolled-up shirtsleeves above his elbows again. I can't help but follow the movement, my eyes lingering along his forearms. And I realize, for the first time, that he doesn't sport any military tattoos like everyone else. I wonder why.

"What difference does it make?" he says. "People can think whatever they like. I don't desire their validation."

"So you don't mind," I ask him, "that people judge you so harshly?"

"I have no one to impress," he says. "No one who cares about what happens to me. I'm not in the business of making friends, love. My job is to lead an army, and it's the only thing I'm good at. No one," he says, "would be proud of the things I've accomplished. My mother doesn't even know me anymore. My father thinks I'm weak and pathetic. My soldiers want me dead. The world is going to hell. And the conversations I have with you are the longest I've ever had."

"What—really?" I ask, eyes wide.

"Really."

"And you trust me with all this information?" I say. "Why share your secrets with me?"

His eyes darken, deaden, all of a sudden. He looks toward the wall. "Don't do that," he says. "Don't ask me questions you already know the answers to. Twice I've laid myself bare for you and all it's gotten me was a bullet wound and a broken heart. Don't torture me," he says, meeting my eyes again. "It's a cruel thing to do, even to someone like me."

"Warner—"

"I don't understand!" He breaks, finally losing his composure, his voice rising in pitch. "What could *Kent*," he says, spitting the name, "possibly do for you?"

I'm so shocked, so unprepared to answer such a question that I'm rendered momentarily speechless. I don't even know what's happened to Adam, where he might be or what our future holds. Right now all I'm clinging to is a hope that he made it out alive. That he's out there somewhere, surviving against the odds. Right now, that certainty would be enough for me.

So I take a deep breath and try to find the right words, the right way to explain that there are so many bigger, heavier issues to deal with, but when I look up I find Warner is still staring at me, waiting for an answer to a question I now realize he's been trying hard to suppress. Something that must be eating away at him.

And I suppose he deserves an answer. Especially after what I did to him.

So I take a deep breath.

"It's not something I know how to explain," I say. "He's . . . I don't know." I stare into my hands. "He was my first friend. The first person to treat me with respect—to love me." I'm quiet a moment. "He's always been so kind to me."

Warner flinches. His eyes widen in shock. "He's always been so *kind* to you?"

"Yes," I whisper.

Warner laughs a harsh, hollow sort of laugh.

"This is incredible," he says, staring at the door, one hand caught in his hair. "I've been consumed by this question for the past three days, trying desperately to understand why you would give yourself to me so willingly, just to rip my heart out at the very last moment for some—some bland, utterly replaceable automaton. I kept thinking there had to be some great reason, something I'd overlooked, something I wasn't able to fathom."

"And I was ready to accept it," he says. "I'd forced myself to accept it because I figured your reasons were deep and beyond my grasp. I was willing to let you go if you'd found something extraordinary. Someone who could know you in ways I'd never be able to comprehend. Because you deserve that," he says. "I told myself you deserved more than me, more than my miserable offerings." He shakes his head. "But this?" he says, appalled. "These words? This explanation? You chose him because he's *kind* to you? Because he's offered you basic *charity*?"

I'm suddenly angry.

I'm suddenly mortified.

I'm outraged by the permission Warner's granted himself to judge my life—that he thought he'd been *generous* by stepping aside. I narrow my eyes, clench my fists. "It's not charity," I snap. "He cares about me—and I care about him!"

Warner nods, unimpressed. "You should get a dog, love. I hear they share much the same qualities."

"You are unbelievable!" I shove myself upward, scrambling to my feet and regretting it. I have to cling to the bed frame to steady myself. "My relationship with Adam is none of your business!"

"Your *relationship*?" Warner laughs, loud. He moves quickly to face me from the other side of the bed, leaving several feet between us. "What relationship? Does he even know anything about you? Does he understand you? Does he know your wants, your fears, the truth you conceal in your heart?"

"Oh, and what? You do?"

"You know damn well that I do!" he shouts, pointing an accusatory finger at me. "And I'm willing to bet my *life* that he has no idea what you're really like. You tiptoe around his feelings, pretending to be a nice little girl for him, don't you? You're afraid of scaring him off. You're afraid of telling him too much—"

"You don't know *anything*!"

"Oh I know," he says, rushing forward. "I understand perfectly. He's fallen for your quiet, timid shell. For who you *used* to be. He has no idea what you're capable of. What you might do if you're pushed too far." His hand slips behind my neck; he leans in until our lips are only inches apart.

What is happening to my lungs.

"You're a coward," he whispers. "You want to be with me and it terrifies you. And you're ashamed," he says. "Ashamed you could ever want someone like me. Aren't you?" He drops his gaze and his nose grazes mine and I can almost count the millimeters between our lips. I'm struggling to focus, trying to remember that I'm mad at him, mad about something, but his mouth is right in front of mine and my mind can't stop trying to figure out how to shove aside the space between us.

"You want me," he says softly, his hands moving up my back, "and it's *killing* you."

I jerk backward, breaking away, hating my body for

reacting to him, for falling apart like this. My joints feel flimsy, my legs have lost their bones. I need oxygen, need a brain, need to find my lungs—

"You deserve so much more than charity," he says, his chest heaving. "You deserve to live. You deserve to be *alive*." He's staring at me, unblinking.

"Come back to life, love. I'll be here when you wake up."

TEN

I wake up on my stomach.

My face is buried in the pillows, my arms hugging their soft contours. I blink steadily, my bleary eyes taking in my surroundings, trying to remember where I am. I squint into the brightness of the day. My hair falls into my face as I lift my head to look around.

"Good morning."

I startle for no good reason, sitting up too quickly and clutching a pillow to my chest for an equally inexplicable reason. Warner is standing at the foot of the bed, fully dressed. He's wearing black pants and a slate-green sweater that clings to the shape of his body, the sleeves pushed up his forearms. His hair is perfect. His eyes are alert, awake, impossibly brightened by the green of his shirt. And he's holding a steaming mug in his hand. Smiling at me.

I offer him a limp wave.

"Coffee?" he asks, offering me the mug.

I stare at it, doubtful. "I've never had coffee before."

"It isn't terrible," he says with a shrug. "Delalieu is obsessed with it. Isn't that right, Delalieu?"

I jerk backward on the bed, my head nearly hitting the wall behind me.

An older, kindly-looking gentleman smiles at me from

the corner of the room. His thin brown hair and twitchy mustache look vaguely familiar to me, as if I've seen him on base before. I notice he's standing next to a breakfast cart. "It's a pleasure to officially meet you, Miss Ferrars," he says. His voice is a little shaky, but not at all intimidating. His eyes are unexpectedly sincere. "The coffee really is quite good," he says. "I have it every day. Though I always have m-mine with—"

"Cream and sugar," Warner says with a wry smile, his eyes laughing as if at some private joke. "Yes. Though I'm afraid the sugar is a bit too much for me. I find I prefer the bitterness." He glances at me again. "The choice is yours."

"What's going on?" I ask.

"Breakfast," Warner says, his eyes revealing nothing. "I thought you might be hungry."

"It's okay that he's here?" I whisper, knowing full well that Delalieu can hear me. "That he knows I'm here?"

Warner nods. Offers me no other explanation.

"Okay," I tell him. "I'll try the coffee."

I crawl across the bed to reach for the mug, and Warner's eyes follow my movements, traveling from my face to the shape of my body to the rumpled pillows and sheets beneath my hands and knees. When he finally meets my eyes he looks away too quickly, handing me the mug only to put an entire room between us.

"So how much does Delalieu know?" I ask, glancing at the older gentleman.

"What do you mean?" Warner raises an eyebrow.

"Well, does he know that I'm leaving?" I raise an eyebrow, too. Warner stares. "You promised you'd get me off base," I say to him, "and I'm hoping Delalieu is here to help you with that. Though if it's too much trouble, I'm always happy to take the window." I cock my head. "It worked out well the last time."

Warner narrows his eyes at me, his lips a thin line. He's still glaring when he nods at the breakfast cart beside him. "This is how we're getting you out of here today."

I choke on my first sip of coffee. "What?"

"It's the easiest, most efficient solution," Warner says. "You're small and lightweight, you can easily fold yourself into a tight space, and the cloth panels will keep you hidden from sight. I'm often working in my room," he says. "Delalieu brings me my breakfast trays from time to time. No one will suspect anything unusual."

I look at Delalieu for some kind of confirmation.

He nods eagerly.

"How did you get me here in the first place?" I ask. "Why can't we just do the same thing?"

Warner studies one of the breakfast plates. "I'm afraid that option is no longer available to us."

"What do you mean?" My body seizes with a sudden anxiety. "How did you get me in here?"

"You weren't exactly conscious," he says. "We had to be a little more . . . creative."

"Delalieu."

The old man looks up at the sound of my voice, clearly

surprised to be addressed so directly. "Yes, miss?"

"How did you get me into the building?"

Delalieu glances at Warner, whose gaze is now firmly fixed on the wall. Delalieu looks at me, offers me an apologetic smile. "We—well, we carted you in," he says.

"How?"

"Sir," Delalieu says suddenly, his eyes imploring Warner for direction.

"We brought you in," Warner says, stifling a sigh, "in a body bag."

My limbs go stiff with fear. "You *what?*"

"You were unconscious, love. We didn't have many options. I couldn't very well carry you onto base in my arms." He shoots me a look. "There were many casualties from the battle," he says. "On both sides. A body bag was easily overlooked."

I'm gaping at him.

"Don't worry." He smiles. "I cut some holes in it for you."

"You're so thoughtful," I snap.

"It was thoughtful," I hear Delalieu say. I look at him to find he's watching me in shock, appalled by my behavior. "Our commander was saving your life."

I flinch.

I stare into my coffee cup, heat coloring my cheeks. My conversations with Warner have never had an audience before. I wonder what our interactions must look like to an outside observer.

"It's all right, Lieutenant," Warner says. "She tends to

get angry when she's terrified. It's little more than a defense mechanism. The idea of being folded into such a small space has likely triggered her claustrophobic tendencies."

I look up suddenly.

Warner is staring directly at me, his eyes deep with an unspoken understanding.

I keep forgetting that Warner is able to sense emotions, that he can always tell what I'm really feeling. And he knows me well enough to be able to put everything into context.

I'm utterly transparent to him.

And somehow—right now, at least—I'm grateful for it.

"Of course, sir," Delalieu says. "My apologies."

"Feel free to shower and change," Warner says to me. "I left some clothes for you in the bathroom—no dresses," he says, fighting a smile. "We'll wait here. Delalieu and I have a few things to discuss."

I nod, untangling myself from the bedsheets and stumbling to my feet. I tug on the hem of my T-shirt, self-conscious all of a sudden, feeling rumpled and disheveled in front of these two military men.

I stare at them for a moment.

Warner gestures to the bathroom door.

I take the coffee with me as I go, wondering all the while who Delalieu is and why Warner seems to trust him. I thought he said all of his soldiers wanted him dead.

I wish I could listen in on their conversation, but they're both careful to say nothing until the bathroom door shuts behind me.

ELEVEN

I take a quick shower, careful not to let the water touch my hair. I already washed it last night, and the temperature feels brisk this morning; if we're headed out, I don't want to risk catching a cold. It's difficult, though, to avoid the temptation of a long shower—and hot water—in Warner's bathroom.

I dress quickly, grabbing the folded clothes Warner left on a shelf for me. Dark jeans and a soft, navy-blue sweater. Fresh socks and underwear. A brand-new pair of tennis shoes.

The sizes are perfect.

Of course they are.

I haven't worn jeans in so many years that at first the material feels strange to me. The fit is so tight, so tapered; I have to bend my knees to stretch the denim a little. But by the time I tug the sweater over my head, I'm finally feeling comfortable. And even though I miss my suit, there's something nice about wearing real clothes. No fancy dresses, no cargo pants, no spandex. Just jeans and a sweater, like a normal person. It's an odd reality.

I take a quick look in the mirror, blinking at my reflection. I wish I had something to tie my hair back with; I got so used to being able to pull it out of my face while I was at Omega Point. I look away with a resigned sigh, hoping to get a start on this day as soon as possible. But the minute I crack open the bathroom door, I hear voices.

I freeze in place. Listening.

"—sure it's safe, sir?"

Delalieu is talking.

"Forgive me," the older man says quickly. "I don't mean to seem impertinent, but I can't help but be concerned—"

"It'll be fine. Just make sure our troops aren't patrolling that area. We should only be gone a few hours at the most."

"Yes, sir."

Silence.

Then

"Juliette," Warner says, and I nearly fall into the toilet. "Come out here, love. It's rude to eavesdrop."

I step out of the bathroom slowly, face flushed with heat from the shower and the shame of being caught in such a juvenile act. I suddenly have no idea what to do with my hands.

Warner is enjoying my embarrassment. "Ready to go?"

No.

No, I'm not.

Suddenly hope and fear are strangling me and I have to remind myself to breathe. I'm not ready to face the death and destruction of all my friends. Of course I'm not.

But "Yes, of course" is what I say out loud.

I'm steeling myself for the truth, in whatever form it arrives.

TWELVE

Warner was right.

Being carted through Sector 45 was a lot easier than I expected. No one noticed us, and the empty space underneath the cart was actually spacious enough for me to sit comfortably.

It's only when Delalieu flips open one of the cloth panels that I realize where we are. I glance around quickly, my eyes taking inventory of the military tanks parked in this vast space.

"Quickly," Delalieu whispers. He motions toward the tank parked closest to us. I watch as the door is pushed open from the inside. "Hurry, miss. You cannot be seen."

I scramble.

I jump out from underneath the cart and into the open door of the tank, clambering up and into the seat. The door shuts behind me, and I turn back to see Delalieu looking on, his watery eyes pinched together with worry. The tank starts moving.

I nearly fall forward.

"Stay low and buckle up, love. These tanks weren't built for comfort."

Warner is smiling as he stares straight ahead, his hands

sheathed in black leather gloves, his body draped in a steel-gray overcoat. I duck down in my seat and fumble for the straps, buckling myself in as best I can.

"So you know how to get there?" I ask him.

"Of course."

"But your father said you couldn't remember anything about Omega Point."

Warner glances over, his eyes laughing. "How convenient for us that I've regained my memory."

"Hey—how did you even get out of there?" I ask him. "How did you get past the guards?"

He shrugs. "I told them I had permission to be out of my room."

I gape at him. "You're not serious."

"Very."

"But how did you find your way out?" I ask. "You got past the guards, fine. But that place is like a labyrinth—I couldn't find my way around even after I'd been living there for a month."

Warner checks a display on the dashboard. Hits a few buttons for functions I don't understand. "I wasn't completely unconscious when I was carried in," he says. "I forced myself to pay attention to the entrance," he says. "I did my best to memorize any obvious landmarks. I also kept track of the amount of time it took to carry me from the entrance to the medical wing, and then from the medical wing to my room. And whenever Castle took me on my rounds to the bathroom," he says, "I studied my surroundings, trying to gauge how far I was from the exit."

"So—" I frown. "You could've defended yourself against the guards and tried to escape much sooner. Why didn't you?"

"I already told you," he says. "It was oddly luxurious, being confined like that. I was able to catch up on weeks of sleep. I didn't have to work or deal with any military issues. But the most obvious answer," he says, exhaling, "is that I stayed because I was able to see you every day."

"Oh."

Warner laughs, his eyes pressed shut for a second. "You really never wanted to be there, did you?"

"What do you mean?"

He shakes his head. "If you're going to survive," he says to me, "you can never be indifferent to your surroundings. You can't depend on others to take care of you. You cannot presume that someone else will do things right."

"What are you talking about?"

"You didn't care," he says. "You were there, underground for over a month, grouped together with these supernaturally inclined rebels spouting big, lofty ideals about saving the world, and you say you couldn't even find your way around. It's because you didn't care," he says. "You didn't want to participate. If you did, you would've taken the initiative to learn as much as possible about your new home. You would've been beside yourself with excitement. Instead, you were apathetic. Indifferent."

I open my mouth to protest but I don't have a chance.

"I don't blame you," he says. "Their goals were unrealistic. I don't care how flexible your limbs are or how many objects you can move with your mind. If you do not understand your opponent—or worse, if you *underestimate* your opponent—you are going to lose." His jaw tightens. "I kept trying to tell you," he says, "that Castle was going to lead your group into a massacre. He was too optimistic to be a proper leader, too hopeful to logically consider the odds stacked against him, and too ignorant of The Reestablishment to truly understand how they deal with voices of opposition.

"The Reestablishment," Warner says, "is not interested in maintaining a facade of kindness. The civilians are nothing more than peons to them. They want power," he says to me, "and they want to be entertained. They are not interested in fixing our problems. They only want to make sure that they are as comfortable as possible as we dig our own graves."

"No."

"Yes," he says. "It is exactly that simple. Everything else is just a joke to them. The texts, the artifacts, the languages. They just want to scare people, to keep them submissive, and to strip them of their individuality—to herd them into a singular mentality that serves no purpose but their own. This is why they can and will destroy all rebel movements. And this is a fact that your friends did not fully understand. And now," he says, "they have suffered for their ignorance."

He stops the tank.
Turns off the engine.
Unlocks my door.
And I'm still not ready to face this.

THIRTEEN

Anyone would be able to find Omega Point now. Any citizen, any civilian, anyone with working vision would be able to tell you where the large crater in Sector 45 is located.

Warner was right.

I unbuckle myself slowly, reaching blindly for the door handle. I feel like I'm moving through fog, like my legs have been formed from fresh clay. I fail to account for the height of the tank above the ground and stumble into the open air.

This is it.

The empty, barren stretch of land I'd come to recognize as the area just around Omega Point; the land Castle told us was once lush with greenery and vegetation. He said it'd been the ideal hiding place for Omega Point. But this was before things started changing. Before the weather warped and the plants struggled to flourish. Now it's a graveyard. Skeletal trees and howling winds, a thin layer of snow powdered over the cold, packed earth.

Omega Point is gone.

It's nothing but a huge, gaping hole in the ground about a mile across and 50 feet deep. It's a bowlful of innards, of death and destruction, silent in the wake of tragedy. Years of effort, so much time and energy spent toward a specific goal, one purpose: a plan to save humanity.

Obliterated overnight.

A gust of wind climbs into my clothes then, wraps itself around my bones. Icy fingers tiptoe up my pant legs, clench their fists around my knees and pull; suddenly I'm not sure how I'm still standing. My blood feels frozen, brittle. My hands are covering my mouth and I don't know who put them there.

Something heavy falls onto my shoulders. A coat.

I look back to find that Warner is watching me. He holds out a pair of gloves.

I take the gloves and tug them on over my frozen fingers and wonder why I'm not waking up yet, why no one has reached out to tell me it's okay, it's just a bad dream, that everything is going to be fine.

I feel as though I've been scooped out from the inside, like someone has spooned out all the organs I need to function and I'm left with nothing, just emptiness, just complete and utter disbelief. Because this is impossible.

Omega Point.

Gone.

Completely destroyed.

"JULIETTE, GET DOWN—"

FOURTEEN

Warner tackles me to the ground just as the sound of gunshots fills the air.

His arms are under me, cradling me to his chest, his body shielding mine from whatever imminent danger we've just gotten ourselves into. My heart is beating so loudly I can hardly hear Warner's voice as he speaks into my ear. "Are you all right?" he whispers, pulling me tighter against him.

I try to nod.

"Stay down," he says. "Don't move."

I wasn't planning on it, I don't say to him.

"STEP AWAY FROM HER, YOU WORTHLESS SACK OF SHIT—"

My body goes stiff.

That voice. I know that voice.

I hear footsteps coming closer, crunching on the snow and ice and dirt. Warner loosens his hold around me, and I realize he's reaching for his gun.

"Kenji—no—," I try to shout, my voice muffled by the snow.

"GET UP!" Kenji bellows, still moving closer. "Stand up, coward!"

I've officially begun to panic.

Warner's lips brush against my ear. "I'll be right back."

Just as I turn to protest, Warner's weight is lifted. His body gone. He's completely disappeared.

I scramble to my feet, spinning around.

My eyes land on Kenji.

He's stopped in place, confused and scanning the area, and I'm so happy to see him that I can't be bothered to care about Warner right now. I'm almost ready to cry. I squeak out Kenji's name.

His eyes lock on to mine.

He charges forward, closing the gap between us and tackling me in a hug so fierce he practically cuts off my circulation. "Holy *shit* it's good to see you," he says, breathless, squeezing me tighter.

I cling to him, so relieved, so stunned. I press my eyes shut, unable to stop the tears.

Kenji pulls back to look me in the eye, his face bright with pain and joy. "What the hell are you doing out here? I thought you were *dead*—"

"I thought *you* were dead!"

He stops then. The smile vanishes from his face. "Where the hell did Warner go?" he says, eyes taking in our surroundings. "You were with him, right? I'm not losing my mind, am I?"

"Yes—listen—Warner brought me here," I tell him, trying to speak calmly, hoping to cool the anger in his eyes. "But he's not trying to fight. When he told me about what happened to Omega Point, I didn't believe him, so I asked him to show me proof—"

"Is that right?" Kenji says, eyes flashing with a kind of hatred I've never seen in him before. "He came to show off what they did? To show you how many people he MURDERED!" Kenji breaks away from me, shaking with fury. "Did he tell you how many children were in there? Did he tell you how many of our men and women were *slaughtered* because of him?" He stops, heaving. "Did he tell you that?" he asks again, screaming into the air. "COME BACK OUT HERE, YOU SICK BASTARD!"

"Kenji, *no*—"

But Kenji's already gone, darting away so quickly he's just a speck in the distance now. I know he's searching the vast space for glimpses of Warner and I need to do something, I need to stop him but I don't know how—

"Don't move."

Warner's whispers are at my ear, his hands planted firmly on my shoulders. I try to spin around and he holds me in place. "I said don't move."

"What are you d—"

"Shhhh," he says. "No one can see me."

"*What?*" I crane my neck to try and glance behind me, but my head knocks against Warner's chin. His *invisible* chin.

"No," I hear myself gasp. "But you're not touching him—"

"Look straight ahead," he whispers. "It won't do us any good for you to be caught talking to invisible people."

I turn my face forward. Kenji is no longer in sight.

"How?" I ask Warner. "How did you—"

Warner shrugs behind me. "I've felt different since we did that experiment with your power. Now that I know exactly what it's like to take hold of another ability, I'm more easily able to recognize it. Like right now," he says. "I feel as though I could quite literally reach forward and take hold of your energy. It was just as simple with Kenji," he says. "He was standing right there. My survival instincts took over."

And even though this is a terrible moment to dwell on these things, I can't help but allow myself to panic. That Warner can so easily project his powers. With no training. No practice.

He can tap into my abilities and use them as he pleases.

This can't possibly be good.

Warner's hands squeeze my shoulders.

"What are you doing?" I whisper.

"I'm trying to see if I can pass the power on to you—if I can retransfer it and make us both invisible—but it seems I'm unable. Once I've taken the energy from someone else, I can *use* it, but I can't seem to share it. After I release the energy, it can only be returned to the owner."

"How do you know so much already?" I ask, astonished. "You just learned about this a few days ago."

"I've been practicing," he says.

"But how? With who?" I pause. *"Oh."*

"Yes," he says. "It's been rather incredible having you stay with me. For so many reasons." His hands fall from my shoulders. "I was worried I might be able to hurt you with your own power. I wasn't sure I could absorb it without accidentally using it against you. But we seem to cancel each other out," he says. "Once I take it from you, I can only ever give it back."

I'm not breathing.

"Let's go," Warner says. "Kenji is moving out of range and I won't be able to hold on to his energy for much longer. We have to get out of here."

"I can't leave," I tell him. "I can't just abandon Kenji, not like this—"

"He's going to try and kill me, love. And while I know I've proved otherwise in your case, I can assure you I'm generally incapable of standing by as someone makes an attempt on my life. So unless you want to watch me shoot him first, I suggest we get out of here as soon as possible. I can feel him circling back."

"No. You can go. You *should* go. But I'm going to stay here."

Warner stills behind me. "What?"

"Go," I tell him. "You have to go to the compounds—you have things to take care of. You should go. But I need to be here. I have to know what's happened to everyone else, and I have to move forward from there."

"You're asking me to leave you here," he says, not bothering to hide his shock. "Indefinitely."

"Yes," I say to him. "I'm not leaving until I get some answers. And you're right. Kenji will definitely shoot first and ask questions later, so it's best that you leave. I'll talk to him, try to tell him what's happened. Maybe we could all work together—"

"What?"

"It doesn't just have to be me and you," I tell him. "You said you wanted to help me kill your father and take down The Reestablishment, right?"

Warner nods slowly against the back of my head.

"Okay. So." I take a deep breath. "I accept your offer."

Warner goes rigid. "You accept my offer."

"Yes."

"Do you understand what you're saying?"

"I wouldn't say it if I didn't mean it. I'm not sure I'll be able to do this without you."

I feel the breath rush out of him, his heart beating hard against my back.

"But I need to know who else is still alive," I insist. "And the group of us can work together. We'll be stronger that way, and we'll all be fighting toward the same goal—"

"No."

"It's the only way—"

"I have to go," he says, spinning me around. "Kenji is almost here." He shoves a hard plastic object into my hand. "Activate this pager," he says, "whenever you're ready. Keep it with you and I'll know where to find you."

"But—"

"You have four hours," he says. "If I don't hear from you before then, I'll assume you are in some kind of danger, and I will come find you myself." He's still holding my hand, the pager still pressed against my palm. It's the craziest feeling, to be touched by someone you can't see. "Do you understand?"

I nod, once. I have no idea where to look.

And then I freeze, every inch of me hot and cold all at once because he presses his lips to the back of my fingers in one soft, tender moment and when he pulls away I'm reeling, heady, unsteady.

Just as I'm regaining my footing, I hear the familiar sound of an electric thrum, and realize Warner has already begun to drive away.

And I'm left to wonder what on earth I've just agreed to.

FIFTEEN

Kenji is stomping toward me, his eyes blazing.

"Where the hell did he go? Did you see where he went?"

I shake my head as I reach forward, grabbing his arms in an attempt to focus his eyes. "Talk to me, Kenji. Tell me what happened—where is everyone—?"

"There is no *everyone*!" he snaps, breaking away. "Omega Point is gone—everything gone—*everything*—" He drops to his knees, heaving as he falls forward, his forehead digging into the snow. "I thought you were dead, too—I thought—"

"No," I gasp. "No, Kenji—they can't all have died—not everyone—"

Not Adam.

Not Adam.

Please please please not *Adam*

I'd been too optimistic about today.

I'd been lying to myself.

I didn't really believe Warner. I didn't believe it could be this bad. But now, to see the truth, and to hear Kenji's agony—the reality of all that happened is hitting me so hard I feel like I'm falling backward into my own grave.

My knees have hit the ground.

"Please," I'm saying, "please tell me there are others—Adam has to be alive—"

"I grew up here," Kenji is saying. He's not listening to me and I don't recognize his raw, aching voice. I want the old Kenji, the one who knew how to take charge, to take control. And this isn't him.

This Kenji is terrifying me.

"This was my whole life," he says, looking toward the crater that used to be Omega Point. "The only place—all those people—" He chokes. "They were my *family*. My only family—"

"Kenji, please . . ." I try to shake him. I need him to snap out of his grief before I succumb to it, too. We need to move out of plain sight and I'm only now beginning to realize that Kenji doesn't care. He *wants* to put himself in danger. He *wants* to fight. He wants to *die*.

I can't let that happen.

Someone needs to take control of this situation right now and right now I might be the only one capable.

"Get up," I snap, my voice harsher than I intended. "You need to get up, and you need to stop acting reckless. You know we're not safe out here, and we have to move. Where are you staying?" I grab his arm and pull, but he won't budge. "Get up!" I shout again. "Get—"

And then, just like that, I remember I'm a whole hell of a lot stronger than Kenji will ever be. It almost makes me smile.

I close my eyes and focus, trying to remember everything

Kenji taught me, everything I've learned about how to control my strength, how to tap into it when I need to. I spent so many years bottling everything up and locking it away that it still takes some time to remember it's there, waiting for me to harness it. But the moment I welcome it, I feel it rush into me. It's a raw power so potent it makes me feel invincible.

And then, just like that, I yank Kenji up off the ground and toss him over my shoulder.

Me.

I do that.

Kenji, of course, unleashes a string of the foulest expletives I've ever heard. He's kicking at me but I can hardly feel it; my arms are wrapped loosely around him, my strength carefully reined in so as not to crush him. He's angry, but at least he's swearing again. This is something I recognize.

I cut him off midexpletive. "Tell me where you're staying," I say to him, "and pull yourself together. You can't fall apart on me now."

Kenji is silent a moment.

"Hey, um, I'm sorry to bother you, but I'm looking for a friend of mine," he says. "Have you seen her? She's a tiny little thing, cries a lot, spends too much time with her feelings—"

"Shut up, Kenji."

"Oh wait!" he says. "It *is* you."

"Where are we going?"

"When are you going to put me down?" he counters, no

longer amused. "I mean, I've got an excellent view of your ass from here, but if you don't mind me staring—"

I drop him without thinking.

"God*dammit*, Juliette—what the *hell*—"

"How's the view from down there?" I stand over his splayed body, arms crossed over my chest.

"I hate you."

"Get up, please."

"When did you learn to do that?" he grumbles, stumbling to his feet and rubbing his back.

I roll my eyes. Squint into the distance. Nothing and no one in sight, so far. "I didn't."

"Oh, right," he says. "Because that makes sense. Because tossing a grown-ass man over your shoulders is just so freaking easy. That shit just comes naturally to you."

I shrug.

Kenji lets out a low whistle. "Cocky as hell, too."

"Yeah." I shade my eyes against the cold sunlight. "I think spending all that time with you really screwed me up."

"Ohhh-ho," he says, clapping his hands together, unamused. "Stand up, princess. You're a comedian."

"I'm already standing up."

"It's called a joke, smart-ass."

"Where are we going?" I ask him again. I start walking in no particular direction. "I really need to know where we're headed."

"Unregulated turf." He falls into step with me, taking my hand to lead the way. We go invisible immediately. "It was the only place we could think of."

"We?"

"Yeah. It's Adam's old place, remember? It's where I first—"

I stop walking, chest heaving. I'm crushing Kenji's hand in mine and he yanks it free, unleashing expletives as he does, making us visible again. "Adam is still alive?" I ask, searching his eyes.

"Of course he's still alive." Kenji shoots me a dirty look as he rubs at his hand. "Have you heard nothing I've been saying to you?"

"But you said everyone was dead," I gasp. "You said—"

"Everyone *is* dead," Kenji says, his features darkening again. "There were over a hundred of us at Omega Point. There are only nine of us left."

SIXTEEN

"Who?" I ask, my heart constricting. "Who survived? How?"

Kenji lets out a long breath, running both hands through his hair as he focuses on a point behind me. "You just want a list?" he asks. "Or do you want to know how it all happened?"

"I want to know everything."

He nods. Looks down, stomps on a clump of snow. He takes my hand again, and we start walking, two invisible kids in the middle of nowhere.

"I guess," Kenji finally says, "that on some level we have you to thank for us still being alive. Because if we'd never gone to find you, we probably would've died on the battlefield with everyone else."

He hesitates.

"Adam and I noticed you were missing pretty quickly, but by the time we fought our way back to the front, we were too late. We were still maybe twenty feet out, and could only see them hauling you into the tank." He shakes his head. "We couldn't just run after you," he says. "We were trying not to get shot at."

His voice gets deeper, more somber as he tells the story.

"So we decided we'd go an alternate route—avoiding all

the main roads—to try and follow you back to base, because that's where we thought you were headed. But just as we got there, we ran into Castle, Lily, Ian, and Alia, who were on their way out. They'd managed to complete their own mission successfully; they broke into Sector 45 and stole Winston and Brendan back. Those two were half dead when Castle found them," Kenji says quietly.

He takes a sharp breath.

"And then Castle told us what they'd heard while they were on base—that the troops were mobilizing for an air assault on Omega Point. They were going to drop bombs on the entire area, hoping that if they hit it with enough firepower, everything underground would just collapse in on itself. There'd be no escape for anyone inside, and everything we'd built would be destroyed."

I feel him tense beside me.

We stop moving for just a moment before I feel Kenji tug on my hand. I duck into the cold and wind, steeling myself against the weather and his words.

"Apparently they'd tortured the location out of our people on the battlefield," he says. "Just before killing them." He shakes his head. "We knew we didn't have much time, but we were still close enough to base that I managed to commandeer one of the army tanks. We loaded up and headed straight for Point, hoping to get everyone out in time. But I think, deep down," he says, "we knew it wasn't going to work. The planes were overhead. Already on their way."

He laughs, suddenly, but the action seems to cause him pain.

"And by some freak miracle of insanity, we intercepted James almost a mile out. He'd managed to sneak out, and was on his way toward the battlefield. The poor kid had pissed the whole front of his pants he was so scared, but he said he was tired of being left behind. Said he wanted to fight with his brother." Kenji's voice is strained.

"And the craziest shit," he says, "is that if James had stayed at Point like we told him to, where we thought he'd be safe, he would've died with everyone else." Kenji laughs a little. "And that was it. There was nothing we could do. We just had to stand there, watching as they dropped bombs on thirty years of work, killed everyone too young or too old to fight back, and then massacred the rest of our team on the field." He clenches his hand around mine. "I come back here every day," he says. "Hoping someone will show up. Hoping to find something to take back." He stops then, voice tight with emotion. "And here you are. This shit doesn't even seem real."

I squeeze his fingers—gently, this time—and huddle closer to him. "We're going to be okay, Kenji. I promise. We'll stick together. We'll get through this."

Kenji tugs his hand out of mine only to slip it around my shoulder, pulling me tight against his side. His voice is soft when he speaks. "What happened to you, princess? You seem different."

"Bad different?"

"Good different," he says. "Like you finally put your big-girl pants on."

I laugh out loud.

"I'm serious," he says.

"Well." I pause. "Sometimes different is better, isn't it?"

"Yeah," Kenji says. "Yeah, I guess it is." He hesitates. "So . . . are you going to tell me what happened? Because last I saw you, you were being shoved into the backseat of an army tank, and this morning you show up all freshly showered and shiny-white-sneakered and you're walking around with *Warner*," he says, releasing my shoulder and taking my hand again. "And it doesn't take a genius to figure out that that shit doesn't make any sense."

I take a deep, steadying breath. It's strange not being able to see Kenji right now; it feels as if I'm making these confessions to the wind. "Anderson shot me," I tell him.

Kenji stills beside me. I can hear him breathing hard. *"What?"*

I nod, even though he can't see me. "I wasn't taken back to base. The soldiers delivered me to Anderson; he was waiting in one of the houses on unregulated turf. I think he wanted privacy," I tell Kenji, carefully omitting any information about Warner's mom. Those secrets are too private, and not mine to share. "Anderson wanted revenge," I say instead, "for what I did to his legs. He was crippled; when I saw him he was using a cane. But before I could figure out what was happening, he pulled out a gun and shot me. Right in the chest."

"Holy shit," Kenji breathes.

"I remember it so well." I hesitate. "Dying. It was the most painful thing I've ever experienced. I couldn't scream because my lungs were torn apart or full of blood. I don't know. I just had to lie there, trying to breathe, hoping to drop dead as quickly as possible. And the whole time," I say, "the whole time I kept thinking about how I'd spent my entire life being a coward, and how it got me nowhere. And I knew that if I had the chance to do it all again, I'd do it differently. I promised myself I'd finally stop being afraid."

"Yeah, that's all super heartwarming," Kenji says, "but how in the hell did you survive a shot to the chest?" he demands. "You should be dead right now."

"Oh." I clear my throat a little. "Yeah, um, Warner saved my life."

"Shut the hell up."

I try not to laugh. "I'm serious," I say, taking a minute to explain how the girls were there and how Warner used their power to save me. How Anderson left me to die and how Warner took me back to base with him, hid me, and helped me recover. "And by the way," I say to Kenji, "Sonya and Sara are almost definitely still alive. Anderson took them back to the capital with him; he wants to force them to serve as his own personal healers. He's probably gotten them to fix his legs by now."

"Okay, you know what"—Kenji stops walking, grabs my shoulders—"you need to just back up, okay, because you are dumping way too much information on me all at once, and I need you to start from the beginning, and I need you to tell me *everything*," he says, his voice rising in pitch. "What the hell is going on? The girls are still alive? And what do you mean, Warner transferred their power to you? How the hell is that possible?"

So I tell him.

I finally tell him the things I've always wanted to confess. I tell him the truth about Warner's ability and the truth about how Kenji was injured outside the dining hall that night. I tell him how Warner had no idea what he was capable of, and how I let him practice with me in the tunnel while everyone was in the medical wing. How together we broke through the floor.

"Holy shit," Kenji whispers. "So that asshole tried to *kill* me."

"Not on purpose," I point out.

Kenji mutters something crude under his breath.

And though I mention nothing about Warner's unexpected visit to my room later that night, I do tell Kenji how Warner escaped, and how Anderson was waiting for Warner to show up before shooting me. Because Anderson knew how Warner felt about me, I tell Kenji, and wanted to punish him for it.

"Wait." Kenji cuts me off. "What do you mean, he knew how Warner *felt* about you? We *all* knew how Warner felt about you. He wanted to use you as a weapon," Kenji says. "That shouldn't have been a revelation. I thought his dad was happy about that."

I go stiff.

I forgot this part was still a secret. That I'd never revealed the truth about my connection to Warner. Because while

Adam might've suspected that Warner had more than a professional interest in me, I'd never told anyone about my intimate moments with Warner. Or any of the things he's said to me.

I swallow, hard.

"Juliette," Kenji says, a warning in his voice. "You can't hold this shit back anymore. You have to tell me what's going on."

I feel myself sway.

"Juliette—"

"He's in love with me," I whisper. I've never admitted that out loud before, not even to myself. I think I hoped I could ignore it. Hide it. Make it go away so Adam would never find out.

"He's—wait—*what?*"

I take a deep breath. I suddenly feel exhausted.

"Please tell me you're joking," Kenji says.

I shake my head, forgetting he can't see me.

"Wow."

"Kenji, I—"

"This is soooo weird. Because I always thought Warner was crazy, you know?" Kenji laughs. "But now, I mean, now there's no doubt."

My eyes fly wide open, shocking me into laughter. I push his invisible shoulder, hard.

Kenji laughs again, half amused, half reeling from disbelief. He takes a deep breath. "So, okay, wait, so, how do you know he's in love with you?"

"What do you mean?"

"I mean, like—what, he took you out on a date or something? Bought you chocolates and wrote you some really shitty poetry? Warner doesn't exactly seem like the affectionate type, if you know what I mean."

"Oh." I bite the inside of my cheek. "No, it was nothing like that."

"Then?"

"He just . . . told me."

Kenji stops walking so abruptly I nearly fall over. "No he didn't."

I don't know how to respond to that.

"He actually said those words? To your face? Like, directly to your face?"

"Yes."

"So—so—so wait, so he tells you he loves you . . . and you said? What?" Kenji demands, dumbfounded. "'Thank you'?"

"No." I stifle a cringe, remembering all too well that I actually shot Warner for it the first time. "I mean I didn't—I mean—I don't know, Kenji, it's all really weird for me right now. I still haven't found a way to deal with it." My voice drops to a whisper. "Warner is really . . . intense," I say, and I'm overcome by a flood of memories, my emotions colliding into one jumble of insanity.

His kisses on my body. My pants on the floor. His desperate confessions unhinging my joints.

I squeeze my eyes shut, feeling too hot, too unsteady,

everything all too suddenly.

"That's definitely one way of putting it," Kenji mutters, snapping me out of my reverie. I hear him sigh. "So Warner still has no idea that he and Kent are brothers?"

"No," I say, immediately sobered.

Brothers.

Brothers who hate each other. Brothers who want to kill each other. And I'm caught in the middle. Good God, what has happened to my life.

"And both of these guys can touch you?"

"Yes? But—well, no, not really." I try to explain. "Adam . . . can't really touch me. I mean, he can, sort of . . . ?" I trail off. "It's complicated. He has to actively work and train to counteract my energy with his own. But with Warner—" I shake my head, staring down at my invisible feet as I walk. "Warner can touch me with no consequences. It doesn't do anything to him. He just absorbs it."

"Damn," Kenji says after a moment. "Damn damn damn. This shit is bananas."

"I know."

"So—okay—you're telling me that Warner saved your life? That he actually begged the girls to help him heal you? And that he then hid you in his own room, and took care of you? Fed you and gave you clothes and shit and let you sleep in his bed?"

"Yes."

"Yeah. Okay. I have a really hard time believing that."

"I know," I say again, this time blowing out an exasperated

breath. "But he's really not what you guys think. I know he seems kind of crazy, but he's actually really—"

"Whoa, wait—are you *defending* him?" Kenji's voice is laced with shock. "We are talking about the same dude who locked you up and tried to make you his military *slave*, right?"

I'm shaking my head, wishing I could try to explain everything Warner's told me without sounding like a naive, gullible idiot. "It's not—" I sigh. "He didn't actually want to use me like that—," I try to say.

Kenji barks out a laugh. "Holy *shit*," he says. "You actually believe him, don't you? You're buying into all the bullshit he's fed you—"

"You don't know him, Kenji, that's not fair—"

"Oh my God," he breathes, laughing again. "You are seriously going to try and tell me that I don't know the man who led me into battle? He was my goddamn commander," Kenji says to me. "I know exactly who he is—"

"I'm not trying to argue with you, okay? I don't expect you to understand—"

"This is hilarious," Kenji says, wheezing through another laugh. "You really don't get it, do you?"

"Get what?"

"Ohhh, *man*," he says suddenly. "Kent is going to be *pissed*," he says, dragging out the word in glee. He actually giggles.

"Wait—what? What does Adam have to do with this?"

"You do realize you haven't asked me a single question

about him, right?" A pause. "I mean, I just told you the whole saga of all the shit that happened to us and you were just like, Oh, okay, cool story, bro, thanks for sharing. You didn't freak out or ask if Adam was injured. You didn't ask me what happened to him or even how he's coping right now, especially seeing as how he thinks you're *dead* and everything."

I feel sick all of a sudden. Stopped in my tracks. Mortified and guilty guilty guilty.

"And now you're standing here, defending *Warner,*" Kenji is saying. "The same guy who tried to *kill Adam,* and you're acting like he's your friend or someshit. Like he's just some normal dude who's a little misunderstood. Like every single other person on the planet got it wrong, and probably because we're all just a bunch of judgmental, jealous assholes who hate him for having such a pretty, pretty face."

Shame singes my skin.

"I'm not an idiot, Kenji. I have reasons for the things I say."

"Yeah, and maybe I'm just saying that you have no idea what you're saying."

"Whatever."

"Don't *whatever* me—"

"*Whatever,*" I say again.

"Oh my God," Kenji says to no one in particular. "I think this girl wants to get her ass kicked."

"You couldn't kick my ass if I had ten of them."

Kenji laughs out loud. "Is that a challenge?"

"It's a warning," I say to him.

"Ohhhhhh, so you're threatening me now? Little crybaby knows how to make threats now?"

"Shut up, Kenji."

"*Shut up, Kenji,*" he repeats in a whiny voice, mocking me.

"How much farther do we have to go?" I ask too loudly, irritated and trying to change the subject.

"We're almost there," he shoots back, his words clipped.

Neither one of us speaks for a few minutes.

Then

"So . . . why did you walk all this way?" I ask. "Didn't you say you had a tank?"

"Yeah," Kenji says with a sigh, our argument momentarily forgotten. "We have two, actually. Kent said he stole one when you guys first escaped; it's still sitting in his garage."

Of course.

How could I forget?

"But I like walking," Kenji continues. "I don't have to worry about anyone seeing me, and I always hope that maybe if I'm on foot, I'll be able to notice things I wouldn't be able to otherwise. I'm still hoping," he says, his voice tight again, "that we'll find more of our own hidden out here somewhere."

I squeeze Kenji's hand again, clinging closer to him. "Me too," I whisper.

SEVENTEEN

Adam's old place is exactly as I remember it.

Kenji and I sneak in from the underground parking garage, and scale a few flights of stairs to the upper levels. I'm suddenly so nervous I can hardly speak. I've had to grieve the loss of my friends twice already, and part of me feels like this can't possibly be happening. But it must be. It has to be.

I'm going to see Adam.

I'm going to see Adam's face.

He's going to be *real*.

"They blasted the door open when they were searching for us that first time," Kenji is saying, "so the door is pretty jammed up—we'd been piling a bunch of furniture against it to keep it closed, but then it got stuck the other way, soo . . . yeah, it might take them a while to open it. But other than that, this little place has been good to us. Kent's still got a ton of food in storage, and all the plumbing still works because he'd paid for almost everything through the end of the year. All in all, we got pretty lucky," he says.

I'm nodding my head, too afraid to open my mouth. That coffee from this morning suddenly doesn't feel very good in my stomach, and I'm jittery from head to toe.

Adam.

I'm about to see Adam.

Kenji bangs on the door. "Open up," he shouts. "It's me."

For a minute all I hear is the sound of heavy movement, creaky wood, screechy metal, and a series of thuds. I watch the doorframe as it shakes; someone on the other side is yanking on the door, trying to get it unjammed.

And then it opens. So slowly. I'm gripping my hands to keep myself steady.

Winston is standing at the door.

Gaping at me.

"Holy shit," he says. He pulls his glasses off—I notice they've been taped together—and blinks at me. His face is bruised and battered, his bottom lip swollen, split open. His left hand is bandaged, the gauze wrapped several times around the palm of his hand.

I offer him a timid smile.

Winston grabs ahold of Kenji's shirt and yanks him forward, eyes still focused on my face. "Am I hallucinating again?" he asks. "Because I'm going to be so pissed if I'm hallucinating again. *Dammit,*" he says, not waiting for Kenji to respond. "If I had any idea how much it would suck to have a concussion, I'd have shot myself in the face when I had a chance—"

"You're not hallucinating." Kenji cuts him off with a laugh. "Now let us inside."

Winston is still blinking at me, eyes wide as he backs away, giving us room to enter. But the minute I step over the threshold I'm thrust into another world, a whole different set of memories. This is Adam's home. The first place I ever found sanctuary. The first place I ever felt safe.

And now it's full of people, the space far too small to house so many large bodies. Castle and Brendan and Lily and Ian and Alia and James—they've all frozen midmovement, midsentence. They're all staring at me in disbelief. And I'm just about to say something, just about to find something acceptable to say to my only group of battered, broken friends, when Adam walks out of the small room I know used to belong to James. He's holding something in his hands, distracted, not noticing the abrupt change in the atmosphere.

But then he looks up.

His lips are parted as if to speak, and whatever he was holding hits the ground, shattering into so many sounds it startles everyone back to life.

Adam is staring at me, eyes locked on my face, his chest heaving, his face fighting so many different emotions. He looks half terrified, half hopeful. Or maybe terrified to be hopeful.

And though I realize I should probably be the first to speak, I suddenly have no idea what to say.

Kenji pulls up beside me, his face splitting into a huge smile. He slips his arm around my shoulder. Squeezes. Says, "Lookie what I found."

Adam begins to move across the room, but it feels strange—like everything has begun to slow down, like this moment isn't real, somehow. There's so much pain in his eyes.

I feel like I've been punched in the gut.

But then there he is, right in front of me, his hands searching my body as if to ensure that I'm real, that I'm still intact. He's studying my face, my features, his fingers weaving into my hair. And then all at once he seems to accept that I'm not a ghost, not a nightmare, and he hauls me against himself so quickly I can't help but gasp in response.

"Juliette," he breathes.

His heart is beating hard against my ear, his arms wrapped tight around me, and I melt into his embrace, relishing the warm comfort, the familiarity of his body, his scent, his skin. My hands reach around him, slip up his back and grip him hard, and I don't even realize silent tears have fallen down my face until he pulls back to look me in the eye. He tells me not to cry, tells me it's okay, that everything is going to be okay and I know it's all a lie but it still feels so good to hear.

He's studying my face again, his hands carefully cradling the back of my head, so careful not to touch my skin. The reminder sends a sharp pain through my heart. "I can't believe you're really here," he says, his voice breaking. "I can't believe this is actually happening—"

Kenji clears his throat. "Hey—guys? Your loin passion is grossing out the little ones."

"I'm not a *little one,*" James says, visibly offended. "And I don't think it's gross."

Kenji spins around. "You're not bothered by all the heavy breathing going on over here?" He makes a haphazard gesture toward us.

I jump away from Adam reflexively.

"No," James says, crossing his arms. "Are you?"

"Disgust was my general reaction, yeah."

"I bet you wouldn't think it was gross if it was you."

A long pause.

"You make a good point," Kenji finally says. "Maybe you should find me a lady in this crappy sector. I'm okay with anyone between the ages of eighteen and thirty-five." He points at James. "So how about you get on that, thanks."

James seems to take the challenge a little too seriously. He nods several times. "Okay," he says. "How about Alia? Or Lily?" he says, immediately pointing out the only other women in the room.

Kenji's mouth opens and closes a few times before he says, "Yeah, no thanks, kid. These two are like my sisters."

"So smooth," Lily says to Kenji, and I realize it's the first time I've really heard her speak. "I bet you win over all the eligible women by telling them they're like sisters to you. I bet the ladies are just lining up to jump into bed with your punkass."

"Rude." Kenji crosses his arms.

James is laughing.

"You see what I have to deal with?" Kenji says to him. "There's no love for Kenji. I give and I give and I give, and I get nothing in return. I need a woman who will appreciate all of this," he says, gesturing to the length of his body. He's clearly overexaggerating, hoping to entertain James with his ridiculousness, and his efforts are appreciated. Kenji is probably their only chance for comedic relief in this cramped space, and it makes me wonder if that's why he sets off on his own every day. Maybe he needs time to grieve in silence, in a place where no one expects him to be the funny one.

My heart starts and stops as I hesitate, wondering at how hard it must be for Kenji to keep it together even when he wants to fall apart. I caught a glimpse of that side of him for the first time today, and it surprised me more than it should have.

Adam squeezes my shoulder, and I turn to face him. He smiles a tender, tortured smile, his eyes heavy with pain and joy.

But of all the things I could be feeling right now, guilt hits me the hardest.

Everyone in this room is carrying such heavy burdens. Brief moments of levity puncture the general gloom shrouding this space, but as soon as the jokes subside, the grief slides back into place. And though I know I should grieve for the lives lost, I don't know how. They were all strangers to me. I was only just beginning to develop a relationship with Sonya and Sara.

But when I look around I see that I'm alone in feeling this way. I see the lines of loss creasing my friends' faces. I see the sadness buried in their clothes, perched atop their furrowed brows. And something in the back of my mind is nagging at me, disappointed in me, telling me I should be one of them, that I should be just as defeated as they are.

But I'm not.

I can't be that girl anymore.

For so many years I lived in constant terror of myself. Doubt had married my fear and moved into my mind, where it built castles and ruled kingdoms and reigned over me, bowing my will to its whispers until I was little more than an acquiescing peon, too terrified to disobey, too terrified to disagree.

I had been shackled, a prisoner in my own mind.

But finally, finally, I have learned to break free.

I *am* upset for our losses. I'm horrified. But I'm also anxious and restless. Sonya and Sara are still alive, living at the mercy of Anderson. They still need our help. So I don't know how to be sad when all I feel is an unrelenting determination to do something.

I am no longer afraid of fear, and I will not let it rule me.

Fear will learn to fear me.

EIGHTEEN

Adam leads me toward the couch, but Kenji intercepts us. "You guys can have your moment, I promise," he says, "but right now we all need to get on the same page, say hello and how are you and whatever whatever and we need to do it fast; Juliette has information everyone needs to hear."

Adam looks from Kenji to me. "What's going on?"

I turn to Kenji. "What are you talking about?"

He rolls his eyes at me. Looks away and says, "Have a seat, Kent."

Adam backs away—just an inch or two—his curiosity winning out for the moment, and Kenji tugs me forward so I'm standing in the middle of this tiny room. Everyone is staring at me like I might pull turnips out of my pants. "Kenji, what—"

"Alia, you remember Juliette," Kenji says, nodding at a slim blond girl sitting in a back corner of the room. She offers me a quick smile before looking away, blushing for no apparent reason. I remember her; she's the one who designed my custom knuckle braces—the intricate pieces I'd worn over my gloves both times we went out to battle. I'd never really paid close attention to her before, and I now realize it's because she tries to be invisible. She's a soft, sweet-looking girl with gentle brown eyes; she also happens to be an exceptional designer. I wonder how she developed her skill.

"Lily—you definitely remember Juliette," Kenji is saying to her. "We all broke into the storage compounds together." He glances at me. "You remember, right?"

I nod. Grin at Lily. I don't really know her, but I like her energy. She mock-salutes me, smiling wide as her springy brown curls fall into her face. "Nice to see you again," she says. "And thanks for not being dead. It sucks being the only girl around here."

Alia's blond head pops up for only a second before she retreats deeper into the corner.

"Sorry," Lily says, looking only slightly remorseful. "I meant the only *talking* girl around here. Please tell me you talk," she says to me.

"Oh, she talks," Kenji says, shooting me a look. "Cusses like a sailor, too."

"I do not cuss like a—"

"Brendan, Winston." Kenji cuts me off, pointing at the two guys sitting on the couch. "These two definitely don't require an introduction, but, as you can see," he says, "they look a little different now. Behold, the transformative powers of being held hostage by a bunch of sadistic bastards!" He flourishes a hand in their direction, his sarcasm accompanied by a brittle smile. "Now they look like a pair of wildebeests. But, you know, by comparison, I look like a damn king. So it's good news all around."

Winston points at my face. His eyes are a little unfocused, and he has to blink a few times before saying, "I like you. It's pretty nice you're not dead."

"I second that, mate." Brendan claps Winston on the shoulder but he's smiling at me. His eyes are still so very light blue, and his hair, so very white blond. But he has a huge gash running from his right temple down to his jawline, and it looks like it's only just beginning to scab up. I can't imagine where else he's hurt. What else Anderson must've done to both him and Winston. A sick, slithery feeling moves through me.

"It's so good to see you again," Brendan is saying, his British accent always surprising me. "Sorry we couldn't be a bit more presentable."

I offer them both a smile. "I'm so happy you're all right."

"Ian," Kenji says, gesturing to the tall, lanky guy perched on the arm of the couch. Ian Sanchez. I remember him as a guy on my assembly team when we broke into the storage compound, but more important, I know him to be one of the four guys who were kidnapped by Anderson's men. He, Winston, Brendan, and another guy named Emory.

We'd managed to get Ian and Emory back, but not Brendan and Winston. I remember Kenji saying that Ian and Emory were so messed up when we brought them in that even with the girls helping to heal them, it'd still taken them a while to recover. Ian looks okay to me now, but he, too, must've undergone some horrific things. And Emory clearly isn't here.

I swallow, hard, offering Ian what I'm hoping is a strong smile.

He doesn't smile back.

"How are you still alive?" he demands, with no preamble. "You don't look like anyone beat the shit out of you, so, I mean, no offense or whatever, but I don't trust you."

"We're getting to that part," Kenji says, cutting Adam off just as he begins to protest on my behalf. "She has a solid explanation, I promise. I already know all the details." He shoots Ian a sharp look, but Ian doesn't seem to notice. He's still staring at me, one eyebrow raised as if in challenge.

I cock my head at him, considering him closely.

Kenji snaps his fingers in front of my face. "Focus, princess, I'm already getting bored." He glances around the room, looking for anyone we might've missed for the reintroductions. "James," he says, his eyes landing on the upturned face of my only ten-year-old friend. "Anything you want to say to Juliette before we get started?"

James looks at me, his blue eyes bright below his sandy-blond hair. He shrugs. "I never thought you were dead," he says simply.

"Is that right?" Kenji says with a laugh.

James nods. "I had a feeling," he says, tapping his head.

Kenji grins. "All right, well, that's it. Let's get started."

"What about Ca—," I begin to say, but stop dead at the flicker of alarm that flits in and out of Kenji's features.

My gaze lands on Castle, studying his face in a way I hadn't when I first arrived.

Castle's eyes are unfocused, his eyebrows furrowed as if he's caught in an endlessly frustrating conversation with himself; his hands are knotted together in his lap. His hair has broken free of its always-perfect ponytail at the nape of his neck, and his dreads have sprung around his face, falling into his eyes. He's unshaven, and looks as though he's been dragged through mud; as though he sat down in that chair the moment he walked in and hasn't left it since.

And I realize that of the group of us, Castle has been hit the hardest.

Omega Point was his life. His dreams were in every brick, every echo of that space. And in one night, he lost everything. His hopes, his vision for the future, the entire community he strove to build. His only family.

Gone.

"He's had it really rough," Adam whispers to me, and I'm startled by his presence, not realizing he was standing beside me again. "Castle's been like that for a little while now."

My heart breaks.

I try to meet Kenji's eyes, try to apologize wordlessly, to tell him I understand. But Kenji won't look at me. It takes him a few moments to pull himself together, and only then does it hit me just how hard all of this must be for him right now. It's not just Omega Point. It's not just everyone he's lost, not just all the work that's been destroyed.

It's Castle.

Castle, who's been like a father to Kenji, his closest confidant, his dearest friend.

He's become a husk of who he was.

My heart feels weighed down by the depth of Kenji's pain; I wish so much that I could do something to help. To fix things. And in that moment I promise myself I will.

I'll do everything I can.

"All right." Kenji claps his hands together, nods a few times before taking a tight breath. "Everyone all warm and fuzzy? Good? Good." He nods again. "Now let me tell you the story of how our friend Juliette was shot in the chest."

NINETEEN

Everyone is gaping at me.

Kenji has just finished giving them every detail I shared with him, taking care to leave out the parts about Warner telling me he loves me, and I'm silently grateful. Even though I told Adam that he and I shouldn't be together anymore, everything between us is still so raw and unresolved. I've tried to move on, to distance myself from him because I wanted to protect him; but I've had to mourn Adam's loss in so many different ways now that I'm not sure I even know how to feel anymore.

I have no idea what he thinks of me.

There are so many things Adam and I need to talk about; I just don't want Warner to be one of them. Warner has always been a tense topic between us—especially now that Adam knows they're brothers—and I'm not in the mood for arguing, especially not on my first day back.

But it seems I won't be able to get off that easily.

"*Warner* saved your life?" Lily asks, not bothering to hide her shock or her repulsion. Even Alia is sitting up and paying attention now, her eyes glued to my face. "Why the hell would he do that?"

"Dude, forget that," Ian cuts in. "What are we going to

do about the fact that Warner can just steal our powers and shit?"

"You don't have any powers," Winston answers him. "So you don't have anything to worry about."

"You know what I mean," Ian snaps, a hint of color flushing up his neck. "It's not safe for a psycho like him to have that kind of ability. It freaks me the hell out."

"He's not a psych—," I try to say, but the room erupts into a cacophony of voices, all vying for a chance to be heard.

"What does this even mean—"

"—dangerous?"

"So Sonya and Sara are still *alive*—"

"—actually saw Anderson? What did he look like?"

"But why would he even—"

"—okay, but that's not—"

"WAIT," Adam cuts everyone off. "Where the hell is he *now*?" He turns to look me in the eye. "You said Warner brought you out here to show you what happened to Omega Point, but then the minute Kenji shows up, he just disappears." A pause. "Right?"

I nod.

"So—what?" he says. "He's done? He's just walking away?" Adam spins around, looks at everyone. "Guys, he knows that at least one of us is still alive! He's probably gone to get backup, to find a way to take the rest of us out—" He stops, shakes his head, hard. "Shit," he says under his breath. "SHIT."

Everyone freezes at the same time. Horrified.

"No," I say quickly, holding up both hands. "No—he's not going to do that—"

Eight pairs of eyes turn on me.

"He doesn't care about killing you guys. He doesn't even like The Reestablishment. And he hates his father—"

"What are you talking about?" Adam cuts me off, alarmed. "Warner is an *animal*—"

I take a steadying breath. I need to remember how little they know Warner, how little they've heard from his point of view; I have to remind myself what I used to think of him just a few days ago.

Warner's revelations are still so recent. I don't know how to properly defend him or how to reconcile these polarizing impressions of him, and for a moment it makes me furious with him and his stupid pretenses, for ever having put me in this position. If only he didn't come across as a sick, twisted psycho, I wouldn't have to stand up for him right now.

"He *wants* to take down The Reestablishment," I try to explain. "And he wants to kill Anderson, too—"

The room explodes into more arguments. Shouts and epithets that all boil down to no one believing me, everyone thinking I'm insane and that Warner's brainwashed me; they think he's a proven murderer who locked me up and tried to use me to torture people.

And they're not wrong. Except that they are.

I want so desperately to tell them they don't understand.

None of them know the truth, and they're not giving me a chance to explain. But just as I'm about to say something else in my own defense, I catch a glimpse of Ian out of the corner of my eye.

He's laughing at me.

Out loud, slapping his knee, head thrown back, howling with glee at what he thinks is my stupidity, and for a moment I seriously begin to doubt myself and everything Warner said to me.

I squeeze my eyes shut.

How will I ever really know if I can trust him? How do I know he wasn't lying to me like he always did, like he claims he has been from the beginning?

I'm so sick of this uncertainty. So sick and tired of it.

But I blink and I'm being pulled out of the crowd, tugged toward James's bedroom door; to the storage closet that used to be his room. Adam pulls me inside and shuts the door on the insanity behind us. He's holding my arms, looking into my eyes with a strange, burning intensity that startles me.

I'm trapped.

"What's going on?" he asks. "Why are you defending Warner? After everything he did to you, you should hate him—you should be furious—"

"I can't, Adam, I—"

"What do you mean you *can't*?"

"I just—it's not that easy anymore." I shake my head, try to explain the unexplainable. "I don't know what to think of him now. There are so many things I misunderstood. Things I couldn't comprehend." I drop my eyes. "He's really . . ." I hesitate, conflicted.

I don't know how to tell the truth without sounding like a liar.

"I don't know," I finally say, staring into my hands. "I don't know. He's just . . . he's not as bad as I thought."

"Wow." Adam exhales, shocked. *"He's not as bad as you thought.* He's not as bad as you thought? How on earth could he be any better than you *thought*—?"

"Adam—"

"What the hell are you *thinking*, Juliette?"

I look up. He can't hide the disgust in his eyes.

I panic.

I need to find a way to explain, to present an irrefutable example—proof that Warner is not who I thought he was—but I can already tell that Adam has lost confidence in me, that he doesn't trust me or believe me anymore, and I flounder.

He opens his mouth to speak.

I beat him to it. "Do you remember that day you found me crying in the shower? After Warner forced me to torture that toddler?"

Adam hesitates before nodding slowly, reluctantly.

"That was one of the reasons I hated him so much. I thought he'd actually put a child in that room—that he'd stolen someone's kid and wanted to watch me torture it. It was just so despicable," I say. "So disgusting, so horrifying. I thought he was inhuman. Completely evil. But . . . it wasn't real," I whisper.

Adam looks confused.

"It was just a simulation," I try to explain. "Warner told me it was a simulation chamber, not a torture room. He said it all happened in my imagination."

"Juliette," Adam says. Sighs. He looks away, looks back at me. "What are you talking about? Of course it was a simulation."

"What?"

Adam laughs a small, confused sort of laugh.

"You knew it wasn't real . . . ?" I ask.

He stares at me.

"But when you found me—you said it wasn't my fault—you told me you'd heard about what happened, and that it wasn't my fault—"

Adam runs a hand through the hair at the back of his neck. "I thought you were upset about breaking down that wall," he says. "I mean, I knew the simulation would probably be scary as hell, but I thought Warner would've told you what it was beforehand. I had no idea you'd walked into something like that thinking it was going to be real." He presses his eyes shut for a second. "I thought you were upset about learning you had this whole new crazy ability. And about the soldiers who were injured in the aftermath."

I'm blinking at him, stunned.

All this time, a small part of me was still holding on to doubt—believing that maybe the torture chamber *was* real and that Warner was just lying to me. Again.

But now, to have confirmation from Adam himself.

I'm floored.

Adam is shaking his head. "That bastard," he's saying. "I can't believe he did that to you."

I lower my eyes. "Warner's done a lot of crazy things," I say, "but he really thought he was helping me."

"But he wasn't helping you," Adam says, angry again. "He was *torturing* you—"

"No. That's not true." I focus my eyes on a crack in the wall. "In some strange way . . . he did help me." I hesitate before meeting Adam's gaze. "That moment in the simulation chamber was the first time I ever allowed myself to be angry. I never knew how much more I could do—that I could be so physically strong—until that moment."

I look away.

Clasp and unclasp my hands.

"Warner puts up this facade," I'm saying. "He acts like he's a sick, heartless monster, but he's . . . I don't know . . ." I trail off, my eyes trained on something I can't quite see. A memory, maybe. Of Warner smiling. His gentle hands wiping away my tears. *It's okay, you're okay,* he'd said to me. "He's really—"

"I don't, um—" Adam breaks away, blows out a strange, shaky breath. "I don't know how I'm supposed to understand this," he says, looking unsteady. "You—what? You like him now? You're friends with him? The same guy who tried to *kill* me?" He's barely able to conceal the pain in his voice. "He had me hung from a conveyor belt in a slaughterhouse, Juliette. Or have you already forgotten that?"

I flinch. Drop my head in shame.

I *had* forgotten about that.

I'd forgotten that Warner almost killed Adam, that he'd shot Adam right in front of my face. He saw Adam as a traitor, as a soldier who held a gun to the back of his head; defied him and stole me away.

It makes me sick.

"I'm just . . . I'm so confused," I finally manage to say. "I want to hate him but I just don't know how anymore—"

Adam is staring at me like he has no idea who I am.

I need to talk about something else.

"What's going on with Castle?" I ask. "Is he sick?"

Adam hesitates before answering, realizing I'm trying to change the subject. Finally, he relents. Sighs. "It's bad," he says to me. "He's been hit worse than the rest of us. And Castle taking it all so hard has really affected Kenji."

I study Adam's face as he speaks, unable to stop myself from searching for similarities to Anderson and Warner.

"He doesn't really leave that chair," Adam is saying. "He sits there all day until he collapses from exhaustion, and even then, he just falls asleep sitting in the same spot. Then he wakes up the next morning and does the same thing again, all day. He only eats when we force him to, and only moves to go to the bathroom." Adam shakes his head. "We're all hoping he'll snap out of it pretty soon, but it's been really weird to just lose a leader like that. Castle was in charge of everything. And now he doesn't seem to care about anything."

"He's probably still in shock," I say, remembering it's

only been three days since the battle. "Hopefully, with time," I tell him, "he'll be all right."

"Yeah," Adam says. Nods. Studies his hands. "But we really need to figure out what we're going to do. I don't know how much longer we can live like this. We're going to run out of food in a few weeks at the most," he says. "We've got ten people to feed now. Plus, Brendan and Winston are still hurting; I've done what I can for them using the limited supplies I have here, but they need actual medical attention and pain medication, if we can swing it." A pause. "I don't know what Kenji's told you, but they were seriously messed up when we brought them in here. Winston's swelling has only just gone down. We really can't stay here for much longer," he says. "We need a plan."

"Yes." I'm so relieved to hear he's ready to be proactive. "Yes. Yes. We need a plan. What are you thinking? Do you already have something in mind?"

Adam shakes his head. "I don't know," he admits. "Maybe we can keep breaking into the storage units like we used to—steal supplies every once in a while—and lie low in a bigger space on unregulated ground. But we'll never be able to set foot on the compounds," he says. "There's too much risk. They'll shoot us dead on sight if we're caught. So . . . I don't know," he says. He looks sheepish as he laughs. "I'm kind of hoping I'm not the only one with ideas."

"But . . ." I hesitate, confused. "That's it? You're not thinking of fighting back anymore? You think we should just find a way to live—like *this*?" I gesture to the door, to what lies beyond it.

Adam looks at me, surprised by my reaction.

"It's not like I *want* this," he says. "But I can't see how we could possibly fight back without getting ourselves killed. I'm trying to be practical." He runs an agitated hand through his hair. "I took a chance," he says, lowering his voice. "I tried to fight back, and it got us all massacred. I shouldn't even be alive right now. But for some crazy reason, I am, and so is James, and God, Juliette, so are you.

"And I don't know," he says, shaking his head, looking away. "I feel like I've been given a chance to live my life. I'll need to think of new ways to find food and put a roof over my head. I have no money coming in, I'll never be able to enlist in this sector again, and I'm not a registered citizen, so I'll never be able to work. Right now all I'm focused on is how I'll be able to feed my family and my friends in a few weeks." His jaw tenses. "Maybe one day another group will be smarter—stronger—but I don't think that's us anymore. I don't think we stand a chance."

I'm blinking at him, stunned. "I can't believe this."

"You can't believe what?"

"You're giving up." I hear the accusation in my voice and I do nothing to hide it. "You're just giving up."

"What choice do I have?" he asks, his eyes hurt, angry. "I'm not trying to be a martyr," he says. "We gave it a shot. We tried to fight back, and it came to shit. Everyone we know is dead, and that battered group of people you saw out there is all that's left of our resistance. How are the nine of us supposed to fight the world?" he demands. "It's not a fair fight, Juliette."

I'm nodding. Staring into my hands. Trying and failing to hide my shock.

"I'm not a coward," he says to me, struggling to moderate his voice. "I just want to protect my family. I don't want James to have to worry that I'm going to show up dead every day. He needs me to be rational."

"But living like this," I say to him. "As fugitives? Stealing to survive and hiding from the world? How is that any better? You'll be worried every single day, constantly looking over your shoulder, terrified of ever leaving James alone. You'll be miserable."

"But I'll be alive."

"That's not being alive," I say to him. "That's not living—"

"How would you know?" he snaps. His mood shifts so suddenly I'm stunned into silence. "What do you know about being alive?" he demands. "You wouldn't say a word when I first found you. You were afraid of your own shadow. You were so consumed by grief and guilt that you'd gone almost completely insane—living so far inside your own head that you had no idea what happened to the world while you were gone."

I flinch, stung by the venom in his voice. I've never seen Adam so bitter or cruel. This isn't the Adam I know. I want him to stop. Rewind. Apologize. Erase the things he's just said.

But he doesn't.

"You think you've had it hard," he's saying to me. "Living

in psych wards and being thrown in jail—you think that was difficult. But what you don't realize is that you've always had a roof over your head, and food delivered to you on a regular basis." His hands are clenching, unclenching. "And that's more than most people will ever have. You have no idea what it's really like to live out here—no idea what it's like to starve and watch your family die in front of you. You have no idea," he says to me, "what it means to truly suffer. Sometimes I think you live in some fantasy land where everyone survives on optimism—but it doesn't work that way out here. In this world you're either alive, about to die, or dead. There's no romance in it. No illusion. So don't try to pretend you have any idea what it means to be alive today. *Right now.* Because you don't."

Words, I think, are such unpredictable creatures.

No gun, no sword, no army or king will ever be more powerful than a sentence. Swords may cut and kill, but words will stab and stay, burying themselves in our bones to become corpses we carry into the future, all the time digging and failing to rip their skeletons from our flesh.

I swallow, hard

one

two

three

and steady myself to respond quietly. Carefully.

He's just upset, I'm telling myself. He's just scared and worried and stressed out and he doesn't mean any of it, not really, I keep telling myself.

He's just upset.

He doesn't mean it.

"Maybe," I say. "Maybe you're right. Maybe I don't know what it's like to live. Maybe I'm still not human enough to know more than what's right in front of me." I stare straight into his eyes. "But I do know what it's like to hide from the world. I know what it's like to live as though I don't exist, caged away and isolated from society. And I won't do it again," I say. "I can't. I've finally gotten to a point in my life where I'm not afraid to speak. Where my shadow no longer haunts me. And I don't want to lose that freedom—not again. I can't go backward. I'd rather be shot dead screaming for justice than die alone in a prison of my own making."

Adam looks toward the wall, laughs, looks back at me.

"Are you even hearing yourself right now?" he asks. "You're telling me you want to jump in front of a bunch of soldiers and tell them how much you hate The Reestablishment, just to prove a point? Just so they can kill you before your eighteenth birthday? That doesn't make any sense," he says. "It doesn't serve anything. And this doesn't sound like you," he says, shaking his head. "I thought you wanted to live on your own. You never wanted to be caught up in war—you just wanted to be free of Warner and the asylum and your crazy parents. I thought you'd be happy to be done with all the fighting."

"What are you talking about?" I say. "I've always said I wanted to fight back. I've said it from the beginning—from the moment I told you I wanted to escape when we were on base. This *is* me," I insist. "This is how I feel. It's the same way I've always felt."

"No," he says. "No, we didn't leave base to start a war. We left to get the hell away from The Reestablishment, to resist in our own way, but most of all to find a life together. But then Kenji showed up and took us to Omega Point and everything changed, and we decided to fight back. Because it seemed like it might actually work—because it seemed like we might actually have a chance. But now"—he looks around the room, at the closed door—"what do we have left? We're all half dead," he says. "We are eight poorly armed men and women and one ten-year-old boy trying to fight entire armies. It's just not *feasible,*" he says. "And if I'm going to die, I don't want it to be for a stupid reason. If I go to war—if I risk my life—it's going to be because the odds are in my favor. Not otherwise."

"I don't think it's stupid to fight for *humanity—*"

"You have no idea what you're saying," he snaps, his jaw tensing. "There's nothing we can do now."

"There's always something, Adam. There has to be. Because I won't live like this anymore. Not ever again."

"Juliette, please," he says, his words desperate all of a sudden, anguished. "I don't want you to get killed—I don't want to lose you again—"

"This isn't about you, Adam." I feel terrible saying it, but he has to understand. "You're so important to me. You've loved me and you were there for me when no one else was. I never want you to think I don't care about you, because

I do," I tell him. "But this decision has nothing to do with you. It's about *me,*" I tell him. "And this life"—I point to the door—"the life on the other side of that wall? That's not what I want."

My words only seem to upset him more.

"Then you'd rather be dead?" he asks, angry again. "Is that what you're saying? You'd rather be dead than try to build a life with me here?"

"I would rather be dead," I say to him, inching away from his outstretched hand, "than go back to being silent and suffocated."

And Adam is just about to respond—he's parting his lips to speak—when the sounds of chaos reach us from the other side of the wall. We share one panicked look before yanking the bedroom door open and rushing into the living room.

My heart stops. Starts. Stops again.

Warner is here.

TWENTY

He's standing at the front door, hands shoved casually in his pockets, no fewer than six different guns pointed at his face. My mind is racing as it tries to process what to do next, how best to proceed. But Warner's face changes seasons as I enter the room: the cold line of his mouth blossoms into a bright smile. His eyes shine as he grins at me, not seeming to mind or even notice the many lethal weapons aimed in his direction.

I can't help but wonder how he found me.

I begin to move forward but Adam grabs my arm. I turn around, wondering at my sudden irritation with him. I'm almost irritated with myself for being irritated with him. This is not how I imagined it would be to see Adam again. I don't want it to be this way. I want to start over.

"What are you doing?" Adam says to me. "Don't go near him."

I stare at his hand on my arm. Look up to meet his gaze.

Adam doesn't budge.

"Let go of me," I say to him.

His face clears all of a sudden, like he's startled, somehow. He looks down at his hand; releases me without a word.

I put as much space between us as I can, the whole time scanning the room for Kenji. His sharp black eyes meet mine immediately and he raises one eyebrow; his head is cocked to the side, the twitch of his lips telling me the next move is mine and I'd better make it count. I part my way through my friends until I'm standing in front of Warner, facing my friends and their guns and hoping they won't fire at me instead.

I make an effort to sound calm. "Please," I say. "Don't shoot him."

"And why the hell not?" Ian demands, his grip tightening around his gun.

"Juliette, love," Warner says, leaning into my ear. His voice is still loud enough for everyone to hear. "I do appreciate you defending me, but really, I'm quite able to handle the situation."

"It's eight against one," I say to him, forgetting my fear in the temptation to roll my eyes. "They've all got guns pointed at your face. I'm pretty sure you need my interference."

I hear him laugh behind me, just once, just before every gun in the room is yanked out of every hand and thrown up against the ceiling. I spin around in shock, catching a glimpse of the astonishment on every face behind me.

"Why do you always hesitate?" Warner asks, shaking his head as he glances around the room. "Shoot if you want to shoot. Don't waste my time with theatrics."

"How the hell did you do that?" Ian demands.

Warner says nothing. He tugs off his gloves carefully,

pulling at each finger before slipping them off his hands.

"It's okay," I tell him. "They already know."

Warner looks up. Raises an eyebrow at me. Smiles a little. "Do they really?"

"Yes. I told them."

Warner's smile changes into something almost self-mocking as he turns away, his eyes laughing as he contemplates the ceiling. Finally he nods at Castle, who's staring at the commotion with a vaguely displeased expression. "I borrowed," Warner says to Ian, "from present company."

"Hot damn," Ian breathes.

"What do you want?" Lily asks, fists clenched, standing in a far corner of the room.

"Nothing from you," Warner says to her. "I'm here to pick up Juliette. I have no wish to disturb your . . . slumber party," he says, looking around at the pillows and blankets piled on the living room floor.

Adam goes rigid with alarm. "What are you talking about? She's not going anywhere with you."

Warner scratches the back of his head. "Do you never get exhausted being so wholly unbearable? You have as much charisma as the rotting innards of unidentified roadkill."

I hear an abrupt wheezing noise and turn toward the sound.

Kenji has a hand pressed to his mouth, desperately trying to suppress a smile. He's shaking his head, holding up a hand in apology. And then he breaks, laughing out loud, snorting as he tries to muffle the sound. "I'm sorry," he says, pressing his lips together, shaking his head again. "This is not a funny moment. It's not. I'm not laughing."

Adam looks like he might punch Kenji in the face.

"So you don't want to kill us?" Winston says. "Because if you're not going to kill us, you should probably get the hell out of here before we kill you first."

"No," Warner says calmly. "I am not going to kill you. And though I wouldn't mind disposing of these two"—he nods at Adam and Kenji—"the idea is little more than exhausting to me now. I am no longer interested in your sad, pathetic lives. I am only here to accompany and transport Juliette safely home. She and I have urgent matters to attend to."

"No," I hear James say suddenly. He clambers to his feet, stares Warner straight in the eye. "*This* is her home now. You can't take her away. I don't want anyone to hurt her."

Warner's eyebrows fly up in surprise. He seems genuinely startled, as though he's only now noticing the ten-year-old. Warner and James have never actually met before; neither one of them knows they're brothers.

I look at Kenji. He looks back.

This is a big moment.

Warner studies James's face with rapt fascination. He bends down on one knee, meets James at eye level. "And who are you?" he asks.

Everyone in the room is silent, watching.

James blinks steadily and doesn't answer right away. He finally shoves his hands into his pockets and stares at the floor. "I'm James. Adam's brother. Who are you?"

Warner tilts his head a little. "No one of consequence," he says. He tries to smile. "But it's very nice to meet you, James. I'm pleased to see your concern for Juliette's safety. You should know, however, that I have no intention of hurting her. It's just that she's made me a promise, and I intend to see it through."

"What kind of promise?" James asks.

"Yeah, what kind of promise?" Kenji cuts in, his voice loud—and angry—all of sudden.

I look up, look around. Everyone is staring at me, waiting for me to answer. Adam's eyes are wide with horror and disbelief.

I meet Warner's gaze. "I'm not leaving," I tell him. "I never promised I would stay on base with you."

He frowns. "You'd rather stay *here*?" he asks. "Why?"

"I need my friends," I tell him. "And they need me. Besides, we're all going to have to work together, so we may as well get started now. And I don't want to have to be smuggled in and out of base," I add. "You can just meet me here."

"Whoa—wait—what do you mean we can all work together?" Ian interrupts. "And why are you inviting him to come back here? What the hell are you guys talking about?"

"What kind of promise did you make him, Juliette?" Adam's voice is loud and accusing.

I turn toward the group of them. Me, standing beside Warner, facing Adam's angry eyes along with the confused, soon-to-be-angry faces of my friends.

Oh how strange all of this has become in such a short period of time.

I take a tight, bracing breath.

"I'm ready to fight," I say, addressing the entire group. "I know some of you might feel defeated; some of you might think there's no hope left, especially not after what happened to Omega Point. But Sonya and Sara are still out there, and they need our help. So does the rest of the world. And I haven't come this far just to turn back now. I'm ready to take action and Warner has offered to help me."

I look directly at Kenji. "I've accepted his offer. I've promised to be his ally; to fight by his side; to kill Anderson and to take down The Reestablishment."

Kenji narrows his eyes at me and I can't tell if he's angry, or if he's really, really angry.

I look at the rest of my friends. "But we can all work together," I say.

"I've been thinking about this a lot," I go on, "and I think the group of us still has a chance, especially if we combine our strengths with Warner's. He knows things about The Reestablishment and his father that we'd never be able to know otherwise."

I swallow hard as I take in the shocked, horrified looks on the faces of those around me. "But," I hurry to say, "if you aren't interested in fighting back anymore, I totally understand. And if you'd rather I didn't stay here among you, I would respect your decision. Either way, I've already made my choice," I tell them. "Whether or not you choose to join me, I've decided to fight. I will take down The Reestablishment or I will die trying. There's nothing left for me otherwise."

TWENTY-ONE

The room is quiet for a long time. I've dropped my eyes, too afraid to see the looks on their faces.

Alia is the first to speak.

"I'll fight with you," she says, her soft voice ringing strong and confident in the silence. I look up to meet her eyes and she smiles, her cheeks flushed with color and determination.

But before I even have a chance to respond, Winston jumps in.

"Me too," he says. "As soon as my head stops hurting, but yeah, me too. I've got nothing left to lose," he says with a shrug. "And I'll kick some ass just to get the girls back, even if we can't save the rest of the world."

"Same," Brendan says, nodding at me. "I'm in, too."

Ian is shaking his head. "How the hell can we trust this guy?" he asks. "How do we know he's not full of shit?"

"Yeah," Lily pipes up. "This doesn't feel right." She focuses her eyes on Warner. "Why would you want to help any of us?" she asks him. "Since when have you ever been trustworthy?"

Warner runs a hand through his hair. Smiles unkindly. Glances at me.

He's not amused.

"I am *not* trustworthy," Warner finally says, looking up to meet Lily's eyes. "And I have no interest in helping you," he says. "In fact, I think I was very clear just a moment ago when I said that I was here for Juliette. I did not sign up to help her friends, and I will make zero guarantees for your survival or your safety. So if you're seeking reassurance," he says, "I can, and will, offer you none."

Ian is actually smiling.

Lily looks a little mollified.

Kenji is shaking his head.

"All right." Ian nods. "That's cool." He rubs his forehead. "So what's the game plan?"

"Have you all lost your *minds*?" Adam explodes. "Are you forgetting who you're talking to? He just busts down our door and demands to take Juliette away and you want to stand by his side and fight with him? The same guy who's responsible for destroying Omega Point?" he says. "Everyone is dead because of him!"

"I am not responsible for that," Warner says sharply, his expression darkening. "That was not my call, nor did I have any idea it was happening. By the time I broke out of Omega Point and found my way back to base, my father's plans were already under way. I was not a part of the battle, nor was I a part of the assault on Omega Point."

"It's true," Lily says. "The supreme is the one who ordered the air strike against Omega Point."

"Yeah, and as much as I hate this guy by default," Winston adds, jerking a thumb at Warner, "I hate his father a whole hell of a lot more. He's the one who kidnapped us. It was his men who held us captive; not the soldiers of Sector 45. So yeah," Winston says, stretching back on the couch, "I'd love to watch the supreme die a slow, miserable death."

"I have to admit," Brendan says, "I'm not often keen on revenge, but it does sound very sweet right now."

"I want to watch that bastard bleed," Ian says.

"How nice that we all have something in common," Warner mutters, irritated. He sighs. Looks at me. "Juliette, a word, please?"

"This is bullshit!" Adam shouts. He looks around. "How can you all so easily forget yourselves? How can you forget what he's done—what he did to me—what he did to Kenji?" Adam pivots to face me then. "How can you even look at him," he says to me, "knowing how he treated us? He nearly murdered me—leaving me to bleed out slowly so he could take his time torturing me to death—"

"Kent, man, please—you need to calm down, okay?" Kenji steps forward. "I understand that you're pissed—I'm not happy about this either—but things get crazy in the aftermath of war. Alliances form in unlikely ways." He shrugs. "If this is the only way to take Anderson out, maybe we should consider—"

"I can't believe this." Adam cuts him off, looking around. "I can't believe this is happening. You've all lost your minds. You're all *insane*," he says, gripping the back of his head. "This guy is a psycho—he's a *murderer*—"

"Adam," I try to say. "Please—"

"What's happened to you?" He turns on me. "I don't

even know who you are anymore. I thought you were dead—I thought *he'd* killed you," he says, pointing at Warner. "And now you're standing here, teaming up with the guy who tried to ruin your life? Talking about fighting back because you have nothing left to live for? What about *me*?" he demands. "What about our relationship? When did that stop being enough for you?"

"This isn't about us," I try to tell him. "Please, Adam—let me explain—"

"I have to get out of here," he says abruptly, moving toward the door. "I can't be here right now—I can't process all of this in one day. It's too much," he says. "It's too much for me—"

"Adam—" I catch his arm in one last attempt, one last effort to try and talk to him, but he breaks away.

"All of this," he says, meeting my eyes, his voice quieting to a raw, aching whisper, "was for you. I left everything I knew because I thought we were in this together. I thought it was going to be me and you." His eyes are so dark, so deep, so hurt. Looking at him makes me want to curl up and die. "What are you doing?" he says, desperate now. "What are you *thinking*?"

And I realize he actually wants an answer.

Because he waits.

He stands there, and he waits. Waits to hear my response while everyone watches us, likely entertained by the spectacle we've made. I can't believe he's doing this to me. Here. Right now. In front of everyone.

In front of *Warner.*

I try to meet Adam's eyes, but find I can't hold his gaze for very long.

"I don't want to live in fear anymore," I say, hoping I sound stronger than I feel. "I have to fight back," I tell him. "I thought we wanted the same things."

"No—I wanted *you,*" he says, struggling to keep his voice steady. "That's all I wanted. From the very beginning, Juliette. You were it. You were all I wanted."

And I can't speak.

I can't speak

I can't cough up the words because I can't break his heart like this but he's waiting, he's waiting and he's looking at me and "I need more," I choke out. "I wanted you, too, Adam, but I need more than that. I need to be free. Please, try to understand—"

"STOP!" Adam explodes. "Stop trying to get me to understand a bunch of *bullshit*! I can't deal with you anymore." And then he grabs the jacket sitting on the sofa, hauls the door open, and slams it shut behind him.

There's a moment of absolute silence.

I try to run after him.

Kenji catches me around the waist, yanks me backward. Gives me a hard, knowing look. "I'll take care of Kent. You stay here and clean up the mess you made," he says, cocking his head at Warner.

I swallow, hard. Don't say a word.

It's only after Kenji has disappeared that I turn around

to face the remaining members of our audience, and I'm still searching for the right thing to say when I hear the one voice I least expected.

"Ah, Ms. Ferrars," Castle says. "It's so good to have you back. Things are always so much more entertaining when you're around."

Ian bursts into tears.

TWENTY-TWO

Everyone crowds around Castle at once; James practically tackles him. Ian shoves everyone else out of the way in his attempt to get closer. Castle is smiling, laughing a little. He finally looks more like the man I remember.

"I'm all right," he's saying. He sounds exhausted, as if the words are costing him a great deal to get out. "Thank you so much for your concern. But I'll be all right. I just need a little more time, that's all."

I meet his eyes. I'm afraid to approach him.

"Please," Castle says to Alia and Winston—the two standing closest on either side of him—"help me up. I'd like to greet our newest visitor."

He's not talking about me.

Castle gets to his feet with some difficulty, even with everyone scrambling to help him. The entire room suddenly feels different: lighter; happier, somehow. I hadn't realized how much of everyone's grief was tied up in Castle's well-being.

"Mr. Warner," Castle says, locking eyes with him from across the room. "How very nice of you to join us."

"I'm not joining anyth—"

"I always knew you would," Castle says. He smiles a little. "And I am pleased."

Warner seems to be trying not to roll his eyes.

"You may let the guns down now," Castle says to him. "I promise I will watch them closely in your absence."

We all glance up at the ceiling. I hear Warner sigh. All at once, the guns float to the floor, settling gently onto the carpet.

"Very good," Castle says. "Now, if you'll excuse me, I think I'm in desperate need of a long shower. I hope you won't mistake my early exit for rudeness," he adds. "It's only that I feel quite certain we'll be seeing a lot of each other in these next weeks."

Warner's jaw tenses by way of response.

Castle smiles.

Winston and Brendan help Castle to the bathroom, while Ian shouts eagerly about grabbing him a change of clothes. Me, Warner, James, Alia, and Lily are the only ones left in the room.

"Juliette?" Warner says.

I glance in his direction.

"A moment of your time, please? In private?"

I hesitate.

"You can use my room," James interjects. "I don't mind."

I look at him, shocked he'd offer up his personal space so freely to the likes of me and Warner; especially after having seen his brother's outburst just now.

"Adam will be okay," James says to me, as if reading my mind. "He's just really stressed out. He's worried about a lot of things. He thinks we're going to run out of food and stuff."

"James—"

"It's really okay," James says. "I'll hang out with Alia and Lily."

I glance at the two girls, but their faces reveal nothing. Alia offers me only the slightest of sympathetic smiles. Lily is staring at Warner, sizing him up.

I finally sigh, relenting.

I follow Warner into the small storage closet, closing the door behind me.

He doesn't waste any time.

"Why are you inviting your friends to join us? I told you I didn't want to work with them."

"How did you find me?" I counter. "I never pressed the button on that pager you gave me."

Warner studies my eyes, his sharp green gaze locked on to mine as if trying to read me for clues. But the intensity of his gaze is always too much for me; I break the connection too soon, feeling untethered, somehow.

"It was simple deductive reasoning," he finally says. "Kent was the only member of your group with a life outside of Omega Point; his old home was the only place they'd have been able to retreat to without causing a disturbance. And, as such," Warner says, "it was the first place I checked." A slight shake of his head. "Contrary to what you might believe, love, I am not an idiot."

"I never thought you were an idiot," I say, surprised. "I thought you were crazy," I tell him, "but not an idiot." I hesitate. "I actually think you're brilliant," I confess. "I wish

I could think like you." I look away and look back at him too quickly, feeling a lot like I need to learn to keep my mouth shut.

Warner's face clears. His eyes crinkle in amusement as he smiles. "I don't want your friends on my team," he says. "I don't like them."

"I don't care."

"They will only slow us down."

"They will give us an advantage," I insist. "I know you don't think they did things the right way at Omega Point, but they did know how to survive. They all have important strengths."

"They're completely broken."

"They're grieving," I tell him, annoyed. "Don't underestimate them. Castle is a natural leader," I say. "Kenji is a genius and an excellent fighter. He acts like an idiot sometimes, but you know better than anyone else that it's just a show. He's smarter than all of us. Plus, Winston and Alia can design anything we need as long as they have the materials; Lily has an incredible photographic memory; Brendan can handle electricity and Winston can stretch his limbs into just about anything. And Ian . . ." I falter. "Well, Ian is . . . good for something, I'm sure."

Warner laughs a little, his smile softening until it disappears altogether. His features settle into an uncertain expression. "And Kent?" Warner finally asks.

I feel my face pale. "What about him?"

"What is he good for?"

I hesitate before answering. "Adam is a great soldier."

"Is that all?"

My heart is pounding so hard. Too hard.

Warner looks away, carefully neutralizes his expression, his tone. "You care for him."

It's not a question.

"Yes," I manage to say. "Of course I do."

"And what does that entail, exactly?"

"I don't know what you mean," I lie.

Warner is staring at the wall, holding himself very still, his eyes revealing nothing of what he's really thinking, what he's feeling. "Do you love him?"

I'm stunned.

I can't even imagine what it must cost him to ask this question so directly. I almost admire him for being brave enough to do it.

But for the first time, I'm not really sure what to say. If this were one week ago, two weeks ago, I would've answered without hesitation. I would've known, definitively, that I loved Adam, and I wouldn't have been afraid to say so. But now I can't help but wonder if I even know what love is; if what I felt for Adam was love or just a mix of deep affection and physical attraction. Because if I loved him—if I really, truly loved him—would I hesitate now? Would I so easily be able to detach myself from his life? His pain?

I've worried so much about Adam these past weeks—the effects of his training, the news of his father—but I don't know if it's been out of love, or if it's been out of guilt. He left everything for me; because he wanted to be with me. But as much as it pains me to admit it, I know I didn't run away to be with him. Adam wasn't my main reason; he wasn't the driving force.

I ran away for me. Because I wanted to be free.

"Juliette?"

Warner's soft whisper brings me back to the present, hauls me up and into myself, jarring my consciousness back to reality. I'm afraid to dwell on the truths I've just uncovered.

I meet Warner's eyes. "Yes?"

"Do you love him?" he asks again, more quietly this time.

And I suddenly have to force myself to say three words I never, ever thought I'd say. "I don't know."

Warner closes his eyes.

He exhales, the tension clear in his shoulders and in the line of his jaw and when he finally looks at me again there are stories in his eyes, thoughts and feelings and whispers of things I've never even seen before. Truths he might never bring himself to say; impossible things and unbelievable things and an abundance of feeling I've never thought him capable of. His whole body seems to relax in relief.

I don't know this boy standing before me. He's a perfect stranger, an entirely different being; the type of person I might never have known if my parents hadn't tossed me away.

"Juliette," he whispers.

I'm only now realizing just how close he is. I could press my face against his neck if I wanted to. Could place my hands on his chest if I wanted to.

If I wanted to.

"I'd really love for you to come back with me," he says.

"I can't," I say to him, heart racing suddenly. "I have to stay here."

"But it's not practical," he says. "We need to plan. We need to talk strategy—it could take days—"

"I already have a plan."

His eyebrows fly up and I tilt my head, fixing him with a hard look before I reach for the door.

TWENTY-THREE

Kenji is waiting on the other side.

"What the *hell* do you two think you're doing?" he says. "Get your asses out here, *right now*."

I head straight into the living room, eager to put distance between me and whatever keeps happening to my head when Warner gets too close. I need air. I need a new brain. I need to jump out of a window and catch a ride with a dragon to a world far from here.

But the moment I look up and try to steady myself, I find Adam staring at me. Blinking like he's starting to see something he wishes he could unsee, and I feel my face flush so fast that for a moment I'm surprised I'm not standing in a toilet.

"Adam," I hear myself say. "No—it's not—"

"I can't even talk to you right now." He's shaking his head, his voice strangled. "I can't even be near you right now—"

"Please," I try to say. "We were just talking—"

"You were just *talking*? Alone? In my brother's bedroom?" He's holding his jacket in his hands. He tosses it onto the couch. Laughs like he might be losing his mind. Runs a hand through his hair and glances up at the ceiling.

Stares back at me. "What the hell is going on, Juliette?" he asks, his jaw tensing. "What is happening right now?"

"Can't we talk about this in private—?"

"No." His chest is heaving. "I want to talk about this right now. I don't care who hears it."

My eyes immediately go to Warner. He's leaning against the wall just outside James's room, arms crossed loosely at his chest. He's watching Adam with a calm, focused interest.

Warner stills suddenly, as if he can feel my eyes on him.

He looks up, looks at me for exactly two seconds before turning away. He seems to be laughing.

"Why do you keep looking at him?" Adam demands, eyes flashing. "Why are you even looking at him at all? Why are you so interested in some demented *psycho*—"

I'm so tired of this.

I'm tired of all the secrets and all my inner turmoil and all the guilt and confusion I've felt over these two brothers. More than anything else, I don't like this angry Adam in front of me.

I try to talk to him and he won't listen to me. I try to reason with him and he attacks me. I try to be honest with him and he won't believe me. I have no idea what else to do.

"What's really going on between you guys?" Adam is still asking me. "What's *really* happening, Juliette? I need you to stop lying to me—"

"Adam." I cut him off. I'm surprised by how calm I sound. "There's so much we need to be discussing right now," I say to him, "and this isn't it. Our personal problems don't need to be shared with everyone."

"So you admit it then?" he says, somehow angrier. "That we have problems, that something is wrong—"

"Something's been wrong for a while," I say, exasperated. "I can't even talk to y—"

"Yeah, ever since we dragged this asshole back to Omega Point," Adam says. He turns to glare at Kenji. "It was *your* idea—"

"Hey, don't pull me into your bullshit, okay?" Kenji counters. "Don't blame me for your issues."

"We were fine until she started spending so much goddamn time with him—," Adam begins to say.

"She spent just as much time with him while we were still on base, genius—"

"*Stop,*" I say. "Please understand: Warner is here to help us. He wants to take down The Reestablishment and kill the supreme just like we do—he's not our enemy anymore—"

"He's going to *help* us?" Adam asks, eyes wide, feigning surprise. "Oh, you mean just like he helped us the last time he said he was going to fight on our side? Right before he broke out of Omega Point and *bailed*?" Adam laughs out loud, disbelieving. "I can't believe you're falling for all of his *bullshit*—"

"This isn't some kind of trick, Adam—I'm not stupid—"

"Are you sure?"

"What?" I can't believe he just insulted me.

"I asked you if you were sure," he snaps. "Because you're

acting pretty damn stupid right now, so I don't know if I can trust your judgment anymore."

"What is *wrong* with you—"

"What's wrong with *you?*" he shouts back, eyes blazing. "You don't do this. You don't act like this," he says. "You're like a completely different person—"

"Me?" I demand, my voice rising. I've been trying so hard to control my temper but I just don't think I can anymore. He says he wants to have this conversation in front of everyone?

Fine.

We'll have this conversation in front of everyone.

"If I've changed," I say to him, "then so have you. Because the Adam I remember is kind and gentle and he'd never insult me like this. I know things have been rough for you lately, and I'm trying to understand, to be patient, to give you space—but these last few weeks have been rough on all of us. We're all going through a hard time but we don't put each other down. We don't hurt each other. But you can't even be nice to Kenji," I tell him. "You used to be *friends* with Kenji, remember? Now every time he so much as cracks a joke you look at him like you want to kill him, and I don't know why—"

"You're going to defend everyone in this room except for me, aren't you?" Adam says. "You love Kenji so much, you spend all your goddamn time with Kenji—"

"He's my friend!"

"I'm your boyfriend!"

"No," I tell him. "You're not."

Adam is shaking, fists clenched. "I can't even believe you right now."

"We broke up, Adam." My voice is steady. "We broke up a month ago."

"Right," Adam says. "We broke up because you said you loved me. Because you said you didn't want to hurt me."

"I don't," I tell him. "I don't want to hurt you. I've never wanted to hurt you."

"What the hell do you think you're doing right now?" he shouts.

"I don't know how to talk to you," I tell him, shaking my head. "I don't understand—"

"No—you don't understand anything," he snaps. "You don't understand me, you don't understand yourself, and you don't understand that you're acting like a stupid child who's allowed herself to be brainwashed by a psychopath."

Time seems to stand still.

Everything I want to say and everything I've wished to say begins to take shape, falling to the floor and scrambling upright. Paragraphs and paragraphs begin building walls around me, blocking and justifying as they find ways to fit together, linking and weaving and leaving no room for escape. And every single space between every unspoken word clambers up and into my open mouth, down my throat and into my chest, filling me with so much emptiness I think I might just float away.

I'm breathing.

So hard.

A throat clears.

"Yes, right, I'm really sorry to interrupt," Warner says, stepping forward. "But Juliette, I need to get going. Are you sure you want to stay here?"

I freeze.

"GET OUT," Adam shouts. "Get the hell out of my house, you piece of shit. And don't come back here."

"Well," Warner says, cocking his head at me. "Never mind. It looks like you don't really have a choice." He holds out his hand. "Shall we?"

"You're not taking her anywhere." Adam turns on him. "She's not leaving with you, and she's not partnering up with you. Now get lost."

"Adam. STOP." My voice is angrier than I mean it to be, but I can't help it anymore. "I don't need your permission. I'm not going to live like this. I'm not hiding anymore. You don't have to come with me—you don't even have to understand," I tell him. "But if you loved me, you wouldn't stand in my way."

Warner is smiling.

Adam notices.

"Is there something you want to say?" Adam turns on him.

"God, no," Warner says. "Juliette doesn't require my assistance. And *you* might not have realized it yet, but it's obvious to everyone else that you've lost this fight, Kent."

Adam snaps.

He charges forward, fist pulled back and ready to swing, and it all happens so quickly I only have time to gasp before I hear a sharp crack.

Adam's fist is frozen only inches from Warner's face. It's caught in Warner's hand.

Adam is shocked into silence, his whole body shaking from the unspent energy. Warner leans into his brother's face, whispers, "You really don't want to fight me, you idiot," and hurls Adam's fist back with so much force that Adam flies backward, catching himself just before hitting the floor.

Adam is up. Bolting across the room. Angrier.

Kenji tackles him.

Adam is shouting for Kenji to let him go, to stop getting involved, and Kenji is yanking Adam across the room against his will. He somehow manages to haul open the front door, and pulls himself and Adam outside.

The door slams shut behind them.

TWENTY-FOUR

James, is my first thought.

I spin around, searching the room for him, hoping he's all right, only to find that Lily has already had the foresight to take him into his room.

Everyone else is staring at me.

"What the hell was that?" Ian is the first to break the silence.

He, Brendan, and Winston are all gaping at me. Alia is standing off to the side, arms wrapped around her body. Castle must still be in the shower.

I flinch as someone touches my shoulder.

Warner.

He leans into my ear, speaking softly so only I can hear him. "It's getting late, love, and I really must get back to base." A pause. "And I'm sorry to keep asking, but are you certain you want to stay here?"

I look up to meet his eyes. Nod. "I need to talk to Kenji," I tell him. "I don't know how everyone else feels anymore, but I don't want to do this without Kenji." I hesitate. "I mean, I can," I say, "if I have to. But I don't want to."

Warner nods. Looks past me at a point behind my head. "Right." He frowns a little. "I expect one day you'll tell me what you find so incredibly appealing about him?"

"Who? Kenji?"

Another nod.

"Oh," I say, blinking in surprise. "He's my best friend."

Warner looks at me. Raises an eyebrow.

I stare back. "Is that going to be a problem?"

He stares into his hands, shakes his head. "No, of course not," he says quietly. He clears his throat. "So, I'll come back tomorrow? Thirteen hundred hours."

"Thirteen hundred hours . . . from *now*?"

Warner laughs. Looks up. "One o'clock in the afternoon."

"Okay."

He looks into my eyes then. Smiles for just a moment too long before he turns around and walks out the door. Without a word to anyone.

Ian is gaping at me. Again.

"I'm—right, I'm so confused," Brendan says, blinking. "Right then—what just happened? Was he *smiling* at you? Genuinely smiling at you?"

"Looked to me like he was in love with you," Winston says, frowning. "But that's probably just because my head is messed up, right?"

I'm doing my best to look at the wall.

Kenji slams the front door open.

Steps inside.

Alone.

"You," he says, pointing at me, eyes narrowed. "Get your ass over here, right now. You and me," he says, "we need to talk."

TWENTY-FIVE

I shuffle over to the door and Kenji grabs my arm to lead me outside. He turns back and shouts, "Get yourselves some dinner" to everyone else, just before we leave.

We're standing on the landing just outside Adam's house, and I realize for the first time that there are more stairwells leading up. To somewhere.

"Come on, princess," Kenji says. "Follow me."

And we climb.

Four, five flights of stairs. Maybe eight. Or fifty. I have no idea. All I know is that by the time we reach the top I'm both out of breath and embarrassed for being out of breath.

When I'm finally able to inhale normally, I chance a look around.

Incredible.

We're on the roof, outside, where the world is pitch-black but for the stars and the sliver of moon someone has hung from the sky. Sometimes I wonder if the planets are still up there, still aligned, still managing to get along after all this time. Maybe we could learn a thing or two from them.

The wind tangles around us and I shiver as my body adjusts to the temperature.

"Come here," Kenji says to me. He motions to the ledge

of the roof, and sits down right on the edge, legs swinging over what would be his fastest path to death. “Don't worry,” he says when he sees my face. “It'll be fine. I sit here a lot.”

When I'm finally sitting next to him, I dare to look down. My feet are dangling from the top of the world.

Kenji drops an arm around me. Rubs my shoulder to keep me warm.

“So,” he says. “When's the big day? Have you set a date yet?”

“What?” I startle. “For what?”

“For the day you're going to stop being such a *dumbass*,” he says, shooting me a sharp look.

“Oh.” I cringe. Kick at the air. “Yeah, that'll probably never happen.”

“Yeah, you're probably right.”

“Shut up.”

“You know,” he says, “I don't know where Adam is.”

I stiffen. Sit up. “Is he okay?”

“He'll be fine,” Kenji says with a resigned sigh. “He's just super pissed off. And hurt. And embarrassed. And all that emotional shit.”

I drop my eyes again. Kenji's arm hangs loosely around my neck, and he pulls me closer, tucking me into his side. I rest my head on his chest.

Moments and minutes and memories build and break between us.

“I really thought you guys were solid,” Kenji finally says to me.

"Yeah," I whisper. "Me too."

A few seconds jump off the roof.

"I'm such a horrible person," I say, so quietly.

"Yeah, well." Kenji sighs.

I groan. Drop my head into my hands.

Kenji sighs again. "Don't worry, Kent was being an asshole, too." He takes a deep breath. "But damn, princess." Kenji looks at me, shakes his head an inch, looks back into the night. "Seriously? *Warner?*"

I look up. "What are you talking about?"

Kenji raises an eyebrow at me. "I know for a fact that you're not stupid, so please don't act like you are."

I roll my eyes. "I really don't want to have this conversation again—"

"I don't care if you don't want to have this conversation again. You have to talk about this. You can't just fall for a guy like Warner without telling me why. I need to make sure he didn't stick a chip in your head or someshit."

I'm silent for almost a full minute.

"I'm not falling for Warner," I say quietly.

"Sure you aren't."

"I'm not," I insist. "I'm just—I don't know." I sigh. "I don't know what's happening to me."

"They're called hormones."

I shoot him a dirty look. "I'm serious."

"Me too." He cocks his head at me. "That's like, biological and shit. Scientific. Maybe your lady bits are scientifically confused."

"My *lady bits?*"

"Oh, I'm sorry"—Kenji pretends to look offended—"would you rather I use the proper anatomical terminology? Because your lady bits do not scare me—"

"Yeah, no thanks." I manage to laugh a little, my sad attempt dissolving into a sigh.

God, everything is changing.

"He's just . . . so different," I hear myself say. "Warner. He's not what you guys think. He's sweet. And kind. And his father is so, so horrible to him. You can't even imagine," I trail off, thinking of the scars I saw on Warner's back. "And more than anything else . . . I don't know," I say, staring into the darkness. "He really . . . believes in me?" I glance up at Kenji. "Does that sound stupid?"

Kenji shoots me a doubtful look. "Adam believes in you, too."

"Yeah," I say, looking into the darkness. "I guess."

"What do you mean, *you guess*? The kid thinks you invented air."

I almost smile. "I don't know which version of me Adam likes. I'm not the same person I was when we were in school. I'm not that girl anymore. I think he wants that," I say, glancing up at Kenji. "I think he wants to pretend I'm the girl who doesn't really speak and spends most of her time being scared. The kind of girl he needs to protect and take care of all the time. I don't know if he likes who I am now. I don't know if he can handle it."

"So the minute you opened your mouth you just shattered all his dreams, huh?"

"I will push you off the roof."

"Yeah, I can definitely see why Adam wouldn't like you."

I roll my eyes.

Kenji laughs. Leans back and pulls me down with him. The concrete is under our heads now, the sky draped all around us. It's like I've been dropped into a vat of ink.

"You know, it actually makes a lot of sense," Kenji finally says.

"What does?"

"I don't know, I mean—you've been locked up basically forever, right? It's not like you were busy touching a bunch of dudes your whole life."

"What?"

"Like—Adam was the first guy who was ever . . . nice to you. Hell, he was probably the first person in the world who was nice to you. And he can touch you. And he's not, you know, disgusting looking." A pause. "I can't blame you, to be honest. It's hard being lonely. We all get a little desperate sometimes."

"Okay," I say slowly.

"I am just saying," Kenji says, "that I guess it makes sense you'd fall for him. Like, by default. Because if not him, who else? Your options were super limited."

"Oh," I say, quietly now. "Right. By *default*." I try to laugh and fail, swallowing hard against the emotion caught in my throat. "Sometimes I'm not sure I even know what's real anymore."

"What do you mean?"

I shake my head. "I don't know," I whisper, mostly to myself.

A heavy pause.

"Did you really love him . . . ?"

I hesitate before answering. "I think so? I don't know?" I sigh. "Is it possible to love someone and then stop loving them? I don't think I even know what love is."

Kenji blows out a breath. Runs a hand through his hair. "Well shit," he mutters.

"Have you ever been in love?" I ask, turning on my side to look at him.

He stares up at the sky. Blinks a few times. "Nope."

I roll back, disappointed. "Oh."

"This is so depressing," Kenji says.

"Yeah."

"We suck."

"Yeah."

"So tell me again why you like Warner so much? Did he, like, take all his clothes off or something?"

"What?" I gasp, so glad it's too dark for him to see me blushing. "No," I say quickly. "No, he—"

"Damn, princess." Kenji laughs, hard. "I had no idea."

I punch him in the arm.

"Hey—be gentle with me!" he protests, rubbing at the sore spot. "I'm weaker than you!"

"You know, I can sort of control it now," I tell him, beaming. "I can moderate my strength levels."

"Good for you. I'll buy you a balloon the minute the world stops shitting on itself."

"Thank you," I say, pleased. "You're a good teacher."

"I'm good at everything," he points out.

"Humble, too."

"And really good-looking."

I choke on a laugh.

"You still haven't answered my question," Kenji says. He shifts, folds his hands behind his head. "Why do you like the rich boy so much?"

I take a tight breath. Focus on the brightest star in the sky. "I like the way I feel about myself when I'm with him," I say quietly. "Warner thinks I'm strong and smart and capable and he actually values my opinion. He makes me feel like his equal—like I can accomplish just as much as he can, and more. And if I do something incredible, he's not even surprised. He *expects* it. He doesn't treat me like I'm some fragile little girl who needs to be protected all the time."

Kenji snorts.

"That's because you're not fragile," Kenji says. "If anything, everyone needs to protect themselves from *you*. You're like a freaking beast," he says. Then adds, "I mean, you know—like, a cute beast. A little beast that tears shit up and breaks the earth and sucks the life out of people."

"Nice."

"I'm here for you."

"I can tell."

"So that's it?" Kenji says. "You just like him for his personality, huh?"

"What?"

"All of this," Kenji says, waving a hand in the air, "has nothing to do with him being all sexy and shit and him being able to touch you all the time?"

"You think Warner is sexy?"

"That is not what I said."

I laugh. "I do like his face."

"And the touching?"

"What touching?"

Kenji looks at me, eyes wide, eyebrows up. "I am not Adam, okay? You can't bullshit me with your innocent act. You tell me this guy can touch you, and that he's into you, and you're clearly into him, and you spent the night in his bed last night, and then I walk in on the two of you in a freaking closet—no wait, I'm sorry, not a closet—a *child's bedroom*—and you're telling me there has been *zero* touching?" He stares at me. "Is that what you're telling me?"

"No," I whisper, face on fire.

"You're just growing up so quickly. You're getting all excited about being able to touch shit for the first time, and I just want to be sure you are observing sanitary regulations—"

"Stop being so disgusting."

"Hey—I'm just looking out for y—"

"Kenji?"

"Yeah?"

I take a deep breath. Try to count the stars. "What am I going to do?"

"About what?"

I hesitate. "About everything."

Kenji makes a strange sound. "Shit if I know."

"I don't want to do this without you," I whisper.

He leans back. "Who said you're going to do anything without me?"

My heart skips a few beats. I stare at him.

"What?" he asks. Raises his eyebrows. "You're surprised?"

"You'll fight with me?" I ask him, hardly breathing. "Fight back with me? Even if it's with Warner?"

Kenji smiles. Looks up at the sky. "Hell yeah," he says.

"Really?"

"I'm here for you, kid. That's what friends are for."

TWENTY-SIX

When we make it back to the house, Castle is standing in the far corner, talking to Winston.

Kenji freezes in the doorframe.

I'd forgotten Kenji hadn't had a chance to see Castle on his feet yet, and I feel a true ache as I look at him. I'm a terrible friend. All I do is dump my problems on him, never thinking to ask him about his own. He must have so much on his mind.

Kenji moves across the room in a daze, not stopping until he reaches Castle. He puts a hand on his shoulder. Castle turns around. The whole room stops to watch.

Castle smiles. Nods, just once.

Kenji pulls him into a fierce hug, holding on for only a few seconds before breaking away. The two stare at each other with some kind of silent recognition. Castle rests a hand on Kenji's arm.

Kenji grins.

And then he spins around and smiles at me, and I'm suddenly so happy, so relieved and thrilled and overjoyed that Kenji gets to sleep with a lighter heart tonight. I feel like I might burst from happiness.

The door slams open.

I turn around.

Adam steps inside.

My heart deflates.

Adam doesn't even look at me as he walks in. "James," he says, crossing the room. "Let's go, buddy. It's time for bed."

James nods and darts into his bedroom. Adam follows him in. The door closes behind them.

"He's home," Castle says. He looks relieved.

No one says anything for a second.

"All right, we should get ready for bed, too," Kenji says, looking around. He walks over to the corner and grabs a stack of blankets. Passes them out.

"Does everyone sleep on the floor?" I ask.

Kenji nods. "Yeah," he says. "Warner wasn't wrong. It really is like a slumber party."

I try to laugh.

Can't.

Everyone gets busy setting up blankets on the ground. Winston, Brendan, and Ian take over one side of the room, Alia and Lily the other. Castle sleeps on the couch.

Kenji points to the middle. "You and me go there."

"Romantic."

"You wish."

"Where does Adam sleep?" I ask, lowering my voice.

Kenji stops midway through tossing down a blanket. Looks up. "Kent's not coming back out," he says to me. "He sleeps with James. Poor kid has really bad nightmares every night."

"Oh," I say, surprised and ashamed of myself for not remembering this. "Of course." Of course he does. Kenji must know this firsthand, too. They all used to room together at Omega Point.

Winston hits a switch. The lights go out. There's a rustle of blankets. "If I hear any of you talk," Winston says, "I will personally send Brendan over to kick you in the face."

"I am not going to kick anyone in the face."

"Kick yourself in the face, Brendan."

"I don't even know why we're friends."

"Please shut up," Lily shouts from her corner.

"You heard the lady," Winston says. "Everyone shut up."

"You're the one talking, dumbass," Ian says.

"Brendan, kick him in the face, please."

"Shut up, mate, I am not kicking any—"

"*Good night,*" Castle says.

Everyone stops breathing.

"Good night, sir," Kenji whispers.

I roll over so I'm face-to-face with Kenji. He grins at me in the dark. I grin back.

"Good night," I mouth.

He winks at me.

My eyes fall shut.

TWENTY-SEVEN

Adam is ignoring me.

He hasn't said a word about yesterday; doesn't betray even a hint of anger or frustration. He talks to everyone, laughs with James, helps get breakfast together. He also pretends I don't exist.

I tried saying good morning to him and he pretended not to hear me. Or maybe he really didn't hear me. Maybe he's managed to train his brain not to hear or see me at all anymore.

I feel like I'm being punched in the heart.

Repeatedly.

"So what do you guys do all day?" I ask, trying desperately to make conversation. We're all sitting on the floor, eating bowls of granola. We woke up late, ate breakfast late. No one has bothered to clean up the blankets yet, and Warner is supposed to be here in about an hour.

"Nothing," Ian says.

"We try not to die, mostly," Winston says.

"It's boring as hell," Lily says.

"Why?" Kenji asks. "You have something in mind?"

"Oh," I say. "No, I just . . ." I hesitate. "Well, Warner's going to be here in an hour, so I wasn't sure if—"

Something crashes in the kitchen. A bowl. In the sink. Silverware flying everywhere.

Adam steps into the living room.

His *eyes*.

"He's not coming back here." These, the first five words Adam says to me.

"But I already told him," I try to say. "He's going to—"

"This is *my* home," he says, eyes flashing. "I won't let him in here."

I'm staring at Adam, heart beating out of my chest. I never thought he'd be capable of looking at me like he hates me. Really, really hates me.

"Kent, man—," I hear Kenji say.

"NO."

"C'mon bro, it doesn't have to be like this—"

"If you want to see him so badly," Adam says to me, "you can get the hell out of my house. But he's not coming back here. Not ever."

I blink.

This isn't really happening.

"Where is she supposed to go?" Kenji says to him. "You want her to stand on the side of the street? So someone can report her and get her killed? Are you out of your mind?"

"I don't give a shit anymore," Adam says. "She can go do whatever the hell she wants." He turns to me again. "You want to be with him?" He points to the door. "Go. Drop dead."

Ice is eating away at my body.

I stumble to my feet. My legs are unsteady. I'm nodding and I don't know why but I can't seem to stop. I make my way to the door.

"Juliette—"

I spin around, even though it's Kenji calling my name, not Adam.

"Don't go anywhere," Kenji says to me. "Don't move. This is ridiculous."

This has spiraled out of control. This isn't just a fight anymore. There is pure, unadulterated hatred in Adam's eyes, and I'm so blindsided by the impossibility of it—so thrown off guard—that I don't know how to react. I never could've anticipated this—never could've imagined things could turn out this way.

The real Adam wouldn't kick me out of his house like this. He wouldn't talk to me like this. Not the Adam I know. The Adam I thought I knew.

"Kent," Kenji says again, "you need to calm down. There is nothing going on between her and Warner, okay? She's just trying to do what she thinks is right—"

"Bullshit!" Adam explodes. "That's bullshit, and you know it, and you're a jackass for denying it. She's been lying to me this whole damn time—"

"You guys aren't even together, man, you can't lay a claim on her—"

"We never broke up!" Adam shouts.

"Of course you did," Kenji snaps back. "Every single person at Point heard your melodramatic ass in the freaking tunnels. We all know you broke up. So stop fighting it."

"That didn't count as a breakup," Adam says, his voice rough. "We still loved each other—"

"Okay, you know what? Whatever. I don't care." Kenji waves his hands, rolls his eyes. "But we're in the middle of a *war* right now. For shit's sake, she was shot in the chest a couple days ago and almost died. Don't you think it's possible she's really trying to think of something bigger than just the two of you? Warner's crazy, but he can help—"

"She looks at that psycho like she's in *love* with him," Adam barks back. "You think I don't know what that look is? You think I wouldn't be able to tell? She used to look at *me* like that. I know her—I know her so well—"

"Maybe you don't."

"Stop defending her!"

"You don't even know what you're saying," Kenji tells him. "You're acting crazy—"

"I was happier," Adam says, "when I thought she was *dead*."

"You don't mean that. Don't say things like that, man. Once you say that kind of shit you can't take it back—"

"Oh, I mean it," Adam says. "I really, really mean it." He finally looks at me. Fists clenched. "Thinking you were dead," he says to me, "was so much better. It hurt so much less than this."

The walls are moving. I'm seeing spots, blinking at nothing.

This isn't really happening, I keep telling myself.

This is just a terrible nightmare, and when I wake up Adam will be gentle and kind and wonderful again. Because he isn't cruel like this. Not to me. Never to me.

"You, of all people," Adam says to me. He looks so disgusted. "I trusted you—told you things I never should've told you—and now you're going out of your way to throw it all back in my face. I can't believe you'd do this to me. That you'd fall for *him*. What the hell is wrong with you?" he demands, his voice rising in pitch. "How sick in the head do you have to be?"

I'm so afraid to speak.

So afraid to move my lips.

I'm so scared that if I move even an inch, my body will snap in half and everyone will see that my insides are made up of nothing but all the tears I'm swallowing back right now.

Adam shakes his head. Laughs a sad, twisted laugh. "You won't even deny it," he says. "Unbelievable."

"Leave her alone, Kent," Kenji says suddenly, his voice deathly sharp. "I'm serious."

"This is *none* of your business—"

"You're being a dick—"

"You think I give a shit what you think?" Adam turns on him. "This isn't your fight, Kenji. Just because she's too much of a coward to say anything doesn't mean you have to defend her—"

I feel like I've stepped outside of myself. Like my body has collapsed onto the floor and I'm looking on, watching as

Adam transforms into a completely different human being. Every word. Every insult he hurls at me seems to fracture my bones. Pretty soon I'll be nothing but blood and a beating heart.

"I'm leaving," Adam is saying. "I'm leaving, and when I come back, I want her gone."

Don't cry, I keep saying to myself.

Don't cry.

This isn't real.

"You and me," Adam is saying to me now, his voice so rough, so angry, "we're *done*. We're finished," he snaps. "I never want to see you again. Not anywhere in this world, and definitely not in my own goddamn house." He stares at me, chest heaving. "So get the hell out. Get out before I get back."

He stalks across the room. Grabs a coat. Yanks the door open.

The walls shake as he slams it shut.

TWENTY-EIGHT

I'm standing in the middle of the room, staring at nothing.

I'm suddenly freezing. My hands, I think, are shaking. Or maybe it's my bones. Maybe my bones are shaking. I move mechanically, so slowly, my mind still fuzzy. I'm vaguely aware that someone might be saying something to me, but I'm too focused on getting my coat because I'm so cold. It's so *cold* in here. I really need my jacket. And maybe my gloves. I can't stop shivering.

I pull my coat on. Shove my hands into the pockets. I feel like someone might be talking to me but I can't hear anything through the weird haze muting my senses. I clench my fists and my fingers fumble against a piece of plastic.

The pager. I'd almost forgotten.

I pull it out of my pocket. It's a tiny little thing; a thin, black rectangle with a button set flush against the length of it. I press it without thinking. I press it over and over and over again, because the action calms me. Soothes me, somehow. *Click click.* I like the repetitive motion. *Click. Click click.* I don't know what else to do.

Click.

Hands land on my shoulders.

I turn around. Castle is standing just behind me, his eyes

heavy with concern. "You're not going to leave," he says to me. "We'll work things out. It'll be all right."

"No." My tongue is dust. My teeth have crumbled away. "I have to go."

I can't stop pressing the button on this pager.

Click.

Click click.

"Come sit down," Castle is saying to me. "Adam is upset, but he'll be okay. I'm sure he didn't mean what he said."

"I'm pretty sure he did," Ian says.

Castle shoots him a sharp look.

"You can't leave," says Winston. "I thought we were going to kick some ass together. You promised."

"Yeah," Lily pipes up, trying to sound upbeat. But her eyes are wary, pulled together in fear or concern and I realize she's terrified for me.

Not *of* me.

For me.

It's the strangest sensation.

Click click click.

Click click.

"If you go," she's saying, trying to smile, "we'll have to live like this forever. And I don't want to live with a bunch of smelly guys for the rest of my life."

Click.

Click click.

"Don't go," James says. He looks so sad. So serious. "I'm sorry Adam was mean to you. But I don't want you to die," he says. "And I don't wish you were dead. I swear I don't."

James. Sweet James. His eyes break my heart.

"I can't stay." My voice sounds strange to me. Broken. "He really meant what he said—"

"We'll be a sad, sorry lot if you leave." Brendan cuts me off. "And I have to agree with Lily. I don't want to live like this for much longer."

"But how—"

The front door flies open.

"JULIETTE—*Juliette*—"

I spin around.

Warner is standing there, face flushed, chest rising and falling, staring at me like I might be a ghost. He strides across the room before I have a chance to say a word and cups my face in his hands, his eyes searching me. "Are you okay?" he's saying. "God—are you okay? What happened? Are you all right?"

He's here.

He's here and all I want to do is fall apart but I don't.

I won't.

"Thank you," I manage to say to him. "Thank you for coming—"

He wraps me up in his arms, not caring about the eight sets of eyes watching us. He just holds me, one arm tight around my waist, the other held to the back of my head. My face is buried in his chest and the warmth of him is so familiar to me now. Oddly comforting. He runs his hand up and down my back, tilts his head toward mine. "What's wrong, love?" he whispers. "What happened? Please tell me—"

I blink.

"Do you want me to take you back?"

I don't answer.

I don't know what I want or need to do anymore. Everyone is telling me to stay, but this isn't their home. This is Adam's home, and it's so clear he hates me now. But I also don't want to leave my friends. I don't want to leave Kenji.

"Do you want *me* to leave?" Warner asks.

"No," I say too quickly. "No."

Warner leans back, just a little. "Tell me what you want," he says desperately. "Tell me what to do," he says, "and I'll do it."

"This is, by far, the craziest shit I have ever seen," Kenji says. "I really never would've believed it. Not in a million years."

"It's like a soap opera." Ian nods. "But with worse acting."

"I think it's kind of sweet," Winston says.

I jerk back, half spinning around. Everyone is staring at us. Winston is the only one smiling.

"What's going on?" Warner asks them. "Why does she look like she's about to cry?"

No one answers.

"Where's Kent?" Warner asks, eyes narrowing as he reads their faces. "What did he do to her?"

"He's out," Lily says. "He left a little bit ago."

Warner's eyes darken as he processes the information.

He turns to me. "Please tell me you don't want to stay here anymore."

I drop my head into my hands. "Everyone wants to help—to fight—except for Adam. But they can't leave. And I don't want to leave them behind."

Warner sighs. Closes his eyes. "Then stay," he says gently. "If that's what you want. Stay here. I can always meet you."

"I can't," I tell him. "I have to go. I'm not allowed to come back here again."

"What?" Anger. In and out of his eyes. "What do you mean you're not *allowed*?"

"Adam doesn't want me to stay here anymore. I have to be gone before he gets back."

Warner's jaw tightens. He stares at me for what feels like a century. I can almost *see* him thinking—his mind working at an impossible rate—to find a solution. "Okay," he finally says. "Okay." He exhales. "Kishimoto," he says all at once, never breaking eye contact with me.

"Present, sir."

Warner tries not to roll his eyes as he turns toward Kenji. "I will set up your group in my private training quarters on base. I will require a day to work out the details, but I will make sure you are granted easy access and clearance to enter the grounds upon arrival. You will make yourself and your team invisible and follow my lead. You are free to stay in these quarters until we are ready to proceed with the first stage of our plan." A pause. "Will this arrangement work for you?"

Kenji actually looks disgusted. "Hell no."

"Why not?"

"You're going to lock us up in your 'private training quarters'?" Kenji says, making air quotes with his fingers. "Why don't you just say you're going to put us in a cage and kill us slowly? You think I'm a moron? What reason would I have to believe that kind of shit?"

"I will make sure you are fed well and regularly," Warner says by way of response. "Your accommodations will be simple, but they will not be simpler than this," he says, gesturing to the room. "The arrangement will provide us ample opportunity to meet and structure our next moves. You must know that you're putting everyone at risk by staying on unregulated territory. You and your friends will be safer with me."

"Why would you do that, though?" Ian asks. "Why would you want to help us and feed us and keep us alive? That doesn't make any sense—"

"It doesn't need to make sense."

"Of course it does," Lily counters. Her eyes are hard, angry. "We're not going to walk onto a military base just to get ourselves killed," she snaps. "This could be some sick trick."

"Fine," Warner says.

"Fine, what?" Lily asks.

"Don't come."

"Oh." Lily blinks.

Warner turns to Kenji. "You are officially refusing my offer, then?"

"Yeah, no thanks," Kenji says.

Warner nods. Looks to me. "Should we get going?"

"But—no—" I'm panicking now, looking from Warner to Kenji and back to Warner again. "I can't just *leave*—I can't just never see them again—"

I turn to Kenji.

"You're just going to stay here?" I ask. "And I'll never see you again?"

"You can stay here with us." Kenji crosses his arms against his chest. "You don't have to go."

"You know I can't stay," I tell him, angry and hurt. "You know Adam meant what he said—he'll go crazy if he comes back and I'm still here—"

"So you're just going to leave, then?" Kenji says sharply. "You're going to walk away from all of us"—he gestures to everyone—"just because Adam decided to be a douchebag? You're trading all of us in for Warner?"

"Kenji—I'm not—I have nowhere else to live! What am I supposed to—"

"Stay."

"Adam will throw me out—"

"No he won't," Kenji says. "We won't let him."

"I won't force myself on him. I won't beg him. Let me at least leave with a shred of dignity—"

Kenji throws his arms in the air in frustration. "This is *bullshit*!"

"Come with me," I say to him. "Please—I want us to stay together—"

"We can't," he says. "We can't risk that, J. I don't know what's going on between you two," he says, gesturing between me and Warner. "Maybe he really is different with you, I don't know, whatever—but I can't put all of our lives at risk based on emotions and an assumption. Maybe he cares about *you*," Kenji says, "but he doesn't give a shit about the rest of us." He looks at Warner. "Do you?"

"Do I what?" Warner asks.

"Do you care about any of us? About our survival—our well-being?"

"No."

Kenji almost laughs. "Well at least you're honest."

"My offer, however, still stands. And you're an idiot to refuse," Warner says. "You'll all die out here, and you know that better than I do."

"We'll take our chances."

"No," I gasp. "Kenji—"

"It'll be all right," he says to me. His forehead is pinched, his eyes heavy. "I'm sure we'll find a way to see each other one day. Do what you need to do."

"No," I'm trying to say. Trying to breathe. My lungs are swelling up, my heart racing so fast I can hear it pounding in my ears. I'm feeling hot and cold and too hot, too cold, and all I can think is *no*, it wasn't supposed to happen like this, it wasn't all supposed to fall apart, not again not again—

Warner grabs my arms. "Please," he's saying, his voice

urgent, panicked. "Please don't do that, love, I need you not to do that—"

"Dammit, Kenji!" I explode, breaking away from Warner. "Please, for the love of God, don't be an idiot. You have to come with me—I need you—"

"I need some kind of guarantee, J"—Kenji is pacing, hands in his hair—"I can't just trust that everything is going to be all right—"

I turn on Warner, chest heaving, fists clenched. "Give them what they want. I don't care what it is," I say to him. "Please, you have to negotiate. You have to make this work. I need him. I need my friends."

Warner looks at me for a long time.

"Please," I whisper.

He looks away. Looks back at me.

He finally meets Kenji's eyes. Sighs. "What do you want?"

"I want a hot bath," I hear Winston say.

And then he giggles.

He actually giggles.

"Two of my men are ill and injured," Kenji says, immediately switching gears. His voice is clipped, sharp. Unfeeling. "They need medicine and medical attention. We don't want to be monitored, we don't want a curfew, and we want to be able to eat more than the Automat food. We want protein. Fruits. Vegetables. Real meals. We want regular access to showers. We'll need new clothes. And we want to remain armed at all times."

Warner is standing so still beside me I can hardly hear him breathing anymore. My head is pounding so hard and my heart is still racing in my chest, but I've calmed down enough that I'm able to breathe a little easier now.

Warner glances down at me.

He holds my gaze for just a moment before he closes his eyes. Exhales a sharp breath. Looks up.

"Fine," he says.

Kenji is staring at him. "Wait—*what?*"

"I will be back tomorrow at fourteen hundred hours to guide you to your new quarters."

"Holy shit." Winston is bouncing on the couch. "Holy shit holy shit holy *shit*."

"Do you have your things?" Warner asks me.

I nod.

"Good," he says. "Let's go."

TWENTY-NINE

Warner is holding my hand.

I only have enough energy to focus on this single, strange fact as he leads me down the stairs and into the parking garage. He opens the door of the tank and helps me in before closing it behind me.

He climbs into the other side.

Turns on the engine.

We're already on the road and I've blinked only six times since we left Adam's house.

I still can't believe what just happened. I can't believe we're all going to be working together. I can't believe I told Warner what to do and he *listened to me.*

I turn to look at him. It's strange: I've never felt so safe or so relieved to be beside him. I never thought I could feel this way with him.

"Thank you," I whisper, grateful and guilty, somehow, about everything that's happened. About leaving Adam behind. I realize now that I've made the kind of choice I can't undo. My heart is still breaking. "Really," I say again. "Thank you so much. For coming to get me. I appreciate—"

"Please," he says. "I'm begging you to stop."

I still.

"I can't stomach your pain," he says. "I can feel it so strongly and it's making me crazy—*please,*" he says to me. "Don't be sad. Or hurt. Or guilty. You've done nothing wrong."

"I'm sorry—"

"Don't be sorry, either," he says. "God, the only reason I'm not going to kill Kent for this is because I know it would only upset you more."

"You're right," I say after a moment. "But it's not just him."

"What?" he asks. "What do you mean?"

"I don't want you to kill anyone at all," I say. "Not just Adam."

Warner laughs a sharp, strange laugh. He looks almost relieved. "Do you have any other stipulations?"

"Not really."

"You don't want to fix me, then? You don't have a long list of things I need to work on?"

"No." I stare out the window. The view is so bleak. So cold. Covered in ice and snow. "There's nothing wrong with you that isn't already wrong with me," I say quietly. "And if I were smart I'd first figure out how to fix myself."

We're both silent awhile. The tension is so thick in this small space.

"Aaron?" I say, still watching the scenery fly by.

I hear the small hitch in his breath. The hesitation. It's the first time I've used his first name so casually.

"Yes?" he says.

"I want you to know," I tell him, "that I don't think you're crazy."

"What?" He startles.

"I don't think you're crazy." The world is blurring away as I watch it through the window. "And I don't think you're a psychopath. I also don't think you're a sick, twisted monster. I don't think you're a heartless murderer, and I don't think you deserve to die, and I don't think you're pathetic. Or stupid. Or a coward. I don't think you're any of the things people have said about you."

I turn to look at him.

Warner is staring out the windshield.

"You don't?" His voice is so soft and so scared I can scarcely hear it.

"No," I say. "I don't. And I just thought you should know. I'm not trying to fix you; I don't think you need to be fixed. I'm not trying to turn you into someone else. I only want you to be who you really are. Because I think I know the real you. I think I've seen him."

Warner says nothing, his chest rising and falling.

"I don't care what anyone else says about you," I tell him. "I think you're a good person."

Warner is blinking fast now. I can hear him breathing.

In and out.

Unevenly.

He says nothing.

"Do you . . . believe me?" I ask after a moment. "Can you sense that I'm telling the truth? That I really mean it?"

Warner's hands are clenched around the steering wheel.

His knuckles are white.

He nods

Just once.

THIRTY

Warner still hasn't said a single word to me.

We're in his room now, courtesy of Delalieu, who Warner was quick to dismiss. It feels strange and familiar to be back here, in this room that I've found both fear and comfort in.

Now it feels right to me.

This is Warner's room. And Warner, to me, is no longer something to be afraid of.

These past few months have transformed him in my eyes, and these past two days have been full of revelations that I'm still recovering from. I can't deny that he seems different to me now.

I feel like I understand him in a way I never did before.

He's like a terrified, tortured animal. A creature who spent his whole life being beaten, abused, and caged away. He was forced into a life he never asked for, and was never given an opportunity to choose anything else. And though he's been given all the tools to kill a person, he's too emotionally tortured to be able to use those skills against his own father—the very man who taught him to be a murderer. Because somehow, in some strange, inexplicable way, he still wants his father to love him.

And I understand that.

I really, really do.

"What happened?" Warner finally says to me.

I'm sitting on his bed; he's standing by the door, staring at the wall.

"What do you mean?"

"With Kent," he says. "Earlier. What did he say to you?"

"Oh." I flush. Embarrassed. "He kicked me out of his house."

"But why?"

"He was mad," I explain. "That I was defending you. That I'd invited you to come back at all."

"Oh."

I can almost hear our hearts beat in the silence between us.

"You were defending me," Warner finally says.

"Yes."

He says nothing.

I say nothing.

"So he told you to leave," Warner says, "because you were defending me."

"Yes."

"Is that all?"

My heart is racing. I'm suddenly nervous. "No."

"There were other things?"

"Yes."

Warner blinks at the wall. Unmoving. "Really."

I nod.

He says nothing.

"He was upset," I whisper, "because I didn't agree that you were crazy. And he was accusing me"—I hesitate—"of being in love with you."

Warner exhales sharply. Touches a hand to the doorframe.

My heart is pounding so hard.

Warner's eyes are glued to the wall. "And you told him he was an idiot."

Breathe. "No."

Warner turns, just halfway. I see his profile, the unsteady rise and fall of his chest. He's staring directly at the door now, and it's clear it's costing him a great deal of effort to speak. "Then you told him he was crazy. You told him he had to be out of his mind to say something like that."

"No."

"No," he echoes.

I try not to move.

Warner takes a hard, shaky breath. "Then what did you say to him?"

Seven seconds die between us.

"Nothing," I whisper.

Warner stills.

I don't breathe.

No one speaks for what feels like forever.

"Of course," Warner finally says. He looks pale, unsteady. "You said nothing. Of course."

"Aaron—" I get to my feet.

"There are a lot of things I have to do before tomorrow," he says. "Especially if your friends will be joining us on base." His hands tremble in the second it takes him to reach for the door. "Forgive me," he says. "But I have to go."

THIRTY-ONE

I decide to take a bath.

I've never taken a bath before.

I poke around the bathroom as the tub fills with hot water, and discover stacks and stacks of scented soaps. All different kinds. All different sizes. Each bar of soap has been wrapped in a thick piece of parchment, and tied with twine. There are small labels affixed to each package to distinguish one scent from another.

I pick up one of the bundles.

HONEYSUCKLE

I clutch the soap and can't help but think how different it was to take a shower at Omega Point. We had nothing so fancy as this. Our soaps were harsh and smelled strange and were fairly ineffective. Kenji used to bring them into our training sessions and break off pieces to pelt at me when I wasn't focusing.

The memory makes me inexplicably emotional.

My heart swells as I remember that my friends will be here tomorrow. This is really going to happen, I think. We'll be unstoppable, all of us together. I can't wait.

I look more closely at the label.

Top notes of jasmine and nuances of grape. Mild notes of lilac, honeysuckle, rose, and cinnamon. Orange-flower and powder base notes complete the fragrance.

Sounds amazing.

I steal one of Warner's soaps.

I'm freshly scrubbed and wearing a clean set of clothes.

I keep sniffing my skin, pleasantly surprised by how nice it is to smell like a flower. I've never smelled like anything before. I keep running my fingers down my arms, wondering at how much of a difference a good bar of soap can make. I've never felt so clean in my life. I didn't realize soap could lather like that or react so well to my body. The only soap I've ever used before always dried up my skin and left me feeling uncomfortable for a few hours. But this is weird. Wonderful. I feel soft and smooth and so refreshed.

I also have absolutely nothing to do.

I sit down on Warner's bed, pull my feet up underneath me. Stare at his office door.

I'm so tempted to see if the door is unlocked.

My conscience, however, overrules me.

I sink into the pillows with a sigh. Kick up the blankets and snuggle beneath them.

Close my eyes.

My mind is instantly flooded with images of Adam's angry face, his shaking fists, his hurtful words. I try to push the memories away and I can't.

My eyes fly open.

I wonder if I'll ever see him and James again.

Maybe this is what Adam wanted. He can go back to his life with his little brother now. He won't have to worry about sharing his rations with eight other people and he'll be able to survive much longer this way.

But then what? I can't help but think.

He'll be all alone. With no food. No friends. No income.

It breaks my heart to imagine it. To think of him struggling to find a way to live, to provide for his brother. Because even though Adam seems to hate me now, I don't think I could ever reciprocate those feelings.

I don't even know that I understand what just happened between us.

It seems impossible that Adam and I could fissure and break apart so abruptly. I care so deeply for him. He was there for me when no one else was; he gave me hope when I needed it most; he loved me when no one else would. He's not anyone I want to erase from my life.

I want him around. I want my friend back.

But I'm realizing now that Kenji was right.

Adam was the first and only person who'd ever shown me compassion. The first, and, at the time, only person who was able to touch me. I was caught up in the impossibility of it, so convinced fate had brought us together. His tattoo was a perfect snapshot of my dreams.

I thought it was about us. About my escape. About our happily-ever-after.

And it was.

And it wasn't.

I want to laugh at my own blindness.

It linked us, I realize. That tattoo. It did bring me and Adam together, but not because we were destined for one another. Not because he was my flight to freedom. But because we have one major connection between the two of us. One kind of hope neither one of us was able to see.

Warner.

A white bird with streaks of gold like a crown atop its head.

A fair-skinned boy with gold hair, the leader of Sector 45.

It was always him. All along.

The link.

Warner, Adam's brother, my captor and now comrade. He inadvertently brought me and Adam together. And being with Adam gave me a new kind of strength. I was still scared and still very broken and Adam cared for me, giving me a reason to stand up for myself when I was too weak to realize I had always been reason enough. It was affection and a desperate desire for physical connection. Two things I'd been so deprived of, and so wholly unfamiliar with. I had nothing to compare these new experiences to.

Of course I thought I was in love.

But while I don't know much, I do know that if Adam really loved me, he wouldn't have treated me the way he did today. He wouldn't prefer that I was dead.

I know this, because I've seen proof of his opposite.

Because I *was* dying.

And Warner could've let me die. He was angry and hurt

and had every reason to be bitter. I'd just ripped his heart out; I'd let him believe something would come of our relationship. I let him confess the depth of his feelings to me; I let him touch me in ways even Adam hadn't. I didn't ask him to stop.

Every inch of me was saying yes.

And then I took it all back. Because I was scared, and confused, and conflicted. Because of Adam.

Warner told me he loved me, and in return I insulted him and lied to him and yelled at him and pushed him away. And when he had the chance to stand back and watch me die, he didn't.

He found a way to save my life.

With no demands. No expectations. Believing full well that I was in love with someone else, and that saving my life meant making me whole again only to give me back to another guy.

And right now, I can't say I know what Adam would do if I were dying in front of him. I'm not sure if he would save my life. And that uncertainty alone makes me certain that something wasn't right between us. Something wasn't real.

Maybe we both fell in love with the illusion of something more.

THIRTY-TWO

My eyes fly open.

It's pitch-black. Quiet. I sit up too fast.

I must've fallen asleep. I have no idea what time it is, but a quick glance around the room tells me Warner isn't here.

I slip out of bed. I'm still wearing socks and I'm suddenly grateful; I have to wrap my arms around myself, shivering as the cold winter air creeps through the thin material of my T-shirt. My hair is still slightly damp from the bath.

Warner's office door is cracked open.

There's a sliver of light peeking through the opening, and it makes me wonder if he really forgot to close it, or if maybe he's only just walked in. Maybe he's not in there at all. But my curiosity beats out my conscience this time.

I want to know where he works and what his desk looks like; I want to know if he's messy or organized or if he keeps personal items around. I wonder if he has any pictures of himself as a kid.

Or of his mother.

I tiptoe forward, butterflies stirring awake in my stomach. I shouldn't be nervous, I tell myself. I'm not doing anything illegal. I'm just going to see if he's in there, and if he's not, I'll leave. I'm only going to walk in for a second. I'm not going to search through any of his things.

I'm not.

I hesitate outside his door. It's so quiet that I'm almost certain my heart is beating loud and hard enough for him to hear. I don't know why I'm so scared.

I knock twice against the door as I nudge it open.

"Aaron, are you—"

Something crashes to the floor.

I push the door open and rush inside, jerking to a stop just as I cross the threshold. Stunned.

His office is enormous.

It's the size of his entire bedroom and closet combined. Bigger. There's so much space in here—room enough to house the huge boardroom table and the six chairs stationed on either side of it. There's a couch and a few side tables set off in the corner, and one wall is made up of nothing but bookshelves. Loaded with books. Bursting with books. Old books and new books and books with spines falling off.

Everything in here is made of dark wood.

Wood so brown it looks black. Clean, straight lines, simple cuts. Nothing is ornate or bulky. No leather. No high-backed chairs or overly detailed woodwork. Minimal.

The boardroom table is stacked with file folders and papers and binders and notebooks. The floor is covered in a thick, plush Oriental rug, similar to the one in his closet. And at the far end of the room is his desk.

Warner is staring at me in shock.

He's wearing nothing but his slacks and a pair of socks,

his shirt and belt discarded. He's standing in front of his desk, clinging to something in his hands—something I can't quite see.

"What are you doing here?" he says.

"The door was open." What a stupid answer.

He stares at me.

"What time is it?" I ask.

"One thirty in the morning," he says automatically.

"Oh."

"You should go back to bed." I don't know why he looks so nervous. Why his eyes keep darting from me to the door.

"I'm not tired anymore."

"Oh." He fumbles with what I now realize is a small jar in his hands. Sets it on the desk behind him without turning around.

He's been so off today, I think. Unlike himself. He's usually so composed, so self-assured. But recently he's been so shaky around me. The inconsistency is unnerving.

"What are you doing?" I ask.

There's about ten feet between us, and neither one of us is making any effort to bridge the gap. We're talking like we don't know each other, like we're strangers who've just found themselves in a compromising situation. Which is ridiculous.

I begin to cross the room, to make my way over to him.

He freezes.

I stop.

"Is everything okay?"

"Yes," he says too quickly.

"What's that?" I ask, pointing to the little plastic jar.

"You should go back to sleep, love. You're probably more tired than you think—"

I walk right up to him, reach around and grab the jar before he can do much to stop me.

"That is a violation of privacy," he says sharply, sounding more like himself. "Give that back to me—"

"Medicine?" I ask, surprised. I turn the little jar around in my hands, reading the label. I look up at him. Finally understanding. "This is for scars."

He runs a hand through his hair. Looks toward the wall. "Yes," he says. "Now please give it back to me."

"Do you need help?" I ask.

He stills. "What?"

"This is for your back, isn't it?"

He runs a hand across his mouth, down his chin. "You won't allow me to walk away from this with even an ounce of self-respect, will you?"

"I didn't know you cared about your scars," I say to him.

I take a step forward.

He takes a step back.

"I don't."

"Then why this?" I hold up the jar. "Where did you even get this from?"

"It's nothing—it's just—" He shakes his head. "Delalieu found it for me. It's ridiculous," he says. "I feel ridiculous."

"Because you can't reach your own back?"

He stares at me then. Sighs.

"Turn around," I tell him.

"No."

"You're being weird about nothing. I've already seen your scars."

"That doesn't mean you need to see them again."

I can't help but smile a little.

"What?" he demands. "What's so funny?"

"You just don't seem like the kind of person who would be self-conscious about something like this."

"I'm not."

"Obviously."

"Please," he says, "just go back to bed."

"I'm wide-awake."

"That's not my problem."

"Turn around," I tell him again.

He narrows his eyes at me.

"Why are you even using this stuff?" I ask him for the second time. "You don't need it. Don't use it if it makes you uncomfortable."

He's quiet a moment. "You don't think I need it?"

"Of course not. Why . . . ? Are you in pain? Do your scars hurt?"

"Sometimes," he says quietly. "Not as much as they used to. I actually can't feel much of anything on my back anymore."

Something cold and sharp hits me in the stomach. "Really?"

He nods.

"Will you tell me where they came from?" I whisper, unable to meet his eyes.

He's silent for so long I'm finally forced to look up.

His eyes are dead of emotion, his face set to neutral. He clears his throat. "They were my birthday presents," he says. "Every year from the time I was five. Until I turned eighteen," he says. "He didn't come back for my nineteenth birthday."

I'm frozen in horror.

"Right." Warner looks into his hands. "So—"

"He *cut* you?" My voice is so hoarse.

"Whip."

"Oh my God," I gasp, covering my mouth. I have to look toward the wall to pull myself together. I blink several times, struggle to swallow back the pain and rage building inside of me. "I'm so sorry," I choke out. "Aaron. I'm so sorry."

"I don't want you to be repulsed by me," he says quietly.

I spin around, stunned. Mildly horrified. "You're not serious."

His eyes say that he is.

"Have you never looked in a mirror?" I ask, angry now.

"Excuse me?"

"You're perfect," I tell him, so overcome I forget myself. "All of you. Your entire body. Proportionally. Symmetrically. You're absurdly, mathematically perfect. It doesn't even make sense that a person could look like you," I say, shaking my head. "I can't believe you would ever say something like that—"

"Juliette, please. Don't talk to me like that."

"What? Why?"

"Because it's *cruel*," he says, losing his composure. "It's cruel and it's heartless and you don't even realize—"

"Aaron—"

"I take it back," he says. "I don't want you to call me Aaron anymore—"

"Aaron," I say again, more firmly this time. "Please—you can't really think you repulse me? You can't really think I would care—that I would be put off by your scars—"

"I don't know," he says. He's pacing in front of his desk, his eyes fixed on the ground.

"I thought you could sense feelings," I say to him. "I thought mine would be so obvious to you."

"I can't always think clearly," he says, frustrated, rubbing his face, his forehead. "Especially when my emotions are involved. I can't always be objective—and sometimes I make assumptions," he says, "that aren't true—and I don't—I just don't trust my own judgment anymore. Because I've done that," he says, "and it's backfired. So terribly."

He looks up, finally. Looks me in the eye.

"You're right," I whisper.

He looks away.

"You've made a lot of mistakes," I say to him. "You did everything wrong."

He runs a hand down the length of his face.

"But it's not too late to fix things—you can make it right—"

"Please—"

"It's not too late—"

"Stop saying that to me!" he explodes. "You don't know me—you don't know what I've done or what I'd need to do to make things right—"

"Don't you understand? It doesn't matter—you can choose to be different now—"

"I thought you weren't going to try and change me!"

"I'm not trying to change you," I say, lowering my voice. "I'm just trying to get you to understand that your life isn't over. You don't have to be who you've been. You can make different choices now. You can be *happy*—"

"Juliette." One sharp word. His green eyes so intense.

I stop.

I glance at his trembling hands; he clenches them into fists.

"Go," he says quietly. "I don't want you to be here right now."

"Then why did you bring me back with you?" I ask, angry. "If you don't even want to see me—"

"Why don't you understand?" He looks up at me and his eyes are so full of pain and devastation it actually takes my breath away.

My hands are shaking. "Understand what—?"

"I *love* you."

He breaks.

His voice. His back. His knees. His face.

He breaks.

He has to hold on to the side of his desk. He can't meet

my eyes. "I love you," he says, his words harsh and soft all at once. "I love you and it isn't enough. I thought it would be enough and I was wrong. I thought I could fight for you and I was wrong. Because I can't. I can't even face you anymore—"

"Aaron—"

"Tell me it isn't true," he says. "Tell me I'm wrong. Tell me I'm blind. Tell me you love me."

My heart won't stop screaming as it breaks in half.

I can't lie to him.

"I don't—I don't know how to understand what I feel," I try to explain.

"Please," he whispers. "Please just go—"

"Aaron, please understand—I thought I knew what love was before and I was wrong—I don't want to make that mistake again—"

"Please"—he's begging now—"for the love of God, Juliette, I have lost my *dignity*—"

"Okay." I nod. "Okay. I'm sorry. Okay."

I back away.

I turn around.

And I don't look back.

THIRTY-THREE

"I have to leave in seven minutes."

Warner and I are both fully dressed, talking to each other like perfect acquaintances; like last night never happened. Delalieu brought us breakfast and we ate quietly in separate rooms. No talk of him or me or us or what might've been or what might be.

There is no us.

There's the absence of Adam, and there's fighting against The Reestablishment. That's it.

I get it now.

"I'd bring you with me," he's saying, "but I think it'll be hard to disguise you on this trip. If you want, you can wait in the training rooms—I'll bring the group of them straight there. You can say hello as soon as they arrive." He finally looks at me. "Is that okay?"

I nod.

"Very good," he says. "I'll show you how to get there."

He leads me back into his office, and into one of the far corners by the couch. There's an exit in here I didn't see last night. Warner hits a button on the wall. The doors slide open.

It's an elevator.

We walk in and he hits the button for the ground floor. The doors close and we start moving.

I glance up at him. "I never knew you had an elevator in your room."

"I needed private access to my training facilities."

"You keep saying that," I tell him. "*Training facilities.* What's a training facility?"

The elevator stops.

The doors slide open.

He holds them open for me. "This."

I've never seen so many machines in my life.

Running machines and leg machines and machines that work your arms, your shoulders, your abdominals. There are even machines that look like bikes. I don't know what any of them are called. I know one of these things is a bench press. I also know what dumbbells look like, and there are racks and racks of those, in all different sizes. Weights, I think. Free weights. There are also bars attached to the ceiling in some places, but I can't imagine what those are for. There are tons of things around this room, actually, that look entirely foreign to me.

And each wall is used for something different.

One wall seems to be made of stone. Or rock. There are little grooves in it that are accented by what look like pieces of plastic in different colors. Another wall is covered in guns. Hundreds of guns resting on pegs that keep them in place. They're pristine. Gleaming as if they've just been cleaned. There's a door in that same wall; I wonder where it goes. The third wall is covered in the same black, sponge-like material that covers the floors. It looks like it might be soft and springy. And the final wall is the one we've just walked through. It houses the elevator, and one other door, and nothing else.

The dimensions are enormous. This space is at least two or three times the size of Warner's bedroom, his closet, and his office put together. It doesn't seem possible that all of this is for one person.

"This is amazing," I say, turning to face him. "You use all of this?"

He nods. "I'm usually in here at least two or three times a day," he says. "I got off track when I was injured," he says, "but in general, yes." He steps forward, touches the spongy black wall. "This has been my life for as long as I've known it. Training," he says. "I've been training forever. And this is where we're going to start with you, too."

"Me?"

He nods.

"But I don't need to train," I tell him. "Not like this."

He tries to meet my eyes and can't.

"I have to go," he says. "If you get bored in here, take the elevator back up. This elevator can only access two levels, so you can't get lost." He buttons his blazer. "I'll return as soon as I can."

"Okay."

I expect him to leave, but he doesn't. "You'll still be here," he finally says, "when I return."

It's not exactly a question.

I nod anyway.

"It doesn't seem possible," he says, so quietly, "that you're not trying to run away."

I say nothing.

He exhales a hard breath. Pivots on one heel. And leaves.

THIRTY-FOUR

I'm sitting on one of the benches, toying with five-pound dumbbells, when I hear his voice.

"Holy shit," he's saying. "This place is legit."

I jump up, nearly dropping the weights on my foot. Kenji and Winston and Castle and Brendan and Ian and Alia and Lily are all walking through the extra door in the gun wall.

Kenji's face lights up when he sees me.

I run forward and he catches me in his arms, hugs me tight before breaking away. "Well, I'll be damned," Kenji says. "He didn't kill you. That's a really good sign."

I shove him a little. Suppress a grin.

I quickly say hi to everyone. I'm practically bouncing I'm so excited to have them here. But they're all looking around in shock. Like they really thought Warner was leading them into a trap.

"There's a locker room through here," Warner is telling them. He points to the door beside the elevator. "There are plenty of showers and bathroom stalls and anything else you might need to keep from smelling like an animal. Towels, soap, laundry machines. All through here."

I'm so focused on Warner I almost don't notice Delalieu standing in the corner.

I stifle a gasp.

He's standing quietly, hands clasped behind his back, watching closely as everyone listens to Warner talk. And not for the first time, I wonder who he really is. Why Warner seems to trust him so much.

"Your meals will be delivered to you three times a day," Warner is saying. "If you don't eat, or if you miss a meal and find yourself hungry, feel free to shed your tears in the shower. And then learn to set a schedule. Don't bring your complaints to me.

"You already have your own weapons," he goes on, "but, as you can see, this room is also fully stocked and—"

"*Sweet,*" Ian says. He looks a little too excited as he heads toward a set of rifles.

"If you touch any of my guns, I will break both of your hands," Warner says to him.

Ian freezes in place.

"This wall is off-limits to you. All of you," he says, looking around the room. "Everything else is available for your use. Do not damage any of my equipment. Leave things the way you found them. And if you do not shower on a regular basis, do not come within ten feet of me."

Kenji snorts.

"I have other work to attend to," Warner says. "I will return at nineteen hundred hours, at which time we can reconvene and begin our discussions. In the interim, take advantage of the opportunity to get situated. You may use the extra mats in the corner to sleep on. I hope for your sake you brought your own blankets."

Alia's bag slips out of her hands and thuds onto the floor. Everyone spins in her direction. She goes scarlet.

"Are there any questions?" Warner asks.

"Yeah," Kenji says. "Where's the medicine?"

Warner nods to Delalieu, who's still standing in the corner. "Give my lieutenant a detailed account of any injuries and illnesses. He will procure the necessary treatments."

Kenji nods, and means it. He actually looks grateful. "Thank you," he says.

Warner holds Kenji's gaze for just a moment. "You're welcome."

Kenji raises his eyebrows.

Even I'm surprised.

Warner looks at me then. He looks at me for just a split second before looking away. And then, without a word, he hits the button for the elevator.

Steps inside.

I watch the doors close behind him.

THIRTY-FIVE

Kenji is staring at me, concerned. "What the hell was that?"

Winston and Ian are looking at me too, making no effort to hide their confusion. Lily is unpacking her things. Castle is watching me closely. Brendan and Alia are deep in conversation.

"What do you mean?" I ask. I'm trying to be nonchalant, but I think my ears have gone pink.

Kenji clasps one hand behind his neck. Shrugs. "You two get into a fight or something?"

"No," I say too quickly.

"Uh-huh." Kenji cocks his head at me.

"How's Adam?" I ask, hoping to change the subject.

Kenji blows out a long breath; looks away; rubs at his eyes just before dropping his bag on the floor. He leans back against the wall. "I'm not gonna lie to you, J," he says, lowering his voice. "This crap with Kent is really stressing me out. Your drama is making things messy. He didn't make it easy for us to leave."

"What? But he said he didn't want to fight back anymore—"

"Yeah, well." Kenji nods. "Apparently that doesn't mean he wants to lose all his friends at once."

I shake my head. "He's not being fair."

"I know," Kenji says. Sighs again. "Anyway, it's good to see you, princess, but I'm tired as hell. And hungry. Grumpy. You know." He makes a haphazard motion with his hand. Slumps to the floor.

He's not telling me something.

"What's wrong?" I sit down across from him and lower my voice.

He looks up, meets my eyes.

"I miss James, okay? I miss that kid." Kenji sounds so tired. I can actually see the exhaustion in his eyes. "I didn't want to leave him behind."

My heart sinks fast.

Of course.

James.

"I'm so sorry. I wish there'd been a way we could've brought him with us."

Kenji flicks an imaginary piece of lint off his shirt. "It's probably safer for him where he is," he says, but it's obvious he doesn't believe a word of it. "I just wish Kent would stop being such a dick."

I cringe.

"This could all be amazing if he would just get his shit together," Kenji says. "But no, he has to go and get all weird and crazy and dramatic." He blows out a breath. "He's so freaking emotional," Kenji says suddenly. "Everything is such a big deal to him. He can't just let things go. He can't just be cool and move on with his life. I just . . . I don't know. Whatever. I just wish James were here. I miss him."

"I'm sorry," I say again.

Kenji makes a weird face. Waves his hand at nothing. "It's fine. I'll be fine."

I look up and find that everyone else has dispersed.

Castle, Ian, Alia, and Lily are heading to the locker room, while Winston and Brendan wander around the facility. They're touching the rock wall right now, having a conversation I can't hear.

I scoot closer to Kenji. Prop my head in my hands.

"So," he says. "I don't see you for twenty-four hours and you and Warner go from let's-hug-in-super-dramatic-fashion to let-me-give-you-an-ice-cold-shoulder, huh?" Kenji is tracing shapes into the mats underneath us. "Must be an interesting story there."

"I doubt it."

"You're seriously not going to tell me what happened?" He looks up, offended. "I tell you everything."

"Sure you don't."

"Don't be fresh."

"What's really going on, Kenji?" I study his face, his weak attempt at humor. "You seem different today. Off."

"Nothing," he mumbles. "I told you. I just didn't want to leave James."

"But that's not all, is it?"

He says nothing.

I look into my lap. "You can tell me anything, you know. You've always been there for me and I'll always be here if you need to talk, too."

Kenji rolls his eyes. "Why do you have to make me feel

all guilty about not wanting to participate in share-your-feelings-story-time?"

"I'm n—"

"I'm just—I'm in a really shitty mood, okay?" He looks off to the side. "I feel weird. Like I just want to be pissed off today. Like I just want to punch people in the face for no reason."

I pull my knees up to my chest. Rest my chin on my knees. Nod. "You've had a hard day."

He grunts. Nods and looks at the wall. Presses a fist into the mat. "Sometimes I just get really tired, you know?" He stares at his fist, at the shapes he makes by pressing his knuckles into the soft, spongy material. "Like I just get really fed up." His voice is suddenly so quiet, it's almost like he's not talking to me at all. I can see his throat move, the emotions caught in his chest. "I keep losing people," he says. "It's like every day I'm losing people. Every goddamn day. I'm so sick of it—I'm so sick and tired of it—"

"Kenji—," I try to say.

"I missed you, J." He's still studying the mats. "I wish you'd been there last night."

"I missed you, too."

"I don't have anyone else to talk to."

"I thought you didn't like talking about your feelings," I tease him, trying to lighten the mood.

He doesn't bite.

"It just gets really heavy sometimes." He looks away. "Too heavy. Even for me. And some days I don't want to laugh," he says. "I don't want to be funny. I don't want to give a shit about anything. Some days I just want to sit on my ass and cry. All day long." His hands stop moving against the mats. "Is that crazy?" he asks quietly, still not meeting my gaze.

I blink hard against the stinging in my eyes. "No," I tell him. "No, that's not crazy at all."

He stares at the floor. "Hanging out with you has made me weird, J. All I do is sit around thinking about my feelings these days. Thanks for that."

I crawl forward and hug him right around the middle and he responds immediately, wrapping me up against him. My face is pressed to his chest and I can hear his heart beating so hard. He's still hurting so badly right now, and I keep forgetting that. I need to not forget that.

I cling to him, wishing I could ease his pain. I wish I could take his burdens and make them mine.

"It's weird, isn't it?" he says.

"What is?"

"If we were naked right now, I'd be dead."

"Shut up," I say, laughing against his chest. We're both wearing long sleeves, long pants. As long as my face and hands don't touch his skin, he's perfectly safe.

"Well, it's true."

"In what alternate universe would I ever be naked with you?"

"I am just *saying*," he says. "Shit happens. You never know."

"I think you need a girlfriend."

"Nah," he says. "I just need a hug. From my friend."

I lean back to look at him. Try to read his eyes. "You're my *best* friend, Kenji. You know that, right?"

"Yeah, kid." He grins at me. "I do. And I can't believe I got stuck with your skinny ass."

I break free of his arms. Narrow my eyes at him.

He laughs. "So how's the new boyfriend?"

My smiles fall away. "He's not my boyfriend."

"Are you sure about that? Because I'm pretty sure Romeo wouldn't have let us come live with him if he weren't a little bit madly in love with you."

I look into my hands. "Maybe one day Warner and I will learn to be friends."

"Seriously?" Kenji looks shocked. "I thought you were super into him?"

I shrug. "I'm . . . attracted to him."

"But?"

"But Warner still has a long way to go, you know?"

"Well, yeah," Kenji says. Exhales. Leans back. "Yeah. Yeah, I do."

We both say nothing for a while.

"This shit is still super freaking weird, though," Kenji says all of a sudden.

"What do you mean?" I glance up. "Which part?"

"Warner," Kenji says. "Warner is so freaking weird to me right now." Kenji looks at me. Really looks at me. "You know—in all my time on base, I never saw him have, like, a single casual conversation with a soldier before. Never. He was ice cold, J. *Ice. Cold,*" he says again. "He never smiled.

Never laughed. Never showed any emotion. And he never, *ever* talked unless he was issuing orders. He was like a machine," Kenji says. "And this?" He points at the elevator. "This guy who just left here? The guy who showed up at the house yesterday? I don't know who the hell that is. I can't even wrap my mind around it right now. Shit is unreal."

"I didn't know that," I say to him, surprised. "I had no idea he was like that."

"He wasn't like that with you?" Kenji asks. "When you first got here?"

"No," I say. "He was always pretty . . . animated with me. Not, like, *nice* animated," I clarify, "but, I mean . . . I don't know. He talked a lot." I'm silent as the memories resurface. "He was always talking, actually. That's kind of all he ever did. And he smiled at me all the time." I pause. "I thought he was doing it on purpose. To make fun of me. Or try to scare me."

Kenji leans back on his hands. "Yeah, no."

"Huh," I say, my eyes focused on a point in the distance.

Kenji sighs. "Is he . . . like . . . nice to you, at least?"

I look down. Stare at my feet. "Yeah," I whisper. "He's really nice to me."

"But you guys are not an item or anything?"

I make a face.

"Okay," Kenji says quickly, holding up both hands. "All right—I was just curious. This is a judgment-free zone, J."

I snort. "Yeah it isn't."

Kenji relaxes a little. "You know, Adam really thinks you

and Warner are, like, a thing now."

I roll my eyes. "Adam is stupid."

"Tsk, tsk, princess. We need to talk about your language—"

"Adam needs to tell Warner they're brothers."

Kenji looks up, alarmed. "Lower your voice," he whispers. "You can't just go around saying that. You know how Kent feels about it."

"I think it's unfair. Warner has a right to know."

"Why?" Kenji says. "You think he and Kent are going to become besties all of a sudden?"

I look at him then, my eyes steady, serious. "James is his brother, too, Kenji."

Kenji's body goes stiff, his face blank. His eyes widen, just a little.

I tilt my head. Raise an eyebrow.

"I didn't even . . . wow," he says. He presses a fist to his forehead. "I didn't even think about that."

"It's not fair to either of them," I say. "And I really think Warner would love to know he has brothers in this world. At least James and Adam have each other," I say. "But Warner has always been alone."

Kenji is shaking his head. Disbelief etched across his features. "This just keeps getting more and more twisted," he says. "It's like you think it couldn't possibly get more convoluted, and then, bam."

"He deserves to know, Kenji," I say again. "You know Warner at least deserves to *know*. It's his right. It's his blood, too."

Kenji looks up. Sighs. "Damn."

"If Adam doesn't tell him," I say, "I will."

"You wouldn't."

I stare at him. Hard.

"That's messed up, J." Kenji looks surprised. "You can't do that."

"Why do you keep calling me J?" I ask him. "When did that even happen? You've already given me, like, fifty different nicknames."

He shrugs. "You should be flattered."

"Oh really?" I say. "Nicknames are flattering, huh?"

He nods.

"Then how about I call you Kenny?"

Kenji crosses his arms. Stares me down. "That's not even a little bit funny."

I grin. "It is, a little bit."

"How about I call your new boyfriend King Stick-Up-His-Ass?"

"He's not my boyfriend, *Kenny*."

Kenji shoots me a warning look. Points at my face. "I am not amused, princess."

"Hey, don't you need to shower?" I ask him.

"So now you're telling me I smell."

I roll my eyes.

He clambers to his feet. Sniffs his shirt. "Damn, I do kind of smell, don't I?"

"Go," I say. "Go and hurry back. I have a feeling this is going to be a long night."

THIRTY-SIX

We're all sitting on benches around the training room. Warner is sitting next to me and I'm doing everything I can to make sure our shoulders don't accidentally touch.

"All right, so, first things first, right?" Winston says, looking around. "We have to get Sonya and Sara back. The question is how." A pause. "We have no idea how to get to the supreme."

Everyone looks at Warner.

Warner looks at his watch.

"*Well?*" Kenji says.

"Well, what?" Warner says, bored.

"Well, aren't you going to help us?" Ian snaps. "This is your territory."

Warner looks at me for the first time all evening. "You're absolutely sure you trust these people?" he asks me. "All of them?"

"Yes," I say quietly. "I really do."

"Very well." Warner takes a deep breath before addressing the group. "My father," he says calmly, "is on a ship. In the middle of the ocean."

"He's on a ship?" Kenji asks, startled. "The capital is a *ship?*"

"Not exactly." Warner hesitates. "But the point is, we have to lure him *here*. Going to him will not work. We have to create a problem big enough for him to be forced to come to us." He looks at me then. "Juliette says she already has a plan."

I nod. Take a deep breath. Study the faces before me. "I think we should take over Sector 45."

Stunned silence.

"I think, together," I tell them, "we'll be able to convince the soldiers to fight on our side. At the end of the day, no one is benefiting from The Reestablishment except for the people in charge. The soldiers are tired and hungry and probably only took this job because there were no other options." I pause. "We can rally the civilians *and* the soldiers. Everyone in the sector. Get them to join us. And they know me," I say. "The soldiers. They've already seen me—they know what I can do. But all of us together?" I shake my head. "That would be amazing. We could show them that we're different. Stronger. We can give them hope—a reason to fight back.

"And then," I say, "once we have their support, news will spread, and Anderson will be forced to come back here. He'll have to try and take us down—he'll have no other choice. And once he's back, we take him out. We fight him and his army and we win. And then we take over the country."

"My goodness."

Castle is the first to speak.

"Ms. Ferrars," he says, "you've given this a great deal of thought."

I nod.

Kenji is looking at me like he's not sure if he should laugh or applaud.

"What do you think?" I ask, looking around.

"What if it doesn't work?" Lily says. "What if the soldiers are too scared to change their allegiance? What if they kill you instead?"

"That's a definite possibility," I say. "But I think if we're strong enough—if the nine of us stand united, with all of our strengths combined—I think they'll believe we can do something pretty amazing."

"Yeah but how will they know what our strengths are?" Brendan asks. "What if they don't believe us?"

"We can show them."

"And if they shoot us?" Ian counters.

"I can do it alone, if you're worried about that. I don't mind. Kenji was teaching me how to project my energy before the war, and I think if I can learn to master that, I could do some pretty scary things. Things that might impress them enough to join us."

"You can *project*?" Winston asks, eyes wide. "You mean you can, like, mass-kill everyone with your life-sucking thing?"

"Um, no," I say. "I mean, well, yes, I suppose I could do that, too, but I'm not talking about that. I mean I can project my strength. Not the . . . life-sucking thing—"

"Wait, what strength?" Brendan asks, confused. "I thought it's your skin that's lethal?"

I'm about to respond when I remember that Brendan and Winston and Ian were all taken hostage before I'd begun to seriously train. I don't know that they knew much about my progress at all.

So I start from the top.

"My . . . power," I say, "has to do with more than just my skin." I glance at Kenji. Gesture to him. "We'd been working together for a while, trying to figure out what it was, exactly, I was capable of, and Kenji realized that my true energy is coming from deep within me, not the surface. It's in my bones, my blood, *and* my skin," I try to explain. "My real power is an insane kind of superstrength.

"My skin is just one element of that," I tell them. "It's like the most heightened form of my energy, and the craziest form of protection; it's like my body has put up a shield. Metaphorical barbed wire. It keeps intruders away." I almost laugh, wondering when it became so easy for me to talk about this stuff. To be comfortable with it. "But I'm also strong enough to break through just about anything," I tell them, "and without even injuring myself. Concrete. Brick. Glass—"

"The earth," Kenji adds.

"Yes," I say, smiling at him. "Even the earth."

"She created an earthquake," Alia says eagerly, and I'm actually surprised to hear her voice. "During the first battle," she tells Brendan and Winston and Ian. "When we were trying to save you guys. She punched the ground and it split open. That's how we were able to get away."

The guys are gawking at me.

"So, what I'm trying to say," I tell them, "is that if I can project my strength, and really learn to control it? I don't know." I shrug. "I could move mountains, probably."

"That's a bit ambitious." Kenji grins, ever the proud parent.

"Ambitious, but probably not impossible." I grin back.

"Wow," Lily says. "So you can just . . . destroy stuff? Like, anything?"

I nod. Glance at Warner. "Do you mind?"

"Not at all," he says. His eyes are carefully inscrutable.

I get to my feet and walk over to the stacks of dumbbells, all the while prepping myself mentally to tap into my energy. This is still the trickiest part for me: learning how to moderate my strength with finesse.

I pick up a fifty-pound free weight and carry it over to the group.

For a moment I wonder if this should feel heavy to me, especially considering how it weighs about half of what I do, but I can't really feel it.

I sit back down on the bench. Rest the weight on the ground.

"What are you going to do with that?" Ian asks, eyes wide.

"What do you want me to do?" I ask him.

"You're telling me you can just, like, rip that apart or whatever?" Winston says.

I nod.

"Do it," Kenji says. He's practically bouncing in his seat. "Do it do it."

So I do.

I pick it up, and literally crush the weight between my hands. It becomes a mangled mess of metal. A fifty-pound lump. I rip it in half and drop the two pieces on the floor.

The benches shake.

"Sorry," I say quickly, looking around. "I didn't mean to toss it like that—"

"God*damn*," Ian says. "That is so cool."

"Do it again," Winston says, eyes bright.

"I'd really rather she didn't destroy all of my property," Warner cuts in.

"Hey, so—wait—," Winston says, realizing something as he stares at Warner. "You can do that, too, can't you? You can just take her power and use it like that, too?"

"I can take all of your powers," Warner corrects him. "And do whatever I want with them."

The terror in the room is a very palpable thing.

I frown at Warner. "Please don't scare them."

He says nothing. Looks at nothing.

"So the two of you"—Ian tries to find his voice—"I mean, together—you two could basically—"

"Take over the world?" Warner is looking at the wall now.

"I was going to say you could kick some serious ass, but yeah, that, too, I guess." Ian shakes his head.

"Are you sure you trust this guy?" Lily asks me, jerking

a thumb at Warner and looking at me like she's seriously, genuinely concerned. "What if he's just using you for your power?"

"I trust him with my life," I say quietly. "I already have, and I'd do it again."

Warner looks at me and looks away, and for a brief second I catch the charge of emotion in his eyes.

"So, let me get this straight," Winston says. "Our plan is to basically seduce the soldiers and civilians of Sector 45 into fighting with us?"

Kenji crosses his arms. "Yeah, it sounds like we're going to go all peacock and hope they find us attractive enough to mate with."

"Gross." Brendan frowns.

"Despite how weird Kenji just made this sound," I say, shooting a stern look in his direction, "the answer is yes, basically. We can provide them with a group to rally around. We take charge of the army, and then take charge of the people. And then we lead them into battle. We really, truly fight back."

"And if you win?" Castle asks. He's been so quiet all this time. "What do you plan to do then?"

"What do you mean?" I ask.

"Let's say you are successful," he says. "You defeat the supreme. You kill him and his men. Then what? Who will take over as the supreme commander?"

"I will."

The room gasps. I feel Warner go stiff beside me.

"Damn, princess," Kenji says quietly.

"And then?" Castle asks, ignoring everyone but me. "After that?" His eyes are worried. Scared, almost. "You're going to kill whoever else stands in your way? All the other sector leaders, all across the nation? That's 554 more wars—"

"Some will surrender," I tell him.

"And the others?" he asks. "How can you lead a nation in the right direction when you've just slaughtered all who oppose you? How will you be any different from those you've defeated?"

"I trust myself," I tell him, "to be strong enough to do what's right. Our world is dying right now. You said yourself that we have the means to reclaim our land—to change things back to the way they were. Once power is in the right place—with *us*—you can rebuild what you started at Omega Point. You'll have the freedom to implement those changes to our land, water, animals, and atmosphere, and save millions of lives in the process—giving the new generations hope for a different future. We have to try," I tell him. "We can't just sit back and watch people die when we have the power to make a difference."

The room goes silent. Still.

"Hell," Winston says. "I'd follow you into battle."

"Me too," Alia says.

"And me." Brendan.

"You know I'm in," Kenji says.

"Me too," Lily and Ian say at the same time.

Castle takes a deep breath. "Maybe," he says. He leans back in his chair, clasps his hands. "Maybe you'll be able to do right what I did wrong." He shakes his head. "I am twenty-seven years your senior and I've never had your confidence, but I do understand your heart. And I trust that you say what you believe to be true." A pause. A careful look. "We will support you. But know now that you are taking on a great and terrifying responsibility. One that may backfire in an irreversible way."

"I do understand that," I say quietly.

"Very well then, Ms. Ferrars. Good luck, and godspeed. Our world is in your hands."

THIRTY-SEVEN

"You didn't tell me what you thought of my plan."

Warner and I have just stepped back into his room and he still hasn't said a word to me. He's standing by the door to his office, his eyes on the floor. "I didn't realize you wanted my opinion."

"Of course I want your opinion."

"I should really get back to work," he says, and turns to go.

I touch his arm.

Warner goes rigid. He stands, unmoving, his eyes trained on the hand I've placed on his forearm.

"Please," I whisper. "I don't want it to be like this with us. I want us to be able to talk. To get to know each other again, *properly*—to be friends—"

Warner makes a strange sound deep in his throat. Puts a few feet between us. "I am doing my best, love. But I don't know how to be just your friend."

"It doesn't have to be all or nothing," I try to tell him. "There can be steps in between—I just need time to understand you like this—as a different person—"

"But that's just it." His voice is worn thin. "You need time to understand me as a *different person*. You need time to fix your perception of me."

"Why is that so wrong—"

"Because I am not a different person," he says firmly. "I am the same man I've always been and I have never tried to be different. You have misunderstood me, Juliette. You've judged me, you've perceived me to be something I am not, but that is no fault of mine. I have not changed, and I will not change—"

"You already have."

His jaw clenches. "You have quite a lot of gall to speak with such conviction on matters you know nothing about."

I swallow, hard.

Warner steps so close to me I'm actually afraid to move. "You once accused me of not knowing the meaning of love," he says. "But you were wrong. You fault me, perhaps, for loving you too much." His eyes are so intense. So green. So cold. "But at least I do not deny my own heart."

"And you think I do," I whisper.

Warner drops his eyes. Says nothing.

"What you don't understand," I tell him, my voice catching, "is that I don't even know my own heart anymore. I don't know how to name what I feel yet and I need time to figure it out. You want more right now but right now what I need is for you to be my friend—"

Warner flinches.

"I do not have friends," he says.

"Why can't you try?"

He shakes his head.

"Why? Why not give it a chance—"

"Because I am afraid," he finally says, voice shaking, "that your friendship would be the end of me."

I'm still frozen in place as his office door slams shut behind him.

THIRTY-EIGHT

I never thought I'd see Warner in sweatpants.

Or sneakers.

And right now, he's wearing both. Plus a T-shirt.

Now that our group is staying in Warner's training facilities, I have a reason to tag along as he starts his day. I always knew he spent a lot of time working, but I never knew how much of his time was spent working out. He's so disciplined, so precise about everything. It amazes me.

He starts his mornings on a stationary bike, ends his evenings with a run on the treadmill. And every weekday he works out a different part of his body.

"Mondays are for legs," I heard him explain to Castle. "Tuesdays I work chest. Wednesdays I work my shoulders and my back. Thursdays are for triceps and deltoids. Fridays are for biceps and forearms. And every day is for abdominals and cardio. I also spend most weekends doing target practice," he said.

Today is Tuesday.

Which means right now, I'm watching him bench-press three hundred and fifteen pounds. Three forty-five-pound plates on each side of what Kenji told me is called an Olympic bar, which weighs an additional forty-five pounds. I can't stop staring. I don't think I've ever been more attracted to him in all the time I've known him.

Kenji pulls up next to me. Nods at Warner. "So this gets you going, huh?"

I'm mortified.

Kenji barks out a laugh.

"I've never seen him in sweatpants before." I try to sound normal. "I've never even seen him in shorts."

Kenji raises an eyebrow at me. "I bet you've seen him in less."

I want to die.

Kenji and I are supposed to spend this next month training. That's the plan. I need to train enough to fight and use my strength without being overpowered ever again. This isn't the kind of situation we can go into without absolute confidence, and since I'm supposed to be leading the mission, I still have a lot of work to do. I need to be able to access my energy in an instant, and I need to be able to moderate the amount of power I exert at any given time. In other words: I need to achieve absolute mastery over my ability.

Kenji is also training in his own way; he wants to perfect his skill in projecting; he wants to be able to do it without having to make direct contact with another person. But he and I are the only ones who have any real work to do. Castle has been in control of himself for decades now, and everyone else has fairly straightforward skills that they've very naturally adapted to. In my case, I have seventeen years of psychological trauma to undo.

I need to break down these self-made walls.

Today, Kenji's starting small. He wants me to move a dumbbell across the room through sheer force of will. But all I've managed to do was make it twitch. And I'm not even sure that was me.

"You're not focusing," Kenji says to me. "You need to connect—find your core and pull from within," he's saying. "You have to, like, *literally* pull it out of yourself and then push it out around you, J. It's only difficult in the beginning," he says, "because your body is so used to containing the energy. In your case it's going to be even harder, because you've spent your whole life bottling it up. You have to give yourself permission to let it go. Let down your guard. Find it. Harness it. Release it."

He gives me the same speech, over and over again.

And I keep trying, over and over again.

I count to three.

I close my eyes and try to really, truly focus this time. I listen to the sudden urge to lift my arms, planting my feet firmly on the floor. I blow out a breath. Squeeze my eyes shut tighter. I feel the energy surging up, through my bones, my blood, raging and rising until it culminates into a mass so potent I can no longer contain it. I know it needs release, and needs it now.

But how?

Before, I always thought I needed to touch something to let the power out.

It never occurred to me to throw the energy into a

stationary object. I thought my hands were the final destination; I never considered using them as a transmitter, as a medium for the energy to pass through. But I'm just now realizing that I can try to push it out *through* my hands—*through* my skin. And maybe, if I'm strong enough, I might be able to learn to manipulate the power in midair, forcing it to move whichever way I want.

My sudden realization gives me a renewed burst of confidence. I'm excited now, eager to see if my theory is correct. I steel myself, feeling the rush of power flood through me again. My shoulders tense as the energy coats my hands, my wrists, my forearms. It feels so warm, so intense, almost like it's a tangible thing; the kind of power that could tangle in my fingers.

I curl my fists.

Pull back my arms.

And then fling them forward, opening my hands at the same time.

Silence.

I squint one eye open, sneaking a look at the dumbbell still sitting in the same spot.

Sigh.

"GET DOWN," Kenji shouts, yanking me backward and shoving me face-first onto the floor.

I can hear everyone shouting and thudding to the ground around us. I crane my neck up only to see that they've all got their hands over their heads, faces covered; I try to look around.

Panic seizes me by the throat.

The rock wall is fissuring into what might be a hundred pieces, creaking and groaning as it falls apart. I watch, horrified, as one huge, jagged chunk trembles just before unhinging from the wall.

Warner is standing underneath.

I'm about to scream before I see him look up, both hands outstretched toward the chaos. Immediately, the wall stops shaking. The pieces hover, trembling only slightly, caught between falling and fitting back into place.

My mouth is still open.

Warner looks to his right. Nods.

I follow his line of sight and see Castle on the other side, using his power to hold up the other end. Together they control the pieces as they fall to the floor, allowing them to float down, settling each broken slab and each jagged bit gently against what remains of the wall.

Everyone begins to pop their heads up, realizing something has changed. We slowly get to our feet, and watch, dumbstruck, as Castle and Warner contain the disaster and confine it to one space. Nothing else is damaged. No one is hurt. I'm still looking on, eyes wide with awe.

When the work is finally done, Warner and Castle share a brief moment of acknowledgment before they head in opposite directions.

Warner comes to find me. Castle to everyone else.

"Are you okay?" Warner asks. His tone is businesslike, but his eyes give him away. "You're not injured?"

I shake my head. "That was incredible."

"I can't take any credit for it," he says. "It was Castle's power I borrowed."

"But you're so *good* at it," I tell him, forgetting for a moment that we're supposed to be mad at each other. "You *just* learned you have this ability, and you can already control it. So naturally. But then when I try to do something, I nearly kill everyone in the process." I drop my head. "I'm the worst at everything," I mutter. "The worst."

"Don't feel bad," he says quietly. "You'll figure it out."

"Was it ever hard for you?" I look up, hopeful. "Figuring out how to control the energy?"

"Oh," he says, surprised. "No. Though I've always been very good at everything I do."

I drop my head again. Sigh.

Warner laughs and I peek up.

He's smiling.

"What?"

"Nothing," he whispers.

I hear a sharp whistle. Spin around.

"Hey—jazz hands!" Kenji barks. "Get your ass back over here." He makes it a point to look as irritated as possible. "Back to work. And this time, *focus*. You're not an ape. Don't just throw your shit everywhere."

Warner actually laughs.

Out loud.

I look back at him, and he's looking toward the wall, trying to suppress a wide smile as he runs a hand through his hair, down the back of his neck.

"At least someone appreciates my sense of humor," Kenji says before tugging at my arm. "Come on, princess. Let's try that again. And please, try not to kill everyone in this room."

THIRTY-NINE

We've been practicing all week.

I'm so exhausted I can't even stand up anymore, but I've made more progress than I ever could've hoped for. Kenji is still working with me directly, and Castle is overseeing my progress, but everyone else spends time training on all the various machines.

Winston and Brendan seem to be in better spirits every day—they look healthier, livelier—and the gash on Brendan's face is starting to fade. I'm so happy to see their progress, and doubly thrilled Delalieu was able to find the right medicines for them.

The two of them spend most days eating and sleeping and jumping from the bikes to the treadmill. Lily has been messing around with a little of everything, and today she's exercising with the medicine balls in the corner. Ian has been lifting weights and looking after Castle, and Alia has spent all week sitting in the corner, sketching things in a notepad. She seems happier, more settled. And I can't help but wonder if Adam and James are okay, too. I hope they're safe.

Warner is always gone during the day.

Every once in a while I glance at the elevator doors,

secretly hoping they'll open and deposit him back inside this room. Sometimes he stops by for a bit—jumps on the bike or goes for a quick run—but mostly he's gone.

I only really see him in the mornings for his early workout, and in the evenings when he does another round of cardio. The end of the night is my favorite part of the day. It's when all nine of us sit down and talk about our progress. Winston and Brendan are healing, I'm getting stronger, and Warner lets us know if there've been any new developments from the civilians, the soldiers, or The Reestablishment—so far, everything is still quiet.

And then Warner and I go back up to his quarters, where we shower and head to separate rooms. I sleep on his bed. He sleeps on the couch in his office.

Every night I tell myself I'll be brave enough to knock on his door, but I never have.

I still don't know what to say.

Kenji tugs on my hair.

"*Ow*—" I jerk back, scowling. "What's wrong with you?"

"You've been hit extra hard with the stupid stick today."

"What? I thought you said I was doing okay—"

"You are. But you're distracted. You keep staring at the elevator like it's about to grant you three wishes."

"Oh," I say. I look away. "Well. Sorry."

"Don't apologize," he sighs. Frowns a little. "What the hell is going on between you guys, anyway? Do I even want to know?"

I sigh. Flop onto the mats. "I have no idea, Kenji. He's hot and cold." I shrug. "I guess it's fine. I just need a little space for now."

"But you like him?" Kenji raises an eyebrow.

I say nothing. Feel my face warm.

Kenji rolls his eyes. "You know, I really never would've thought Warner could make you happy."

"Do I *look* happy?" I counter.

"Good point." He sighs. "I just mean that you always seemed so happy with Kent. This is a little hard for me to process." He hesitates. Rubs his forehead. "Well. Actually, you were a hell of a lot weirder when you were with Kent. Super whiny. And so dramatic. And you cried. All. The. Damn. Time." He screws up his face. "Jesus. I can't decide which one of them is worse."

"You think *I'm* dramatic?" I ask him, eyes wide. "Do you even know yourself at all?"

"I am not dramatic, okay? My presence just commands a certain kind of attention—"

I snort.

"Hey," he says, pointing at my face. "I am just saying that I don't know what to believe anymore. I've already been on this merry-go-round. First Adam. Now Warner. Next week you're going to try and hook up with me."

"You really wish that were true, don't you?"

"Whatever," he says, looking away. "I don't even like you."

"You think I'm pretty."

"I think you're delusional."

"I don't even know what this is, Kenji." I meet his eyes. "That's the problem. I don't know how to explain it, and I'm not sure I understand the depth of it yet. All I know is that whatever this is, I never felt it with Adam."

Kenji's eyes pull together, surprised and scared. He says nothing for a second. Blows out a breath. "Seriously?"

I nod.

"*Seriously*, seriously?"

"Yeah," I say. "I feel so . . . *light*. Like I could just . . . I don't know . . ." I trail off. "It's like I feel like, for the first time in my life, I'm going to be okay. Like I'm going to be strong."

"But that sounds like it's just *you*," he says. "That has nothing to do with Warner."

"That's true," I tell him. "But sometimes people can weigh us down, too. And I know Adam didn't mean to, but he was weighing me down. We were two sad people stuck together."

"Huh." Kenji leans back on his hands.

"Being with Adam was always overshadowed by some kind of pain or difficulty," I explain, "and Adam was always so serious. He was intense in a way that exhausted me sometimes. We were always hiding, or sneaking around, or on the run, and we never found enough uninterrupted moments to be together. It was almost like the universe was trying to tell me I was trying too hard to make things work with him."

"Kent wasn't that bad, J." Kenji frowns. "You're not giving him enough credit. He's been acting kind of dickish lately, but he's a good guy. You know he is. Shit is just really rough for him right now."

"I know," I sigh, feeling sad, somehow. "But this world is still falling apart. Even if we win this war, everything is going to get much, much worse before it gets better." I pause. Stare into my hands. "And I think people become who they really are when things get rough. I've seen it firsthand. With myself, my parents, with society, even. And yeah, Adam is a good guy. He really is. But just because he's a good guy doesn't make him the right guy for me."

I look up.

"I'm so different now. I'm not right for him anymore, and he's not right for me."

"But he still loves you."

"No," I say. "He doesn't."

"That's a pretty heavy accusation."

"It's not an accusation," I say. "One day Adam will realize that what he felt for me was just a crazy kind of desperation. We were two people who really needed someone to hold on to, and we had this past that made us seem so compatible. But it wasn't enough. Because if it were, I wouldn't have been able to walk away so easily." I drop my eyes, my voice. "Warner didn't seduce me, Kenji. He didn't steal me away. I just . . . I reached a point where everything changed for me.

"Everything I thought I knew about Warner was wrong. Everything I thought I believed about myself was wrong.

And I knew *I* was changing," I say to him. "I wanted to move forward. I wanted to be angry and I wanted to scream for the first time in my life and I couldn't. I didn't want people to be afraid of me, so I tried to shut up and disappear, hoping it would make them more comfortable. But I hate that I let myself be so passive my whole life, and I see now how differently things could've been if I'd had faith in myself when it mattered. I don't want to go back to that," I tell him. "I won't. Not ever."

"You don't have to," Kenji points out. "Why would you? I don't think Kent wanted you to be passive."

I shrug. "I still wonder if he wants me to be the girl he first fell for. The person I was when we met."

"And that's bad?"

"That's not who I *am* anymore, Kenji. Do I still seem like that girl to you?"

"How the hell should I know?"

"You *don't* know," I say, exasperated. "That's why you don't understand. You don't know what I used to be like. You don't know what it was like in my head. I lived in a really dark place," I say to him. "I wasn't safe in my own mind. I woke up every morning hoping to die and then spent the rest of the day wondering if maybe I was already dead because I couldn't even tell the *difference*," I say, more harshly than I mean to. "I had a small thread of hope and I clung to it, but the majority of my life was spent waiting around to see if someone would take pity on me."

Kenji is just staring at me, his eyes tight.

"Don't you think I've realized," I say to him, angrier now, "that if I'd allowed myself to get mad a long time ago, I would've discovered I had the strength to break through that asylum with my own two hands?"

Kenji flinches.

"Don't you think that I think about that, all the time?" I ask him, my voice shaking. "Don't you think it *kills* me to know that it was my own unwillingness to recognize myself as a human being that kept me trapped for so long? For two hundred and sixty-four days, Kenji," I say, swallowing hard. "Two hundred and sixty-four days I was in there and the whole time, I had the power to break myself out and I didn't, because I had no idea I could. Because I never even tried. Because I let the world teach me to hate myself. I was a *coward*," I say, "who needed someone else to tell me I was worth something before I took any steps to save myself.

"This isn't about Adam or Warner," I tell him. "This is about me and what I want. This is about me finally understanding where I want to be in ten years. Because I'm going to be alive, Kenji. I will be alive in ten years, and I'm going to be happy. I'm going to be strong. And I don't need anyone to tell me that anymore. I am enough, and I always will be."

I'm breathing hard now, trying to calm my heart.

Kenji is staring at me, mildly terrified.

"I want Adam to be happy, Kenji, I really do. But he and I would end up like water going nowhere."

"What do you mean . . . ?"

"Water that never moves," I say to him. "It's fine for a little while. You can drink from it and it'll sustain you. But if it sits too long it goes bad. It grows stale. It becomes toxic." I shake my head. "I need waves. I need waterfalls. I want rushing currents."

"Damn," Kenji says. He laughs nervously, scratches the back of his head. "I think you should write that speech down, princess. Because you're going to have to tell him all of that yourself."

"What?" My body goes rigid.

"Yeah." Kenji coughs. "Adam and James are coming here tomorrow."

"*What?*" I gasp.

"Yeah. Awkward, right?" He tries to laugh. "Sooo awkward."

"Why? Why would he come here? How do you even know?"

"I've, um, kind of been going back?" He clears his throat. "To, you know, check up on them. Mostly James. But you know." He looks away. Looks around.

"To check up on them?"

"Yeah. Just to make sure they're doing okay." He nods at nothing. "Like, I told him that we had a really awesome plan in place," Kenji says, pointing at me. "Thanks to you, of course. Really awesome plan. So. And I told him the food was good," Kenji adds. "And the showers are hot. So, like, he knows Warner didn't cheap out on us or anything. And yeah, you know, some other stuff."

"What other stuff?" I ask, suspicious now. "What did you say to him?"

"Hmm?" Kenji is studying the hem of his shirt, pulling at it.

"Kenji."

"Okay, listen," Kenji says, holding up both hands. "Just—don't get mad, okay?"

"I'm already getting mad—"

"They were going to *die* out there. I couldn't just let them stay in that crappy little space all by themselves—especially not James—and especially not now that we've got a solid plan in place—"

"What did you tell him, Kenji?" My patience is wearing thin.

"Maybe," he says, backing away now, "maybe I told him how you were a calm, rational, very nice person who does not like to hurt people, especially not her very good-looking friend Kenji—"

"Dammit, Kenji, tell me what you did—"

"I need five feet," he says.

"What?"

"Five feet. Of space," he says. "Between us."

"I will give you five inches."

Kenji swallows, hard. "Okay, well, maybe," he says, "maybe I told him . . . that . . . um, you missed him. A lot."

I nearly rock backward, reeling from the impact of his words.

"You did what?" My voice drops to a whisper.

"It was the only way I could get him here, okay? He thought you were in love with Warner, and his pride is such a freaking *issue* with him—"

"What the hell is wrong with you?" I shout. "They're going to *kill* each other!"

"This could be their chance to make up," Kenji says. "And then we can all be friends, just like you wanted—"

"Oh my God," I say, running a hand over my eyes. "Are you *insane*? Why would you do that? I'll have to break his heart all over again!"

"Yeah, you know, I was thinking maybe you could pretend to be, like, *not* interested in Warner? Just until after this war is over? Because that would make things a little less stressful. And then we'd all get along, and Adam and James wouldn't die out there all alone. You know? Happy ending."

I'm so mad right now I'm shaking.

"You told him something else, didn't you?" I ask, my eyes narrowing. "You said something else to him. About me. *Didn't you?*"

"What?" Kenji is moving backward now. "I don't—"

"Is that all you told him?" I demand. "That I missed him? Or did you tell him something else, too?"

"Oh. Well, now that you mention it, yeah, um, I might've told him, um, that you were still in love with him?"

My brain is screaming.

"And . . . that maybe you talk about him all the time? And maybe I told him that you cry a lot about how much you miss him. Maybe. I don't know, we talked about a lot of things, so—"

"I am going to MURDER YOU—"

"No," he says, pointing at me as he shifts backward again. "Bad Juliette. You don't like to kill people, remember? You're against that, remember? You like to talk about feelings and rainbows—"

"Why, Kenji?" I drop my head into my hands. "Why? Why would you lie to him?"

"Because," he snaps, frustrated. "This is *bullshit*. Everyone is already dying in this world. Everyone has lost their homes, their families—everything they've ever loved. And you and Kent should be able to work out your stupid high school drama like two adults. We shouldn't have to lose each other like this. We've already lost everyone else," he says, angry now.

"They're *alive*, J. They're still alive." He looks at me, eyes bright with barely restrained emotion. "That's reason enough for me to try and keep them in my life." He looks away. Lowers his voice. "Please," he says. "This is such crap. This whole thing. I feel like I'm the kid caught in the middle of a divorce. And I didn't want to lie to him, okay? I didn't. But at least I convinced him to come back. And maybe once he gets here, he'll want to stay."

I glare at him. "When are they going to be here?"

Kenji takes a beat to breathe. "I'm getting them in the morning."

"You know I'm going to tell Warner, right? You know

you can't just keep them here and make them invisible."

"I know," he says.

"Fine." I'm so furious I don't even know what to say anymore. I can't even look at him right now.

"So . . . ," Kenji says. "Good talk?"

I spin around. My voice is deathly soft, my face only inches from his. "If they kill each other," I say to him, "I will break your neck."

"Damn, princess. When did you get so violent?"

"I'm not kidding, Kenji. They've tried to kill each other before, and they almost succeeded. I hope you didn't forget that detail when you were making your happy rainbow plans." I stare him down. "This isn't just the story of two guys who don't like each other. They want each other *dead*."

Kenji sighs. Looks toward the wall. "It'll be okay," he says. "We'll figure it out."

"No," I say to him. "*You'll* figure it out."

"Can't you try to see where I'm coming from?" he asks. "Can't you see how much better it would be for us to all be together? There's no one left, J. It's just us. We shouldn't all have to suffer just because you and Kent aren't making out anymore. We shouldn't be living like this."

I close my eyes. Sigh deeply and try to calm down.

"I do," I say quietly. "I do see where you're coming from. I really, really do. And I love you for wanting everyone to be okay, and I love you for looking out for me, and for wanting me and Adam to be together again. I know how much you're going through right now. And I'm so sorry, Kenji. I really am. I know this isn't easy for you. But that's also exactly why I don't understand why you'd force the two of them together. You want to stick them in the same room. In a confined space. I thought you *didn't* want them to die."

"I think you're being a little pessimistic about this."

"Dammit, Kenji!" I throw my arm out, exasperated, and don't even realize what I've done until I hear a crash. I look toward the sound. I've managed to knock down an entire rack of free weights. From across the room.

I am a walking catastrophe.

"I need to cool off," I tell him, trying to moderate my voice. "I'll be back to shave your head while you're sleeping."

Kenji looks genuinely terrified for the first time. "You wouldn't."

I head toward the opposite wall. Hit the button for the elevator. "You're a heavy sleeper, right?"

"That's not funny, J—that's not even a little bit funny—"

The elevator pings open. I step inside. "Good night, Kenji."

I can still hear him shouting at me as the doors close.

FORTY

Warner is in the shower when I get back up to the room.

I glance at the clock. This would be about the time he'd start heading down to the training rooms; I usually meet him there for our nightly recap.

Instead I fall face-first onto the bed.

I don't know what I'm going to do.

Adam is going to show up here tomorrow thinking I still want to be with him. I don't want to have to walk away again, to see the hurt in his eyes. I don't want to hurt him. I really don't. I never have.

I'm going to *kill* Kenji.

I shove my head under the pillows, stacking them on my head and squishing them down around my ears until I've managed to shut out the world. I don't want to think about this right now. Now, of all the times to be thinking about this. Why do things always have to be so complicated? *Why?*

I feel a hand on my back.

I jerk up, pillows flying everywhere, and I'm so stupidly startled I actually fall off the bed. A pillow topples over and hits me in the face.

I groan, clutching the pillow to my chest. I press my

forehead to the soft cushion of it, squeezing my eyes shut. I've never had such a terrible headache.

"Juliette?" A tentative voice. "Are you okay?"

I lower the pillow. Blink up.

Warner is wearing a towel.

A *towel.*

I want to roll under the bed.

"Adam and James are coming here tomorrow," I say to him, all at once. I just say it, just like that.

Warner raises his eyebrows. "I didn't realize they'd received an invitation."

"Kenji is bringing them here. He's been sneaking out to go check on them, and now he's bringing them here. Tomorrow morning."

Warner's face is carefully neutral, his voice unaffected. He might be talking about the color of the walls. "I thought he wasn't interested in joining your resistance anymore."

For a moment I can't believe I'm still lying on the ground, clutching a pillow to my chest, staring at Warner who's wearing a towel and nothing else. I can't even take myself seriously.

"Kenji told Adam I'm still in love with him."

There it is.

A flash of anger. In and out. Warner's eyes spark and fade. He looks to the wall, silent a moment. "I see." His voice is quiet, controlled.

"He knew it was the only way to get Adam back here."

Warner says nothing.

"But I'm not, you know. In love with him." I'm surprised at how easily the words leave my lips, and even more surprised that I feel the need to say them out loud. That I'd need to reassure Warner, of all people. "I care about Adam," I say to him, "in the way that I'll always care about the few people who've shown me kindness in my life, but everything else is just . . . gone."

"I understand," he says.

I don't believe him.

"So what do you want to do?" I ask. "About tomorrow? And Adam?"

"What do you think should be done?"

I sigh. "I'm going to have to talk to him. I'll have to break up with him for the third time," I say, groaning again. "This is so stupid. So *stupid*."

I finally drop the pillow. Drop my arms to my sides.

But when I look up again, Warner is gone.

I sit up, alert. Glance around.

He's standing in the corner, putting on a pair of pants.

I try not to look at him as I climb back onto the bed.

I kick off my shoes and sink under the blankets, burrowing into the pillows until my head is buried beneath them. I feel the weight shift on the bed, and realize Warner must be sitting beside me. He plucks one of the pillows off my head. Leans in. Our noses are only inches apart.

"You don't love him at all?" Warner asks me.

My voice is being stupid. "Romantically?"

He nods.

"No."

"You're not attracted to him?"

"I'm attracted to you."

"I'm serious," he says.

"So am I."

Warner's still staring at me. He blinks, once.

"Don't you believe me?" I ask.

He looks away.

"Can't you tell?" I ask him. "Can't you feel it?"

And I am either losing my mind or Warner just blushed.

"You give me too much credit, love." His eyes are focused on the blanket, his words soft. "I will disappoint you. I am every bit the defective human being you don't think I am."

I sit up. Look at him closely. "You're so different," I whisper. "So different and exactly the same."

"What do you mean?"

"You're so gentle now. You're very . . . calm," I tell him. "Much more than you were before."

He says nothing for a long time. And then he stands up. His tone is curt when he says, "Yes, well, I'm sure you and Kishimoto will find a way to sort this situation out. Excuse me."

And then he leaves. Again.

I have no idea what to make of him anymore.

FORTY-ONE

Adam is already here.

Warner was completely uninterested in dealing with Adam. So he's gone about his day and his duties, having skipped his morning workout.

And now I'm here.

I've just stepped out of the elevator, and the pinging sound that signals the opening of the doors has alerted everyone to my presence. Adam was standing in the corner, talking to James. He's now staring at me.

It's weird, how I feel when I look at him now. There is no extreme emotion in me. No excess of happiness or sadness. Not upset. Not overjoyed. His face is familiar to me; his body, familiar to me. His unsteady smile, as he looks at me, is familiar to me.

How strange that we can go from friends to inseparable to hateful then casual all in one lifetime.

"Hi," I say.

"Hey." He looks away.

"Hi, James." I smile.

"Hi!" He waves, buoyant. He's standing just next to Adam, eyes lit up, clearly thrilled to be back among us. "This place is so cool."

"It is," I agree. "Have you had a chance to take a shower yet? The water is warm here."

"Oh, right," he says, shyly now. "Kenji told me about that."

"Why don't you get washed up? Delalieu will be bringing lunch down soon. I'm sure Brendan can show you around the locker room—and where to put all your stuff. You can have your own locker," I tell him, glancing at Brendan as I do. He nods, taking the hint and jumping to his feet right away.

"Really?" James is saying. "That's so cool. So they just bring the food to you? And you get to shower whenever you want? Is there a curfew?"

"Yes, yes, and no," Brendan answers him. He takes James's hand. Grabs his little bag. "We can stay up as late as we like," he tells him. "Maybe after dinner I'll show you how to use the bicycles in here," he says, his voice fading to an echo as he and James disappear into the locker room.

Once James is gone, everyone seems to exhale.

I steel myself. Step forward.

"I'm really sorry," Adam says first, crossing the room to meet me. "You have no idea—"

"Adam." I cut him off, anxious. Nervous. I have to say this and I have to say it now. "Kenji lied to you."

Adam stops. Stills.

"I haven't been crying over you," I say, wondering if it's even possible to deliver this kind of information without both humiliating him and breaking his heart. I feel like such a monster. "And I'm really, really happy you're here, but I don't think we should be together anymore."

"Oh," he says. Rocks back on his heels. Drops his eyes. Runs both hands through his hair. "Right."

Out of the corner of my eye, I see Kenji looking at me. He's waving his hand, trying to get my attention, but I'm still too mad at him right now. I don't want to talk to him until I've fixed this.

"Adam," I say. "I'm sorry—"

"No," he says, holding up a hand to stop me. He looks dazed, sort of. Strange. "It's okay. Really. I already knew you were going to say that to me." He laughs a little, but awkwardly. "I guess I thought knowing in advance would make it feel a lot less like I was being punched in the gut." He cringes. "But nope. Still hurts like hell." He backs up against the wall. Slides down to the floor.

He's not looking at me.

"How did you know?" I ask. "How did you know what I was going to say?"

"I told him before you got here," Kenji says, stepping forward. He shoots me a sharp look. "I came clean. I told him what we talked about yesterday. All the things you said."

"Then why is he still here?" I ask, stunned. I turn to face Adam. "I thought you said you never wanted to see me again."

"I never should've said that." Adam is still looking at the floor.

"So . . . you're okay?" I ask him. "With Warner?"

Adam looks up in disgust, so different in an instant.

"Are you out of your mind? I want to put his head through a goddamn wall."

"Then why are you still here?" I ask again. "I don't understand—"

"Because I don't want to *die*," he says to me. "Because I've been racking my brain trying to figure out how to feed my little brother and I've come up with exactly jack and shit in the way of solutions. Because it's cold as hell outside, and he's hungry, and because our electricity is going to get shut off soon." Adam is breathing hard. "I didn't know what else to do. So now I'm here, my pride in the toilet, hoping I can stay in my ex-girlfriend's new *boyfriend's* bachelor pad, and I want to kill myself." He swallows. "And I can suffer through that," he says, "if it means James will be safe. But right now I'm still waiting for your shithead of a boyfriend to show up and try to kill me."

"He's not my boyfriend," I say quietly. "And he's not going to kill you. He doesn't even care that you're here."

Adam laughs out loud. "Bullshit," he says.

"I'm serious."

Adam gets to his feet. Studies my eyes. "You're telling me I can stay here, in his room, and eat his food, and he's just going to *let* me?" Adam's eyes are wide, incredulous. "You still don't understand this guy. He doesn't operate the way you think he does, Juliette. He doesn't think like a normal human being. He's a freaking sociopath. And you really are insane," he says, "if you think it's okay to be with someone like that."

I flinch, stung. "Be very careful how you speak to me, Adam. I won't tolerate your insults again."

"I can't even believe you," he says. "I can't believe you can stand there and treat me like this." His face is twisted into something so intensely unattractive.

Anger.

"I'm not trying to hurt you—"

"Maybe you should've remembered that before you ran into the arms of some psycho!"

"Calm your ass down, Kent." I hear Kenji's sharp warning from the corner of the room. "I thought you said you were going to be cool."

"I am being cool," he says, his voice rising, eyes on fire. "I'm a freaking saint. I don't know anyone else who would be as generous as I am right now." He looks back at me. "You were lying to me the whole time we were together. You were *cheating* on me—"

"No I wasn't."

"This kind of shit doesn't just happen overnight," he shouts. "You don't just fall out of love with someone like that—"

"We're *done,* Adam. I'm not doing this again. You're welcome to stay here," I tell him. "Especially for James's sake. But you can't stay here and insult me. You have no right."

Adam tenses his jaw. Grabs his things. And charges into the locker room.

FORTY-TWO

"I am going to kill you."

"He wasn't like that when I went to visit," Kenji says to me. "I swear. He was fine. He was *sad*."

"Yeah, well, obviously seeing my face isn't bringing back happy memories for him."

Kenji sighs. Looks away. "I'm really sorry," he says. "I swear. But he wasn't lying, J. They were down to practically nothing the last time I went back there. Kent said half their supplies went bad because he didn't realize the blast had broken some of the shelves in their storage room. Some of the jars had cracked open and there were rodents and shit eating their food. And they were all alone out there. It's cold as all hell and you have no idea how depressing it was, seeing them like that, and James—"

"I get it, Kenji." I blow out a breath. Fold myself onto the floor. "I really do."

I look up, look around. Everyone is busying themselves with some kind of task. Running or sketching or training or lifting weights. I think we're all exhausted by this drama. No one wants to deal with it anymore.

Kenji sits down across from me.

"He can't keep treating me like that," I finally say. "And

I won't keep having the same conversation with him." I look up. "You brought him here. He's your responsibility. We have three weeks before we initiate this plan, and we're already cutting it really close. I need to be able to come down here and train every day, and I don't want to have to worry about him freaking out on me."

"I know," he says. "I know."

"Good."

"Hey, so—were you serious?" Kenji asks. "When you said Warner doesn't care about him being here?"

"Yeah. Why?"

Kenji raises his eyebrows. "That's . . . weird."

"One day," I say to him, "you'll realize that Warner is not as crazy as you think he is."

"Yeah," Kenji says. "Or maybe one day we'll be able to reprogram that chip in your head."

"Shut up." I laugh, shoving him a little.

"All right. Up. Let's go. It's time to work."

FORTY-THREE

Alia has designed me a new suit.

We're sitting on the mats like we always do in the evenings, and right now, Alia is showing us her designs.

I've never seen her this animated before.

She's more confident talking about the contents of her sketchbook than she is the weather. She's talking fast and fluid, describing the details and the dimensions, even outlining the materials we'll need in order to make it.

It's built with carbon.

Carbon fibers, to be precise. She explained that carbon fibers are so stiff and abrasive that they'll need to be bonded with something very flexible in order to become wearable, so she's planning on experimenting with several different materials. Something about polymers. And synthetic something. And a bunch of other words I didn't really understand. Her sketches show how the carbon fibers are literally woven into a textile, creating a durable and lightweight material that will serve as a stronger basis for what I need.

Her idea was inspired by the knuckle braces she made for me.

She said she originally wanted the suit to be made of thousands of pieces of gunmetal, but then she realized she'd never have the tools to make the pieces as thin as she'd like them, and therefore, the suit would be too heavy. But this is sounding just as amazing.

"It'll complement and enhance your strength," she's saying to me. "The carbon fibers will give you an added level of protection; they won't damage easily, so you'll be able to move more freely through different terrains. And when you're in a dangerous environment, you must remember to maintain a state of *electricum* at all times; that way your body will become virtually indestructible," she says.

"What do you mean . . . ?" I look from her to Castle for clarification. "How can that be possible?"

"Because," Alia explains. "In the same way that you can break through concrete without hurting yourself, you should also be able to sustain an attack—from a bullet, for example—without harm." She smiles. "Your powers make you functionally invincible."

Wow.

"This suit is a precaution more than anything else," she goes on. "We've seen in the past that you *can*, in fact, damage your skin if you're not wholly in control of your power. When you broke the ground in the research rooms," she says, "we thought it was the enormity of the act that injured you. But after examining the situation and your abilities more thoroughly, Castle and I found this deduction to be inaccurate."

"Our energies are never inconsistent," Castle jumps in, nodding at Alia. "They follow a pattern—an almost mathematical precision. If you cannot injure yourself while breaking through a concrete wall, it does not then follow that you should be able to injure yourself by breaking the ground, only to remain *un*injured after breaking the ground a second time." He looks at me. "Your injuries have to do with your hold on your ability. If you ever slip out of *electricum*—if you dial it back for even a moment—you will be vulnerable. Remember to be *on*, at all times. If you do, you cannot be defeated."

"I hate you so hard right now," Kenji mutters under his breath. "Functionally invincible my ass."

"Jealous?" I grin at him.

"I can't even look at you."

"You shouldn't be surprised." Warner has just walked in. I spin around to find he's heading toward our group, smiling a brittle smile at no one in particular. He sits down across from me. Meets my eyes as he says, "I always knew your powers, once harnessed, would be unmatched."

I try to breathe.

Warner finally breaks eye contact with me to glance around the room. "Good evening, everyone," he says. He nods at Castle. A special sort of acknowledgment.

Adam has a special sort of acknowledgment of his own.

He's staring at Warner with an intense, unmasked hatred, looking as though he truly wants to murder Warner, and I'm suddenly more anxious than I've been all day. I'm looking from Adam to Warner and back again and I don't know what to do. I don't know if something is about to happen and I'm so desperate for things to be civil that I—

"Hi," James says, so loudly it startles all of us. He's looking at Warner. "What are you doing here?"

Warner raises an eyebrow. "I live here."

"This is your *house*?" James asks.

Strange. I wonder what Adam and Kenji told him about where they were going.

Warner nods. "In some capacity, yes," he says. "It serves as my home. I live upstairs."

"That's so cool," James says, grinning. "This whole place is so cool." He frowns. "Hey I thought we were supposed to hate you, though."

"*James,*" Adam says, shooting his brother a warning glance.

"What?" James asks.

"You are free to hate me," Warner says. "If you want to. I don't mind."

"Well you *should* mind," James says, surprised. "I'd be really upset if someone hated me."

"You are young."

"I'm almost twelve," James says to him.

"I was told you were ten."

"I said *almost* twelve." James rolls his eyes. "How old are you?"

Everyone is watching. Listening. Too fascinated to look away.

Warner studies James. Takes his time answering. "I'm nineteen years old."

James's eyes go wide. "You're only a year older than Adam," he says. "How do you have so many nice things if you're only a year older than Adam? I don't know anyone your age who has nice things."

Warner looks over at me. Looks back at James. Looks at me again. "Is there nothing you want to add to this conversation, love?"

I shake my head. Smiling.

"Why do you call her 'love'?" James asks. "I've heard you say that before, too. A lot. Are you in love with her? I think Adam's in love with her. Kenji's not in love with her, though. I already asked him."

Warner blinks at him.

"Well?" James asks.

"Well what?"

"Are you in love with her?"

"Are *you* in love with her?"

"What?" James blushes. "No. She's like a million years older than me."

"Would anyone like to take over this conversation?" Warner asks, looking around the group.

"You never answered my question," James says. "About why you have so many things. I'm not trying to be rude," he says. "Really. I'm just wondering. I've never taken a shower with hot water before. And you have so much food. It must be really nice to have so much food all the time."

Warner flinches, unexpectedly. He looks more carefully at James. "No," he says slowly. "It is not a terrible thing to have food and hot water all the time."

"So then are you going to answer my question? About where you got all this stuff?"

Warner sighs.

"I am the commander and regent of Sector 45," he says. "We are currently on an army base, where it is my job to oversee our soldiers and all the civilians who live on the accompanying compounds. I am paid to live here."

"Oh." James goes pale in an instant; he suddenly looks inhumanly terrified. "You work for The Reestablishment?"

"Hey, it's okay, buddy," Kenji says to James. "You're safe here. Okay? No one's going to hurt you."

"This is the kind of guy you're into, huh?" Adam snaps at me. "The kind of guy who petrifies children?"

"It's nice to see you again, Kent." Warner is watching Adam now. "How are you enjoying your stay?"

Adam seems to be fighting back the urge to say a lot of unkind things.

"So you really work for them?" James is asking Warner again, his words just a breath, his eyes still frozen on Warner's face. He's shaking so hard it breaks my heart. "You work for The Reestablishment?"

Warner hesitates. Looks away and looks back again. "Theoretically," he says. "Yes."

"What do you mean?" James asks.

Warner is looking into his hands.

"What do you mean, *theoretically*?" James demands.

"Are you asking," Warner says with a sigh, "because you are actually seeking clarification? Or is it because you don't know what the word *theoretically* means?"

James hesitates, his panic dissolving into frustration for a moment. He screws up his face, annoyed. "Fine. What does *theoretically* mean?"

"Theoretically," Warner says, "I'm supposed to work for The Reestablishment. But, obviously, as I'm hosting a group of rebels on this government-owned military base—in my private quarters, no less—and sustaining said rebels so that they might overthrow our current regime, I would say no. I am not, exactly, working for The Reestablishment. I have committed treason," he says to James. "A crime that is punishable by death."

James stares at him for a long time. "*That's* what *theoretically* means?"

Warner looks up at the wall. Sighs again.

I bite back a laugh.

"So, wait—then you're not the bad guy," James says all of a sudden. "You're on our side, right?"

Warner turns slowly to meet James's eyes. Says nothing.

"Well?" James asks, impatient. "Aren't you on our side?"

Warner blinks. Twice. "So it seems," he says, looking as though he can hardly believe he's saying it.

"Perhaps we should get back to the suit," Castle cuts in. He's looking at Warner, smiling triumphantly. "Alia has spent a long time designing it, and I know she has more details to share."

"Yeah," Kenji says, excited. "This looks badass, Alia. I want one. Can I have one?"

I wonder if I'm the only person who notices that Warner's hands are shaking.

FORTY-FOUR

"Punch me."

Warner is standing directly across from me, head cocked to the side. Everyone is watching us.

I shake my head, fast.

"Don't be afraid, love," he says to me. "I just want you to try."

His arms are relaxed at his sides. His stance so casual. It's Saturday morning, which means he has time off from his daily workout routine. Which means he's decided to work with me, instead.

I shake my head again.

He laughs. "Your training with Kenji is good," he says, "but this is just as important. You need to learn how to fight. You have to be able to defend yourself."

"But I can defend myself," I say to him. "I'm strong enough."

"Strength is excellent," he says, "but it's worth nothing without technique. If you can be overpowered, you are not strong *enough*."

"I don't think I could be overpowered," I say to him. "Not really."

"I admire your confidence."

"Well, it's true."

"When you met my father for the first time," he says, "were you not initially overpowered?"

My blood runs cold.

"And when you set out to fight after I left Omega Point," he says to me, "were you not overpowered again?"

I clench my fists.

"And even after you were captured," he says quietly, "was my father not able to overpower you once more?"

I drop my head.

"I want you to be able to defend yourself," Warner says, his voice gentle now. "I want you to learn how to fight. Kenji was right the other day, when he said you can't just throw your energy around. You have to be able to project with precision. Your moves must always be deliberate. You have to be able to anticipate your opponent in every possible way, both mentally and physically. Strength is only the first step."

I look up, meet his eyes.

"Now punch me," he says.

"I don't know how," I finally admit, embarrassed.

He's trying so hard not to smile.

"Are you looking for volunteers?" I hear Kenji ask. He steps closer. "Because I'll gladly kick your ass if Juliette isn't interested."

"Kenji," I snap, spinning around. I narrow my eyes.

"What?"

"Come on, love," Warner says to me. He's unfazed by Kenji's comment, looking at me as if no one else in this room exists. "I want you to try. Use your strength. Tap into every bit of power you have. And then punch me."

"I'm afraid I'm going to hurt you."

Warner laughs again. Looks away. Bites his lip as he stifles another smile. "You're not going to hurt me," he says. "Trust me."

"Because you'll absorb the power?"

"No," he says. "Because you won't be *able* to hurt me. You don't know how."

I frown, annoyed. "Fine."

I swing my fist in what I assume a punch is supposed to look like. But my motion is limp and wobbly and so humiliatingly bad I almost give up halfway.

Warner catches my arm. He meets my eyes. "Focus," he says to me. "Imagine you are terrified. You are cornered. You are fighting for your life. *Defend* yourself," he demands.

I pull my arm back with more intensity, ready to try harder this time, when Warner stops me. He grabs my elbow. Shakes it a little. "You are not playing baseball," he says. "You do not wind up for a punch, and you do not need to lift your elbow up to your ear. Do not give your opponent advance notice of what you're about to do," he says. "The impact should be unexpected."

I try again.

"My face is in the center, love, right here," he says, tapping a finger against his chin. "Why are you trying to hit my shoulder?"

I try again.

"Better—control your arm—keep your left fist up—protect your face—"

I punch hard, a cheap shot, an unexpected hit even though I know he isn't ready.

His reflexes are too fast.

His fist is clenched around my forearm in an instant. He yanks, hard, pulling my arm forward and down until I'm off-balance and toppling toward him. Our faces are an inch apart.

I look up, embarrassed.

"That was cute," he says, unamused as he releases me. "Try again."

I do.

He blocks my punch with the back of his hand, slamming into the space just inside my wrist, knocking my arm sideways.

I try again.

He uses the same hand to grab my arm in midair and pull me close again. He leans in. "Do not allow anyone to catch your arms like this," he says. "Because once they do, they'll be able to control you." And, as if to prove it, he uses his hold on my arm to pull me in and then shove me backward, hard.

Not too hard.

But still.

I'm starting to get irritated, and he can tell.

He smiles.

"You really want me to hurt you?" I ask him, eyes narrowing.

"I don't think you can," he says.

"I think you're pretty cocky about that."

"Prove me wrong, love." He raises an eyebrow at me. "Please."

I swing.

He blocks.

I strike again.

He blocks.

His forearms are made of *steel*.

"I thought this was about *punching*," I say to him, rubbing at my arms. "Why do you keep hitting my forearms?"

"Your fist does not carry your strength," he says. "It's just a tool."

I swing again, faltering at the last minute, my confidence failing me.

He catches my arm. Drops it.

"If you're going to hesitate," he says, "do it on purpose. If you're going to hurt someone, do it on purpose. If you're going to lose a fight," he says, "do it on *purpose*."

"I just—I can't do this right," I tell him. "My hands are shaking and my arms are starting to hurt—"

"Watch what I do," he says. "Watch my form."

His feet are planted about shoulder-width apart, his legs slightly bent at the knees. His left fist is up and held back, protecting the side of his face, and his right fist is leading, sitting higher and slightly diagonal from his left. Both elbows are tucked in, hovering close to his chest.

He swings at me, slowly, so I can study the movement.

His body is tensed, his aim focused, every movement controlled. The power comes from somewhere deep inside of him; it's the kind of strength that is a consequence of years of careful training. His muscles know how to move. Know how to fight. His power is not a gimmick of supernatural coincidence.

His knuckles gently graze the edge of my chin.

He makes it look so easy to punch someone. I had no idea it was this difficult.

"Do you want to switch?" he asks.

"What?"

"If I try to punch you," he says. "Can you defend yourself?"

"No."

"Try," he says to me. "Just try to block me."

"Okay," I say, not actually wanting to. I feel stupid and petulant.

He swings again, slowly, for my sake.

I slap his arm out of the way.

He drops his hands. Tries not to laugh. "You are so much worse at this than I thought you'd be."

I scowl.

"Use your forearms," he says. "Block my swing. Knock it out of the way and shift your body with it. Remember to move your head when you block. You want to move yourself *away* from danger. Don't just stand there and slap."

I nod.

He starts to swing.

I block too quickly, my forearm hitting his fist. Hard.

I wince.

"It's good to anticipate," he says to me, his eyes sharp. "But don't get eager."

Another swing.

I catch his forearm. Stare at it. I try to pull it down like he did with mine, but he literally does not budge. At all. Not even an inch. It's like tugging on a metal pole buried in concrete.

"That was . . . okay," he says, smiling. "Try again. Focus." He's studying my eyes. "*Focus,* love."

"I *am* focused," I insist, irritated.

"Look at your feet," he says. "You're putting your weight on the front of your feet and you look like you're about to tip over. Plant yourself in place," he says. "But be ready to move. Your weight should rest on the heels of your feet," he says, tapping the back of his own foot.

"Fine," I snap, angry now. "I'm standing on the heels of my feet. I'm not tipping over anymore."

Warner looks at me. Captures my eyes. "Never fight when you're angry," he says quietly. "Anger will make you weak and clumsy. It will divert your focus. Your instincts will fail you."

I bite the inside of my cheek. Frustrated and ashamed.

"Try again," he says slowly. "Stay calm. Have faith in yourself. If you don't believe you can do it," he says, "you won't."

I nod, slightly mollified. Try to concentrate.

I tell him I'm ready.

He swings.

My left arm bends at the elbow in a perfect ninety-degree angle that slams into his forearm so hard it stops his swing. My head has shifted out of the way, my feet turned in the direction of his punch; I'm still standing steady.

Warner is amused.

He swings with his other fist.

I grab his forearm in midair, my fist closed around the space above his wrist, and I take advantage of his surprise to throw him off-balance, pulling his arm down and yanking him forward. He almost crashes into me. His face is right in front of mine.

And I'm so surprised that for a moment I don't know what to do. I'm caught in his eyes.

"Push me," he whispers.

I tighten my hold around his arm, and then shove him across the room.

He flies back, catching himself before hitting the floor.

I'm frozen in place. Shocked.

Someone whistles.

I turn around.

Kenji is clapping. "Well done, princess," he says, trying not to laugh. "I didn't know you had it in you."

I grin, half embarrassed and half absurdly proud of myself.

I meet Warner's eyes across the room. He nods, smiling so wide. "Good," he says. "Very good. You're a fast learner. But we still have a lot of work to do."

I finally look away, catching a glimpse of Adam in the process.

He looks pissed.

FORTY-FIVE

The days have flown by, kites carrying them off into the distance.

Warner's been working with me every morning now. After his workout, and after my training with Kenji, he's carved out two hours a day to spend with me. Seven days a week.

He's an extraordinary teacher.

So patient with me. So pleasant. He's never frustrated, never bothered by how long it takes me to learn something new. He takes the time to explain the logic behind every detail, every motion, every position. He wants me to understand what I'm doing on an elemental level. He makes sure I'm internalizing the information and replicating it on my own, not just mimicking his movements.

I'm finally learning how to be strong in more ways than one.

It's strange. I never thought knowing how to throw a punch could make a difference, but the simple knowledge of understanding how to defend myself has made me so much more confident.

I'm so much more aware of myself now.

I walk around feeling the strength in my limbs. I'm able

to name the individual muscles in my body, knowing exactly how to use them—and how to abuse them, if I do things wrong. My reflexes are getting better, my senses are heightened. I'm beginning to understand my surroundings, to anticipate danger, and to recognize the subtle shifts in body language that indicate anger and aggression.

And my projection is almost too easy now.

Warner collected all sorts of things for me to destroy, just for target practice. Scraps of wood and metal, old chairs and tables. Blocks of concrete. Anything that would test my strength. Castle uses his energy to toss the objects into the air and it's my job to destroy them from across the room. At first it was nearly impossible; it's an extremely intense exercise that requires me to be wholly in control of myself.

But now, it's one of my favorite games.

I can stop and crush anything in the air. From any distance across the room. All I need are my hands to control the energy. I can move my own power in any direction, focusing it on small objects and then widening the scope for a larger mass.

I can move everything in the training room now. Nothing is difficult anymore.

Kenji thinks I need a new challenge.

"I want to take her outside," Kenji says. He's talking directly to Warner—so casually—something that's still strange for me to see. "I think she needs to start experimenting with natural materials. We're too limited in here."

Warner looks at me. "What do you think?"

"Will it be safe?" I ask.

"Well," he says, "it doesn't really matter, does it? In one week we'll be outing ourselves anyway."

"Good point." I try to smile.

Adam has been unusually quiet these past couple weeks.

I don't know if it's because Kenji talked to him and told him to be careful, or if it's because he's really resigned himself to this situation. Maybe he's realized there's nothing romantic happening between me and Warner. Which both pleases and disappoints me.

Warner and I seem to have reached some kind of understanding. A civil, oddly formal relationship that balances precariously between friendship and something else that has never been defined.

I can't say I enjoy it.

Adam doesn't interfere, however, when James speaks to Warner, and Kenji told me it's because Adam doesn't want to traumatize James by giving him a reason to be afraid of living here.

Which means James is constantly talking to Warner.

He's a curious kid, and Warner is so naturally private that he's the most obvious target for James's questions. Their exchanges are always entertaining for all of us. James is thoroughly unapologetic, and bolder than most anyone would ever be when talking to Warner.

It's kind of cute, actually.

Other than that, everyone has been progressing well.

Brendan and Winston are back to perfect, Castle is in better spirits every day, and Lily is a self-sufficient kind of girl who doesn't need much to be entertained—though she and Ian seem to have found a sort of solace in each other's company.

I suppose it makes sense that this kind of isolation would bring people together.

Like Adam and Alia.

He's been spending a lot of time with her lately, and I don't know what that means; it might be nothing more than friendship. But for most of the time I've been down in the training room, I've seen him sitting next her, just watching her sketch, asking the occasional question.

She's always blushing.

In some ways, she reminds me a lot of how I used to be.

I adore Alia, but sometimes watching them together makes me wonder if this is what Adam's always wanted. A sweet, quiet, gentle girl. Someone who would compensate for all the roughness he's seen in his life. He said that to me once, I remember. He said he loved that about me. That I was so *good*. So sweet. That I was the only good thing left in this world.

I think I always knew that wasn't true.

Maybe he's starting to see it, too.

FORTY-SIX

"I have to visit my mother today."

These are the seven words that begin our morning.

Warner has just walked out of his office, his hair a golden mess around his head, his eyes so green and so simultaneously transparent that they defy true description. He hasn't bothered to button his rumpled shirt and his slacks are unbelted and hanging low on his waist. He looks completely disoriented. I don't think he's slept all night and I want so desperately to know what's been happening in his life but I know it's not my place to ask. Worse still, I know he wouldn't even tell me if I did.

There's no level of intimacy between us anymore.

Everything was moving so quickly between us and then it halted to a complete stop. All those thoughts and feelings and emotions frozen in place. And now I'm so afraid that if I make the wrong move, everything will break.

But I miss him.

He stands in front of me every day and I train with him and work alongside him like a colleague and it's not enough for me anymore. I miss our easy conversations, his open smiles, the way he always used to meet my eyes.

I miss him.

And I need to talk to him, but I don't know how. Or when. Or what to say.

Coward.

"Why today . . . ?" I ask tentatively. "Did something happen?"

Warner says nothing for a long time, just stares at the wall. "Today is her birthday."

"Oh," I whisper, heart breaking.

"You wanted to practice outdoors," he says, still staring straight ahead. "With Kenji. I can take you with me when I leave, as long as he promises to keep you invisible. I'll drop you off somewhere on unregulated territory and pick you up when I'm heading back. Will that be all right?"

"Yes."

He says nothing else, but his eyes are wild and unfocused. He's looking at the wall like it might be a window.

"Aaron?"

"Yes, love."

"Are you scared?"

He takes a tight breath. Exhales it slowly.

"I never know what to expect when I visit her," he says quietly. "She's different each time. Sometimes she's so drugged up she doesn't even move. Sometimes her eyes are open and she just stares at the ceiling. Sometimes," he says, "she's completely hysterical."

My heart twists.

"It's good that you still visit her," I say to him. "You know that, right?"

"Is it?" He laughs a strange, nervous sort of laugh. "Sometimes I'm not so sure."

"Yes. It is."

"How can you know?" He looks at me now, looks at me as though he's almost afraid to hear the answer.

"Because if she can tell, for even a second, that you're in the room with her, you've given her an extraordinary gift. She is not gone completely," I tell him. "She knows. Even if it's not all the time, and even if she can't show it. She knows you've been there. And I know it must mean so much to her."

He takes in another shaky breath. He's staring at the ceiling now. "That is a very nice thing to say."

"I really mean it."

"I know," he says. "I know you do."

I look at him a little longer, wondering if there's ever an appropriate time to ask questions about his mother. But there's one thing I've always wanted to ask. So I do.

"She gave you that ring, didn't she?"

Warner goes still. I think I can hear his heart racing from here. "What?"

I walk up to him and take his left hand. "This one," I say, pointing to the jade ring he's always worn on his left pinkie finger. He never takes it off. Not to shower. Not to sleep. Not ever.

He nods, so slowly.

"But . . . you don't like to talk about it," I say, remembering the last time I asked him about his ring.

I count exactly ten seconds before he speaks again.

"I was never allowed," he says very, very quietly, "to receive presents. From anyone. My father hated the idea of presents. He hated birthday parties and holidays. He never let anyone give anything to me, and especially not my mother. He said that accepting gifts would make me weak. He thought they would encourage me to rely on the charity of others.

"But we were hiding one day," he says. "My mother and I." His eyes are up, off, lost in another place. He might not be talking to me at all. "It was my sixth birthday and she was trying to hide me. Because she knew what he wanted to do to me." He blinks. His voice is a whisper, half dead of emotion. "I remember her hands were shaking," he says. "I remember because I kept looking at her hands. Because she was holding mine to her chest. And she was wearing this ring." He quiets, remembering. "I'd never seen much jewelry in my life. I didn't know what it was, exactly. But she saw me staring and she wanted to distract me," he says. "She wanted to keep me entertained."

My stomach is threatening to be sick.

"So she told me a story. A story about a boy who was born with very green eyes, and the man who was so captivated by their color that he searched the world for a stone in exactly the same shade." His voice is fading now, falling into whispers so quiet I can hardly hear him. "She said the boy was me. That this ring was made from that very same stone, and that the man had given it to her, hoping one day she'd be able to give it to me. It was his gift, she said, for my birthday." He stops. Breathes. "And then she took it off, slipped it on my index finger, and said, 'If you hide your heart, he will never be able to take it from you.'"

He looks toward the wall.

"It's the only gift," he says, "anyone has ever given to me."

My tears fall backward, burning as they singe their way down my throat.

FORTY-SEVEN

I feel strange, all day.

I feel off, somehow. Kenji is thrilled to be getting off base, excited about testing my strength in new places, and everyone else is jealous that we get to leave. So I should be happy. I should be eager.

But I feel strange.

My head is in a weird place, and I think it's because I haven't been able to shake Warner's story from my mind. I can't stop trying to imagine him as he was. As a small, terrified child.

No one knows where he's headed today. No one knows the depth of it. And he does nothing to betray how he's really feeling. He's been as calm as ever, controlled and careful in his words, his actions.

Kenji and I are meeting him again in just a moment.

We're slipping through the door in the gun wall, and I'm finally able to see firsthand how Warner sneaked them inside. We're crossing through a shooting range.

There are gun stations and little cubicles with targets set hundreds of feet away, and right now, the entire place is deserted. This must be another one of Warner's practice rooms.

There's a door at the end of the walkway, and Kenji pushes it open. He doesn't need to touch me at all anymore in order to keep me invisible, and it's so much more convenient this way. We can move freely as long as I'm within fifty feet of him, which gives us the flexibility we need to be able to work outside today.

We're now on the other side of the door.

Standing in an enormous storage facility.

The space is at least five hundred feet across, and maybe twice as high. I've never seen more boxes in my entire life. I have no idea what they contain, and no time to wonder.

Kenji is pulling me through the maze.

We sidestep boxes of all different sizes, careful not to trip over electrical cords and the machinery used to move the heavier items. There are rows and rows and more rows divided into even more rows that house everything in very organized sections. I notice there are labels on every shelf and in all the aisles, but I can't get close enough to read them.

When we finally make it to the end of the storage room, there are two huge, fifty-foot doors that lead to the exit. This is clearly a loading zone for trucks and tanks. Kenji grabs my arm and keeps me close as we pass several guards stationed by the exit. We dart through the trucks parked all around the loading zone, until we finally get to the meeting point where we're supposed to find Warner.

I wish Kenji could've been around to make me invisible when I first tried to get on and off base. It would've been so nice to just walk out like a human being, instead of being carted through the halls, jolting and teetering and clinging to the legs of a wheeling tray table.

Warner is leaning against a tank.

Both doors are open, and he's looking around like he might be overseeing the work being done with the loading units. He nods to several soldiers as they pass.

We clamber into the passenger side unnoticed.

And just as I'm about to whisper a notification to Warner, he walks around to the passenger side, says, "Watch your legs, love," and shuts the door.

And then he climbs into the other side. Starts driving.

We're still invisible.

"How did you know we were in here?" Kenji asks immediately. "Can you, like, see invisible people, too?"

"No," Warner says to him, eyes focused in front of him. "I can feel your presence. Hers, most of all."

"Really?" Kenji says. "That's some weird shit. What do I feel like? Peanut butter?"

Warner is unamused.

Kenji clears his throat. "J, I think you should switch spots with me."

"Why?"

"I think your boyfriend is touching my leg."

"You flatter yourself," Warner says.

"Switch spots with me, J. He's making me feel all goosebumpy and shit, like maybe he's about to knife me."

"Fine." I sigh. I try clambering over him, but it's difficult, considering I can see neither my own body nor his.

"Ow—*dammit*—you almost kicked me in the face—"

"Sorry!" I say, trying to scramble over his knees.

"Just move," he says. "God, how much do you weigh—"

He shifts, all at once, slipping out from under me, and gives me a small shove to move me over.

I fall face-first into Warner's lap.

I hear Warner's brief, sharp intake of breath, and I scramble upright, blushing so hard, and I'm suddenly so relieved no one can see me right now.

I want to punch Kenji in the nose.

No one talks much after that.

As we get closer to unregulated territory, the scenery starts to change. The simple, signless, semipaved roads give way to the streets of our old world. The houses are painted in shades that promised to be colorful once upon a time, and the roads are lined with sidewalks that might've carried children safely home from school. The houses are all falling apart now.

Everything is broken, dilapidated. The windows boarded up. The lawns overgrown and iced over. The winter bite looks fresh in the air, and it casts a gloom over the scene in a way that says this all might be different in another season. Who knows.

Warner stops the tank.

He climbs out and walks over to our door, just in case anyone is still out here, and makes it seem as though he's opening it for a specific reason. To check the interior. To examine a problem.

It doesn't matter.

Kenji jumps out first, and Warner seems to be able to tell that he's gone.

I reach for Warner's hand, because I know he can't see me. His fingers immediately tighten around mine. His eyes are focused on the floor.

"It's going to be okay," I tell him. "Okay?"

"Yes," he says. "I'm sure you're right."

I hesitate. "Will you be back soon?"

"Yes," he whispers. "I'll return for you in exactly two hours. Will that be sufficient time?"

"Yes."

"Good. I'll meet you back here, then. In this exact location."

"Okay."

He says nothing for a second. Then, "Okay."

I squeeze his hand.

He smiles at the ground.

I stand up and he shifts to the side, allowing me room to get by. I touch him as I move past, just briefly. Just as a reminder. That I'm here for him.

He flinches, startled, and steps back.

And then he climbs into the tank, and leaves.

FORTY-EIGHT

Warner is late.

Kenji and I had a semisuccessful session, one that consisted mainly of us arguing over where we were standing and what we were looking at. We're going to have to come up with much better signals next time, because trying to coordinate a training session between two invisible people is a lot more difficult than it sounds. Which is saying a lot.

So now we're tired and slightly disappointed, having accomplished little in the way of progress, and we're standing in exactly the same place Warner dropped us off.

And Warner is late.

This is unusual for many reasons. The first of which is that Warner is never late. Not for anything. And the second is that if he were going to be late, it definitely wouldn't be for something like this. This situation is far too dangerous to be casual about. He wouldn't have taken it lightly. I know he wouldn't have.

So I'm pacing.

"I'm sure it's fine," Kenji is saying to me. "He probably just got hung up doing whatever it is he's doing. You know, commandering and shit."

"*Commandering* is not a word."

"It has letters, doesn't it? Sounds like a word to me."

I'm too nervous to banter right now.

Kenji sighs. I hear him stomp his feet against the cold. "He'll be here."

"I don't feel right, Kenji."

"I don't feel right, either," he says. "I'm hungry as hell."

"Warner wouldn't be late. It's not like him to be late."

"How would you know?" Kenji shoots back. "You've known him for how long, exactly? Five months? And you think you know him so well? Maybe he's in a secret jazz club where he sings a cappella and wears sparkly vests and thinks it's cool to do the cancan."

"Warner wouldn't wear sparkly vests," I snap.

"But you think he'd be down with the cancan."

"Kenji, I love you, I really do, but right now I'm so anxious, and I feel so sick, that the more you speak, the more I want to kill you."

"Don't talk sexy to me, J."

I huff, irritated. God, I'm so worried. "What time is it?"

"Two forty-five."

"This isn't right. We should go find him."

"We don't even know where he is."

"I do," I say. "I know where he is."

"*What?* How?"

"Do you remember where we met Anderson for the first time?" I ask him. "Do you remember how to get back to Sycamore Street?"

"Yeah . . . ," Kenji says slowly. "Why?"

"He's about two streets down from there."

"Um. What the hell? Why is he down there?"

"Will you go with me?" I ask, nervous. "Please? Now?"

"Okay," he says, unconvinced. "But only because I'm curious. And because it's cold as hell out here and I need to move my legs before I freeze to death."

"Thank you," I say. "Where are you?"

We follow the sounds of each other's voices until we bump right into one another. Kenji slips his arm into mine. We huddle together against the cold.

He leads the way.

FORTY-NINE

This is it.

The robin's-egg-blue house. The one I woke up in. The one Warner lived in. The one his mother is stored in. We're standing in front of it and it looks exactly as it did the last two times I was here. Beautiful and terrifying. Wind chimes whipping back and forth.

"Why the hell would Warner be here?" Kenji asks. "What is this place?"

"I can't really tell you," I say to him.

"Why not?"

"Because it's not my secret to tell."

Kenji is silent a moment. "So what do you want me to do?"

"Can you wait here?" I ask him. "Will I be able to stay invisible if I go inside? Or will I get out of range?"

Kenji sighs. "I don't know. You can definitely try. I've never tried to do this from outside a house before." He hesitates. "But if you're going to go in without me, can you please hurry the hell up? I'm already freezing my ass off."

"Yes. I promise. I'll be fast. I just want to make sure he's all right—or that he's even in here. Because if he's not inside, he might be waiting for us back at the drop-off."

"And all of this will have been a huge waste of time."

"I'm sorry," I say to him. "I'm really sorry. But I just have to make sure."

"Go," he says. "Go and come back fast."

"Okay," I whisper. "Thank you."

I break away and climb up the stairs to the little porch. Test the handle. It's unlocked. I turn it, push the door open. Step inside.

This is where I was shot.

The bloodstain from where I was lying on the ground has already been cleaned up. Or maybe the carpet was changed. I'm not sure. Either way, the memories still surround me. I can't walk back into this house without feeling sick to my stomach. Everything is wrong in here. Everything is so wrong. So off.

Something has happened.

I can feel it.

I'm careful to shut the door gently behind me. I creep up the stairs, remembering how the floorboards squeaked when I was first captured and brought here, and I'm able to sidestep the noisiest parts; the rest of it, thankfully, just sounds like it could be the wind.

When I'm upstairs, I count three doors. Three rooms.

On the left: Warner's old room. The one I woke up in.

In the middle: the bathroom. The one I was bathed in.

On the far end of the hall, all the way to the right: his mother's room. The one I'm looking for.

My heart is racing in my chest.

I can hardly breathe as I tiptoe closer. I don't know what I'm expecting to find. I don't know what I'm hoping will come of this trip. I don't have any idea, even, if Warner is still in here.

And I have no idea what it'll be like to see his mother.

But something is pulling me forward, urging me to open the door and check. I need to know. I just have to know. My mind won't rest otherwise.

So I inch forward. Take several deep breaths. I grasp the doorknob and turn, so slowly, not even realizing I've lost invisibility until I see my feet crossing the threshold.

I panic in an instant, my brain calculating contingency plans, and though I briefly consider turning around and bolting out the door, my eyes have already scanned the room.

And I know I can't turn back now.

FIFTY

There's a bed in here.

A single bed. Surrounded by machines and IVs and bottles and brand-new bedpans. There are stacks of bedsheets and stacks of blankets and the most beautiful bookcases and embroidered pillows and adorable stuffed animals piled everywhere. There are fresh flowers in five different vases and four brightly painted walls and there's a little desk in the corner with a little matching chair and there's a potted plant and a set of old paintbrushes and there are picture frames, everywhere. On the walls, on the desk, sitting on the table beside the bed.

A blond woman. A little blond boy. Together.

They never age, I notice. The pictures never move past a certain year. They never show the evolution of this child's life. The boy in these photos is always young, and always startled, and always holding fast to the hand of the lady standing beside him.

But that lady is not here. And her nurse is gone, too.

The machines are off.

The lights are out.

The bed is empty.

Warner has collapsed in the corner.

He's curled into himself, knees pulled up to his chest, arms wrapped around his legs, his head buried in his arms. And he's shaking.

Tremors are rocking his entire body.

I've never, ever seen him look like a child before. Never, not once, not in all the time I've known him. But right now, he looks just like a little boy. Scared. Vulnerable. All alone.

It doesn't take much to understand why.

I fall to my knees in front of him. I know he must be able to sense my presence, but I don't know if he wants to see me right now. I don't know how he's going to react if I reach out.

But I have to try.

I touch his arms, so gently. I run my hand down his back, his shoulders. And then I dare to wrap myself around him until he slowly breaks apart, unfolding in front of me.

He lifts his head.

His eyes are red-rimmed and a startling, striking shade of green, shining with barely restrained emotion. His face is the picture of so much pain.

I almost can't breathe.

An earthquake hits my heart then, cracks it right down the middle. And I think here, in him, there is more feeling than any one person should ever have to contain.

I try to hold him closer but he wraps his arms around my hips instead, his head falling into my lap. I bend over him instinctively, shielding his body with my own.

I press my cheek to his forehead. Press a kiss to his temple.

And then he breaks.

Shaking violently, shattering in my arms, a million gasping, choking pieces I'm trying so hard to hold together. And I promise myself then, in that moment, that I will hold him forever, just like this, until all the pain and torture and suffering is gone, until he's given a chance to live the kind of life where no one can wound him this deeply ever again.

And we are quotation marks, inverted and upside down, clinging to one another at the end of this life sentence. Trapped by lives we did not choose.

It's time, I think, to break free.

FIFTY-ONE

Kenji is waiting in the tank when we get back. He managed to find it.

He's sitting in the passenger side, invisibility off, and he doesn't say a single word as Warner and I climb inside.

I try to meet his eyes, already prepared to concoct some crazy story for why it took me an hour to get Warner out of the house, but then Kenji looks at me. Really looks at me.

And I close my mouth forever.

Warner doesn't say a single word. He doesn't even breathe loudly. And when we get back to base, he lets me and Kenji leave the tank under our guise of invisibility and he still says nothing, not even to me. As soon as we're out of the tank, he closes our door, and climbs back inside.

I'm watching him drive off again when Kenji slips his arm into mine.

We weave back through the storage facility without a problem. Cross through the shooting range without a problem. But just before we reach the door to Warner's training facility, Kenji pulls me aside.

"I followed you in," he says, with no preamble. "You took too long and I got worried and I followed you up there." A pause. A heavy pause. "I saw you guys," he says, so quietly. "In that room."

Not for the first time today, I'm glad he can't see my face. "Okay," I whisper, not knowing what else to say. Not knowing what Kenji will do with the information.

"I just—" Kenji takes a deep breath. "I'm just confused, okay? I don't need to know all the details—I realize that whatever was happening in there was none of my business—but are you okay? Did something happen?"

I exhale. Close my eyes as I say, "His mom died today."

"What?" Kenji asks, stunned. "What—h-how? His mom was in there?"

"She'd been sick for a long time," I say, the words rushing out of me. "Anderson kept her locked in that house and he abandoned her. He left her to die. Warner had been trying to help her, and he didn't know how. She couldn't be touched, just like I can't touch anyone, and the pain of it was killing her every day." I'm losing control now, unable to keep my feelings contained any longer. "Warner never wanted to use me as a weapon," I say to him. "He made that up so he had a story to tell his father. He found me by accident. Because he was trying to find a solution. To help *her*. All these years."

Kenji takes a sharp breath. "I had no idea," he says. "I didn't even know he was close to his mom."

"You don't know him at all," I say, not caring how desperate I sound. "You think you do but you really don't." I feel raw, like I've been sanded down to the bone.

He says nothing.

"Let's go," I say. "I need some time to breathe. To think."

"Yeah," he says. He exhales. "Yeah, sure. Of course."

I turn to go.

"J," he says, stopping me, his hand still on my arm.

I wait.

"I'm sorry. I'm really sorry. I didn't know."

I blink fast against the burning in my eyes. Swallow back the emotion building in my throat. "It's okay, Kenji. You were never supposed to."

FIFTY-TWO

I finally manage to pull myself together long enough to head back to the training rooms. It's getting late, but I don't anticipate seeing Warner down here tonight. I think he'll want the time alone.

I'm making myself scarce on purpose.

I've had enough.

I came so close to killing Anderson once, and I'll make sure I have that chance again. But this time, I'll follow through.

I wasn't ready last time. I wouldn't have known what to do even if I'd killed him then. I would've handed control over to Castle and I would've watched quietly as someone else tried to fix our world again. But I see now that Castle was wrong for this job. He's too tender. Too anxious to please everyone.

I, on the other hand, am left with no concerns at all.

I will be unapologetic. I will live with no regrets. I will reach into the earth and rip out the injustice and I will crush it in my bare hands. I want Anderson to fear me and I want him to beg for mercy and I want to say no, not for you. Never for you.

And I don't care if that's not nice enough.

FIFTY-THREE

I get to my feet.

Adam is standing across the room, talking to Winston and Ian. Everyone falls silent as I approach. And if Adam is thinking or feeling anything at all about me, he doesn't show it.

"You have to tell him," I say.

"What?" Adam startles.

"You have to tell him the truth," I say. "And if you don't, I will."

All at once Adam's eyes are a frozen ocean, cold and closed off. "Don't push me, Juliette. Don't say stupid things you're going to regret."

"You have no right to keep this from him. He has no one in this world, and he deserves to know."

"This is *none* of your business," Adam says. He's towering over me, his fists clenched. "Stay out of it. Don't force me to do something I don't want to do."

"Are you actually threatening me?" I ask. "Are you insane?"

"Maybe you've forgotten," he says, "that I'm the only one in this room who can shut you off. But I haven't. You have no power against me."

"Of course I have power against you," I tell him. "My touch was *killing you* when we were together—"

"Yeah, well, things have changed a lot since then." He grabs my hand, yanking so hard I nearly fall forward. I try to pull away and I can't.

He's too strong.

"Adam, let go of me—"

"Can you feel that?" he asks, eyes a crazy, stormy shade of blue.

"What?" I ask. "Feel what?"

"Exactly," he says. "There's nothing there. You're empty. No power, no fire, no superstrength. Just a girl who can't throw a punch to save her life. And I'm perfectly fine. Unharmed."

I swallow hard and meet his cold gaze. "So you've done it, then?" I ask. "You managed to control it?"

"Of course I did," he says angrily. "And you couldn't wait—even though I told you I could do it—you couldn't wait even though I told you I was training so we could be together—"

"It doesn't matter anymore." I'm staring at my hand in his, his refusal to let go. "We would've ended up in the same place sooner or later."

"That's not true—this is proof!" he says, holding up my hand. "We could've made it work—"

"We're too different now. We want different things. And this?" I say, nodding at our hands. "All this managed to prove is that you are extremely good at turning me off."

Adam's jaw clenches.

"Now let go of my hand."

"Hey—can we please refrain from putting on a shitshow tonight?" Kenji's voice booms from across the room. He's heading toward us. Pissed.

"Stay out of this," Adam snaps at him.

"It's called *consideration*. There are other people living in this room, jackass," Kenji says once he's close enough. He grabs Adam's arm. "So knock it off."

Adam breaks away angrily. "Don't touch me."

Kenji shoots him a sharp look. "Let go of her."

"You know what?" Adam says, his anger taking over. "You're so obsessed with her—jumping to her defense all the time, getting involved in our conversations all the time—you like her so much? Fine. You can have her."

Time freezes all around us.

The stage is set:

Adam and his wild eyes, his rage and his red face.

Kenji standing next to him, annoyed, slightly confused.

And me, my hand still locked in Adam's viselike grip, his touch so quickly and easily reducing me back to who I was when we first met.

I'm completely powerless.

But then, in one movement, everything changes:

Adam grabs Kenji's bare hand and presses it into my empty one.

For just long enough.

FIFTY-FOUR

It takes a couple of seconds for the two of us to register what's just happened before Kenji rips his hand away, and in a moment of perfect spontaneity, uses it to punch Adam in the face.

Everyone else in the room is now up and alert. Castle runs forward immediately, and Ian and Winston—who were already standing close by—hurry to join him. Brendan rushes out of the locker room in a towel, eyes searching for the source of the commotion; Lily and Alia jump off the bikes and crowd around us.

We're lucky it's so late; James is already sleeping quietly in the corner.

Adam was thrown back by Kenji's punch, but he quickly regained his footing. He's breathing hard, dragging the back of his hand across his now-bloody lip. He does not apologize.

No sound escapes my open, horrified mouth.

"What in God's name is wrong with you?" Kenji's voice is soft but deathly sharp, his right fist still clenched. "Were you trying to get me killed?"

Adam rolls his eyes. "I knew it wouldn't kill you. Not that quickly. I've felt it before," he says. "It just burns a little."

“Pull yourself together, dickhead,” Kenji snaps. “You’re acting insane.”

Adam says nothing. He actually laughs, flips Kenji off, and heads in the direction of the locker room.

“Hey—are you okay?” I ask Kenji, trying to catch a glimpse of his hand.

“I’m fine,” he sighs, glancing at Adam’s retreating figure before looking back at me. “But his jaw is hard as hell.” He flexes his fist a little.

“But my touch—it didn’t hurt you?”

Kenji shakes his head. “Nah, I didn’t feel anything,” he says. “And I’d know if I did.” He almost laughs, and frowns instead. I cringe at the memory of the last time this happened. “I think Kent was deflecting your power somehow,” Kenji says.

“No he wasn’t,” I whisper. “He let go of my other hand. I felt the energy come back into me.”

We both look at Adam’s retreating figure.

Kenji shrugs.

“But then how—”

“I don’t know,” Kenji says again. He sighs. “I guess I just got lucky. Listen”—he looks around at everyone—“I don’t want to talk right now, okay? I’m going to go sit down. I need to cool off.”

The group breaks up slowly, everyone going back to their corners.

But I can’t walk away. I’m rooted in place.

I felt my skin touch Kenji’s, and that’s not something I

can ignore. Those kinds of moments are so rare for me that I can't just shake them off; I never get to be that close to people without serious consequences. And I felt the power inside my body. Kenji should've felt *something.*

My mind is working fast, trying to solve an impossible equation, and a crazy theory takes root inside of me, crystallizing in a way I'd never thought it could.

This whole time I've been training to control my power, to contain it, to focus it—but I never thought I'd be able to turn it *off.* And I don't know why.

Adam had a similar problem: he'd been running on *electricum* his whole life. But now he's learned how to control it. To power it down when he needs to.

Shouldn't I be able to do the same?

Kenji can go visible and invisible whenever he likes—it was something he had to teach himself after training for a long time, after understanding how to shift from one state of being to another. I remember the story he told me from when he was little: he turned invisible for a couple of days without knowing how to change back. But eventually he did.

Castle, Brendan, Winston, Lily—they can all turn their abilities on and off. Castle doesn't move things with his mind by accident. Brendan doesn't electrocute everything he touches. Winston can tighten and loosen his limbs at will, and Lily can look around normally, without taking snapshots of everything with her eyes.

Why am I the only one without an off switch?

My mind is overwhelmed as I process the possibilities. I

begin to realize that I never even *tried* to turn my power off, because I always thought it would be impossible. I assumed I was fated to this life, to an existence in which my hands—my skin—would always, always keep me away from others.

But now?

"Kenji!" I cry out as I run toward him.

Kenji glances over his shoulder at me, but doesn't have the chance to turn all the way around before I crash into him, grabbing his hands and squeezing them in my own. "Don't let go," I tell him, eyes filling fast with tears. "Don't let go. You don't have to let go."

Kenji is frozen, shock and amazement all over his face. He looks at our hands. Looks back up at me.

"You learned how to control it?" he asks.

I can hardly speak. I manage to nod, tears spilling down my cheeks. "I think I've had it contained, all this time, and just didn't know it. I never would've risked practicing it on anyone."

"Damn, princess," he says softly, his own eyes shining. "I'm so proud of you."

Everyone is crowding around us now.

Castle pulls me into a fierce hug, and Brendan and Winston and Lily and Ian and Alia jump on top of him, crushing me all at once. They're cheering and clapping and shaking my hand and I've never felt so much support or so much strength in our group before. No moment in my life has ever been more extraordinary than this.

But when the congratulations ebb and the good-nights

begin, I pull Kenji aside for one last hug.

"So," I say to him, rocking on my heels. "I can touch anyone I want now."

"Yeah, I know." He laughs, cocking an eyebrow.

"Do you know what that means?"

"Are you asking me out?"

"You know what this *means*, right?"

"Because I'm flattered, really, but I still think we're much better off as friends—"

"Kenji."

He grins. Musses my hair. "No," he says. "I don't know. What does it mean?"

"It means a million things," I say to him, standing on tiptoe to look him in the eye. "But it also means that now I will never end up with anyone by default. I can do anything I want now. Be with anyone I want. And it'll be my choice."

Kenji just looks at me for a long time. Smiles. Finally, he drops his eyes. Nods.

And says, "Go do what you gotta do, J."

FIFTY-FIVE

When I get off the elevator and step into Warner's office, all the lights are off. Everything is swimming in an inky sort of black, and it takes me several tries to adjust my eyes to the darkness. I pad my way through the office carefully, searching for any sign of its owner, and find none.

I head into the bedroom.

Warner is sitting on the edge of the mattress, his coat thrown on the floor, his boots kicked off to the side. He's sitting in silence, palms up on his lap, looking into his hands like he's searching for something he cannot find.

"Aaron?" I whisper, moving forward.

He lifts his head. Looks at me.

And something inside of me shatters.

Every vertebra, every knuckle, both kneecaps, both hips. I am a pile of bones on the floor and no one knows it but me. I am a broken skeleton with a beating heart.

Exhale, I tell myself.

Exhale.

"I'm so sorry," are the first words I whisper.

He nods. Gets to his feet.

"Thank you," he says to no one at all as he walks out the door.

I follow him across the bedroom and into his office. Call out his name.

He stops in front of the boardroom table, his back to me, his hands gripping the edge. "Please, Juliette, not tonight, I can't—"

"You're right," I finally say. "You've always been right."

He turns around, so slowly.

I'm looking into his eyes and I'm suddenly petrified. I'm suddenly nervous and suddenly worried and suddenly so sure I'm going to do this all wrong but maybe wrong is the only way to do it because I can't keep it to myself anymore. There are so many things I need to tell him. Things I've been too much of a coward to admit, even to myself.

"Right about what?" His green eyes are wide. Scared.

I hold my fingers to my mouth, still so afraid to speak.

I do so much with these lips, I think.

I taste and touch and kiss and I've pressed them to the tender parts of his skin and I've made promises and told lies and touched lives all with these two lips and the words they form, the shapes and sounds they curve around. But right now my lips wish he would just read my mind because the truth is I've been hoping I'd never have to say any of it, these thoughts, out loud.

"I do want you," I say to him, my voice shaking. "I want you so much it scares me."

I see the movement in his throat, the effort he's making to keep still. His eyes are terrified.

"I lied to you," I tell him, words tripping and stumbling

out of me. "That night. When I said I didn't want to be with you. I lied. Because you were right. I was a coward. I didn't want to admit the truth to myself, and I felt so guilty for preferring you, for wanting to spend all my time with you, even when everything was falling apart. I was confused about Adam, I was confused about who I was supposed to be and I didn't know what I was doing and I was stupid," I say. "I was stupid and inconsiderate and I tried to blame it on you and I hurt you, so badly." I try to breathe. "And I'm so, so sorry."

"What—" Warner is blinking fast. His voice is fragile, uneven. "What are you saying?"

"I love you," I whisper. "I love you exactly as you are."

Warner is looking at me like he might be going deaf and blind at the same time. "No," he gasps. One broken, broken word. Barely even a sound. He's shaking his head and he's looking away from me and his hand is caught in his hair, his body turned toward the table and he says "No. No, no—"

"Aaron—"

"No," he says, backing away. "No, you don't know what you're saying—"

"I love you," I tell him again. "I love you and I want you and I wanted you then," I say to him, "I wanted you so much and I still want you, I want you right now—"

Stop.

Stop time.

Stop the world.

Stop everything for the moment he crosses the room and pulls me into his arms and pins me against the wall and I'm spinning and standing and not even breathing but I'm alive so alive so very very alive

and he's kissing me.

Deeply, desperately. His hands are around my waist and he's breathing so hard and he hoists me up, into his arms, and my legs wrap around his hips and he's kissing my neck, my throat, and he sets me down on the edge of the boardroom table.

He has one hand under my neck, the other under my shirt and he's running his fingers up my back and suddenly his thigh is between my legs and his hand is slipping behind my knee and up, higher, pulling me closer, and when he breaks the kiss I'm breathing so fast, head spinning as I try to hold on to him.

"Up," he says, gasping for air. "Lift your arms up."

I do.

He tugs up my shirt. Pulls it over my head. Tosses it to the floor.

"Lie back," he says to me, still breathing hard, guiding me onto the table as his hands slide down my spine, under my backside. He unbuttons my jeans. Unzips them. Says, "Lift your hips for me, love," and hooks his fingers around the waist of my pants and my underwear at the same time. Tugs them down.

I gasp.

I'm lying on his table in nothing but my bra.

Then that's gone, too.

His hands are moving up my legs and the insides of my

thighs and his lips are making their way down my chest, and he's undoing what little is left of my composure and every bit of my sanity and I'm aching, everywhere, tasting colors and sounds I didn't even know existed. My head is pressed back against the table and my hands are gripping his shoulders and he's hot, everywhere, gentle and somehow so urgent, and I'm trying not to scream and he's already moving down my body, he's already chosen where to kiss me. How to kiss me.

And he's not going to stop.

I'm beyond rational thought. Beyond words, beyond comprehensible ideas. Seconds are merging into minutes and hearts are collapsing and hands are grasping and I've tripped over a planet and I don't know anything anymore, I don't know anything because nothing will ever be able to compare to this. Nothing will ever capture the way I'm feeling right now.

Nothing matters anymore.

Nothing but this moment and his mouth on my body, his hands on my skin, his kisses in brand-new places making me absolutely, certifiably insane. I cry out and cling to him, dying and somehow being brought back to life in the same moment, the same breath.

He's on his knees.

I bite back the moan caught in my throat just before he lifts me up and carries me to the bed. He's on top of me in an instant, kissing me with a kind of intensity that makes me wonder why I haven't died or caught on fire or woken up from this dream yet. He's running his hands down my body only to bring them back up to my face and he kisses me once, twice, and his teeth catch my bottom lip for just a second and I'm clinging to him, wrapping my arms around his neck and running my hands through his hair and pulling him into me. He tastes so sweet. So hot and so sweet and I keep trying to say his name but I can't even find the time to breathe, much less to say a single word.

I shove him up, off me.

I undo his shirt, my hands shaking and fumbling with the buttons and I get so frustrated I just rip it open, buttons flying everywhere, and I don't have a chance to push the fabric off his body before he pulls me into his lap. He wraps my legs around his hips and dips me backward until the mattress is under my head and he leans over me, cupping my face in his hands, his thumbs two parentheses around my mouth and he pulls me close and he kisses me, kisses me until time topples over and my head spins into oblivion.

It's a heavy, unbelievable kiss.

It's the kind of kiss that inspires stars to climb into the sky and light up the world. The kind that takes forever and no time at all. His hands are holding my cheeks, and he pulls back just to look me in the eye and his chest is heaving and he says, "I think," he says, "my heart is going to explode," and I wish, more than ever, that I knew how to capture moments like these and revisit them forever.

Because this.

This is everything.

FIFTY-SIX

Warner has been asleep all morning.

He didn't wake up to work out. Didn't wake up to shower. Didn't wake up to do anything. He's just lying here, on his stomach, arms wrapped around a pillow.

I've been awake since 8:00 a.m., and I've been staring at him for two hours.

He's usually up at five thirty. Sometimes earlier.

I worry that he might've missed a lot of important things by now. I have no idea if he has meetings or specific places to be today. I don't know if he's ruined his schedule by being asleep so late. I don't know if anyone will come to check on him. I have no idea.

I do know that I don't want to wake him.

We were up very late last night.

I run my fingers down his back, still confused by the word IGNITE tattooed on his skin, and train my eyes to see his scars as something other than the terrifying abuse he's suffered his whole life. I can't handle the horrible truth of it. I curl my body around his, rest my face against his back, my arms holding fast to his sides. I drop a kiss on his spine. I can feel him breathing, in and out, so evenly. So steadily.

Warner shifts, just a little.

I sit up.

He rolls over slowly, still half asleep. Uses the back of one fist to rub his eyes. Blinks several times. And then he sees me.

Smiles.

It's a sleepy, sleepy smile.

I can't help but smile back. I feel like I've been split open and stuffed with sunshine. I've never seen a sleepy Warner before. Never woken up in his arms. Never seen him be anything but awake and alert and sharp.

He looks almost lazy right now.

It's adorable.

"Come here," he says, reaching for me.

I crawl into his arms and cling, and he holds me tight against him. Drops a kiss on the top of my head. Whispers, "Good morning, sweetheart."

"I like that," I say quietly, smiling even though he can't see it. "I like it when you call me sweetheart."

He laughs then, his shoulders shaking as he does. He rolls onto his back, arms stretched out at his sides.

God, he looks so good without his clothes on.

"I have never slept so well in my entire life," he says softly. He grins, eyes still closed. Dimples on both cheeks. "I feel so strange."

"You slept for a long time," I tell him, lacing his fingers in mine.

He peeks at me through one eye. "Did I?"

I nod. "It's late. It's already ten thirty."

He stiffens. "Really?"

I nod again. "I didn't want to wake you."

He sighs. "I'm afraid I should get going then. Delalieu has likely had an aneurysm."

A pause.

"Aaron," I say tentatively. "Who is Delalieu, exactly? Why is he so trustworthy with all of this?"

A deep breath. "I've known him for many, many years."

"Is that all . . . ?" I ask, leaning back to look him in the eye. "He knows so much about us and what we're doing and it worries me sometimes. I thought you said all your soldiers hated you. Shouldn't you be suspicious? Trust him less?"

"Yes," he says quietly, "you'd think I would."

"But you don't."

Warner meets my eyes. Softens his voice. "He's my mother's father, love."

I stiffen in an instant, jerking back. "What?"

Warner looks up at the ceiling.

"He's your *grandfather*?" I'm sitting up in bed now.

Warner nods.

"How long have you known?" I don't know how to stay calm about this.

"My entire life." Warner shrugs. "He's always been around. I've known his face since I was a child; I used to see him around our house, sitting in on meetings for The Reestablishment, all organized by my father."

I'm so stunned I hardly know what to say. "But . . . you treat him like he's . . ."

"My lieutenant?" Warner stretches his neck. "Well, he is."

"But he's your *family*—"

"He was assigned to this sector by my father, and I had no reason to believe he was any different from the man who gave me half my DNA. He's never gone to visit my mother. Never asks about her. Has never shown any interest in her. It's taken Delalieu nineteen years to earn my trust, and I've only just allowed myself this weakness because I've been able to sense his sincerity with regular consistency throughout the years." Warner pauses. "And even though we've reached some level of familiarity, he has never, and will never, acknowledge our shared biology."

"But why not?"

"Because he is no more my grandfather than I am my father's son."

I stare at Warner for a long time before I realize there's no point in continuing this conversation. Because I think I understand. He and Delalieu have nothing more than an odd, formal sort of respect for each other. And just because you're bound by blood does not make you a family.

I would know.

"So do you have to go now?" I whisper, sorry I even brought up the topic of Delalieu.

"Not just yet." He smiles. Touches my cheek.

We're both silent a moment.

"What are you thinking?" I ask him.

He leans in, kisses me so softly. Shakes his head.

I touch the tip of my finger to his lips. "There are secrets in here," I say. "I want them out."

He tries to bite my finger.

I steal it back.

"Why do you smell so good?" he asks, still smiling as he avoids my question. He leans in again, leaves light kisses along my jawline, under my chin. "It's making me crazy."

"I've been stealing your soaps," I tell him.

He raises his eyebrows at me.

"Sorry." I feel myself blush.

"Don't feel bad," he says, serious so suddenly. "You can have anything of mine you want. You can have all of it."

I'm caught off guard, so touched by the sincerity in his voice. "Really?" I ask. "Because I do love that soap."

He grins at me then. His eyes are wicked.

"What?"

He shakes his head. Breaks away. Slips out of bed.

"Aaron—"

"I'll be right back," he says.

I watch him walk into the bathroom. I hear the sound of a faucet, the rush of water filling a tub.

My heart starts racing.

He walks back into the room and I'm clinging to the sheets, already protesting what I think he's about to do.

He tugs on the blanket. Tilts his head at me. "Let go, please."

"No."

"Why not?"

"What are you going to do?" I ask.

"Nothing."

"Liar."

"It's okay, love." His eyes are teasing me. "Don't be embarrassed."

"It's too bright in here. Turn the lights off."

He laughs out loud. Yanks the covers off the bed.

I bite back a scream. "Aaron—"

"You are perfect," he says. "Every inch of you. Perfect," he says again. "Don't hide from me."

"I take it back," I say, panicked, clutching a pillow to my body. "I don't want your soap—I take it back—"

But then he plucks the pillow out of my arms, scoops me up, and carries me away.

FIFTY-SEVEN

My suit is ready.

Warner made sure Alia and Winston would have everything they needed in order to create it, and though I'd seen them tackling the project a little more every day, I never would've thought all those different materials could turn into this.

It looks like snakeskin.

The material is both black and gunmetal gray, but it looks almost gold in certain flashes of light. The pattern moves when I do, and it's dizzying how the threads seem to converge and diverge, looking as though they swim together and come apart.

It fits me in a way that's both uncomfortable and reassuring; it's skintight and a little stiff at first, but once I start moving my arms and legs I begin to understand just how much hidden flexibility it holds. It all seems strangely counterintuitive. This suit is even lighter than the one I had before—it hardly feels like I'm wearing anything at all—and yet it feels so much more durable, so much stronger. I feel like I could block a knife in this suit. Like I could be dragged across a mile of pavement in this suit.

I also have new boots.

They're very similar to my old ones, but these cut off at my calf, not my ankle. They're flat, springy, and soundless as I walk around in them.

I didn't ask for any gloves.

I'm flexing my bare hands, walking the length of the room and back, bending my knees and familiarizing myself with the sensation of wearing a new kind of outfit. It serves a different purpose. I'm not trying to hide my skin from the world anymore. I'm only trying to enhance the power I already have.

It feels so good.

"These are for you, too," Alia says, beaming as she blushes. "I thought you might like a new set." She holds out exact replicas of the knuckle braces she made for me once before.

The ones I lost. In a battle we lost.

These, more than anything else, represent so much to me. It's a second chance. An opportunity to do things right. "Thank you," I tell her, hoping she knows how much I mean it.

I fit the braces over my bare knuckles, flexing my fingers as I do.

I look up. Look around.

Everyone is staring at me. "What do you think?" I ask.

"Your suit looks just like mine." Kenji frowns. "I'm supposed to be the one with the black suit. Why can't you have a pink suit? Or a yellow suit—"

"Because we're not the freaking Power Rangers,"

Winston says, rolling his eyes.

"What the hell is a Power Ranger?" Kenji shoots back.

"I think it looks awesome," James says, grinning big. "You look way cooler than you did before."

"Yeah, that is seriously badass," Lily says. "I love it."

"It's your best work, mates," Brendan says to both Winston and Alia. "Really. And the knuckle—things . . . ," he says, gesturing to my hands. "Those are just . . . they bring the whole thing together, I think. It's brilliant."

"You look very sharp, Ms. Ferrars," Castle says to me. "I think it quite suits you," he says, "if you'll forgive the pun."

I grin.

Warner's hand is on my back. He leans in, whispers, "How easy is it to take this thing off?" and I force myself not to look at him and the smile he's surely enjoying at my expense. I hate that he can still make me blush.

My eyes try to find a new focus around the room.

Adam.

He's staring at me, his features unexpectedly relaxed. Calm. And for one moment, one very brief moment, I catch a glimpse of the boy I once knew. The one I first fell for.

He turns away.

I can't stop hoping he'll be okay; he only has twelve hours to pull himself together. Because tonight, we go over the plan, one last time.

And tomorrow, it all begins.

FIFTY-EIGHT

"Aaron?" I whisper.

The lights are out. We're lying in bed. I'm stretched out across his body, my head pillowed on his chest. My eyes are on the ceiling.

He's running his hand over my hair, his fingers occasionally combing through the strands. "Your hair is like water," he whispers. "It's so fluid. Like silk."

"Aaron."

He leaves a light kiss on top of my head. Rubs his hands down my arms. "Are you cold?" he asks.

"You can't avoid this forever."

"We don't have to avoid it at all," he says. "There's nothing to avoid."

"I just want to know you're okay," I say. "I'm worried about you." He still hasn't said a single thing to me about his mother. He never said a word the entire time we were in her room, and he hasn't spoken about it since. Hasn't even alluded to it. Not once.

Even now, he says nothing.

"Aaron?"

"Yes, love."

"You're not going to talk about it?"

He's silent again for so long I'm about to turn around to face him. But then.

"She's no longer in pain," he says softly. "This is a great consolation to me."

I don't push him to speak after that.

"Juliette," he says.

"Yes?"

I can hear him breathing.

"Thank you," he whispers. "For being my friend."

I turn around then. Press close to him, my nose grazing his neck. "I will always be here if you need me," I say, the darkness catching and hushing my voice. "Please remember that. Always remember that."

More seconds drown in the darkness. I feel myself drifting off to sleep.

"Is this really happening?" I hear him whisper.

"What?" I blink, try to stay awake.

"You feel so real," he says. "You sound so real. I want so badly for this to be real."

"This is real," I say. "And things are going to get better. Things are going to get so much better. I promise."

He takes a tight breath. "The scariest part," he says, so quietly, "is that for the first time in my life, I actually believe that."

"Good," I say softly, turning my face into his chest. I close my eyes.

Warner's arms slip around me, pulling me closer. "Why are you wearing so many clothes?" he whispers.

"Mmm?"

"I don't like these," he says. He tugs on my pants.

I touch my lips to his neck, just barely. It's a feather of a kiss. "Then take them off."

He pulls back the covers.

I only have a second to bite back a shiver before he's kneeling between my legs. He finds the waistband of my pants and tugs, pulling them off, over my hips, down my thighs. So slowly.

My heart is asking me all kinds of questions.

He bunches my pants in one fist and throws them across the room.

And then his arms slip behind my back, pulling me up and against his chest. His hands move under my shirt, up my spine.

Soon my shirt is gone.

Tossed in the same direction as my pants.

I shiver, just a little, and he eases me back onto the pillows, careful not to crush me under his weight. His body heat is so welcome, so warm. My head tilts backward. My eyes are still closed.

My lips part for no reason at all.

"I want to be able to feel you," he whispers, his words at my ear. "I want your skin against mine." His gentle hands move down my body. "God, you're so soft," he says, his voice husky with emotion.

He's kissing my neck.

My head is spinning. Everything goes hot and cold and

something is stirring to life inside of me and my hands reach for his chest, looking for something to hold on to and my eyes are trying and failing to stay open and I'm only just conscious enough to whisper his name.

"Yes, love?"

I try to say more but my mouth won't listen.

"Are you asleep now?" he asks.

Yes, I think. I don't know. Yes.

I nod.

"That's good," he says quietly. He lifts my head, pulls my hair away from my neck so my face falls more easily onto the pillow. He shifts so he's beside me on the bed. "You need to sleep more," he says.

I nod again, curling onto my side. He pulls the blankets up around my arms.

He kisses the curve of my shoulder. My shoulder blade. Five kisses down my spine, one softer than the next. "I will be here every night," he whispers, his words so soft, so tortured, "to keep you warm. I will kiss you until I can't keep my eyes open."

My head is caught in a cloud.

Can you hear my heart? I want to ask him.

I want you to make a list of all of your favorite things, and I want to be on it.

But I'm falling asleep so fast I've lost my grasp on reality, and I don't know how to move my mouth. Time has fallen all around me, wrapped me in this moment.

And Warner is still talking. So quietly, so softly. He

thinks I'm asleep now. He thinks I can't hear him.

"Did you know," he's whispering, "that I wake up, every morning, convinced you'll be gone?"

Wake up, I keep telling myself. *Wake up. Pay attention.*

"That all of this," he says, "these moments, will be confirmed as some kind of extraordinary dream? But then I hear you speak to me," he says. "I see the way you look at me and I can feel how real it is. I can feel the truth in your emotions, and in the way you touch me," he whispers, the back of his hand brushing my cheek.

My eyes flicker open. I blink once, twice.

His lips are set in a soft smile.

"Aaron," I whisper.

"I love you," he says.

My heart no longer fits in my chest.

"Everything looks so different to me now," he says. "It feels different. It tastes different. You brought me back to life." He's quiet a moment. "I have never known this kind of peace. Never known this kind of comfort. And sometimes I am afraid," he says, dropping his eyes, "that my love will terrify you."

He looks up, so slowly, gold lashes lifting to reveal more sadness and beauty than I've ever seen in the same moment. I didn't know a person could convey so much with just one look. There's extraordinary pain in him. Extraordinary passion.

It takes my breath away.

I take his face in my hands and kiss him, so slowly.

His eyes fall closed. His mouth responds to mine. His hands reach up to pull me closer and I stop him.

"No," I whisper. "Don't move."

He drops his hands.

"Lie back," I whisper.

He does.

I kiss him everywhere. His cheeks. His chin. The tip of his nose and the space between his eyebrows. All across his forehead and along his jawline. Every inch of his face. Small, soft kisses that say so much more than I ever could. I want him to know how I feel. I want him to know it the way only he can, the way he can sense the depth of emotion behind my movements. I want him to know and never doubt.

And I want to take my time.

My mouth moves down to his neck and he gasps, and I breathe in the scent of his skin, take in the taste of him and I run my hands down his chest, kissing my way across and down the line of his torso. He keeps trying to reach for me, keeps trying to touch me, and I have to tell him to stop.

"Please," he says, "I want to feel you—"

I gentle his arms back down. "Not yet. Not now."

My hands move to his pants. His eyes fly open.

"Close your eyes," I have to tell him.

"No." He can hardly speak.

"Close your eyes."

He shakes his head.

"Fine."

I unbutton his pants. Unzip.

"Juliette," he breathes. "What—"

I'm pulling off his pants.

He sits up.

"Lie down. Please."

He's staring at me, eyes wide.

He finally falls back.

I tug his pants off all the way. Toss them to the floor.

He's in his underwear.

I trace the stitching on the soft cotton, following the lines on the overlapping pieces of his boxer-briefs as they intersect in the middle. He's breathing so fast I can hear him, can see his chest moving. His eyes are squeezed shut. His head tilted back. His lips parted.

I touch him again, so gently.

He stifles a moan, turns his face into the pillows. His whole body is trembling, his hands clutching at the sheets. I run my hands down his legs, gripping them just above his knees and inching them apart to make room for the kisses I trail up the insides of his thighs. My nose skims his skin.

He looks like he's in pain. So much pain.

I find the elastic waist of his underwear. Tug it down.

Slowly.

Slowly.

The tattoo is sitting just below his hip bone.

h e l l i s e m p t y

a n d a l l t h e d e v i l s a r e h e r e

I kiss my way across the words.

Kissing away the devils.

Kissing away the pain.

FIFTY-NINE

I'm sitting on the edge of the bed, elbows propped up on my knees, face dropped into my hands.

"Are you ready?" he asks me.

I look up. Stand up. Shake my head.

"Breathe, sweetheart." He stands in front of me, slips his hands around my face. His eyes are bright, intense, steady, and so full of confidence. In me. "You are magnificent. You are extraordinary."

I try to laugh and it comes out all wrong.

Warner leans his forehead against mine. "There is nothing to fear. Nothing to worry about. Grieve nothing in this transitory world," he says softly.

I tilt back, a question in my eyes.

"It's the only way I know how to exist," he says. "In a world where there is so much to grieve and so little good to take? I grieve nothing. I take everything."

I stare into his eyes for what feels like forever.

He leans into my ear. Lowers his voice. "Ignite, my love. Ignite."

Warner has called for an assembly.

He says it's a fairly routine procedure, one wherein the

soldiers are required to wear a standard black uniform. "And they will be unarmed," Warner said to me.

Kenji and Castle and everyone else are coming to watch, care of Kenji's invisibility, but I'm the only one who's going to speak today. I told them I wanted to lead. I told them I'd be willing to take the first risk.

So here I am.

Warner walks me out of his bedroom door.

The halls are abandoned. The soldiers patrolling his quarters are gone, already assembled and awaiting his presence. The reality of what I'm about to do is only just starting to sink in.

Because no matter the outcome today, I am putting myself on display. It is a message from me to Anderson. A message I know he'll receive.

I am alive.

I will use your own armies to hunt you down.

And I will kill you.

Something about this thought makes me absurdly happy.

We walk into the elevator and Warner takes my hand. I squeeze his fingers. He smiles straight ahead. And suddenly we're walking out of the elevator and through another door and right into the open courtyard I've only ever stood in once before.

How odd, I think, that I should return to this roof not as a captive. No longer afraid. And clinging fast to the hand of the same blond boy who brought me here before.

How very strange this world is.

Warner hesitates before moving into view. He looks at me for confirmation. I nod. He releases my hand.

We step forward together.

SIXTY

There's an audible gasp from the soldiers standing just below.

They definitely remember me.

Warner pulls a square piece of mesh out of his pocket and presses it to his lips, just once, before holding it in his fist. His voice is amplified across the crowd when he speaks.

"Sector 45," he says.

They shift. Their right fists rise up to fall on their chests, their left fists released, dropping to their sides.

"You were told," he says, "a little over a month ago, that we'd won the battle against a resistance group by the name of Omega Point. You were told we decimated their home base and slaughtered their remaining men and women on the battlefield. You were told," he says, "never to doubt the power of The Reestablishment. We are unbeatable. Unsurpassed in military power and land control. You were told that we are the future. The only hope."

His voice rings out over the crowd, his eyes scanning the faces of his men.

"And I hope," he says, "that you did not believe it."

The soldiers are staring, stunned, as Warner speaks. They seem afraid to step out of line in case this turns out to be some kind of elaborate joke, or perhaps a test from The Reestablishment. They do nothing but stare, no longer taking care to make their faces appear as stoic as possible.

"Juliette Ferrars," he says, "is not dead. She is here, standing beside me, despite the claims made by our supreme commander. He did, in fact, shoot her in the chest. And he did leave her to die. But she was able to survive his attack on her life, and she has arrived here today to make you an offer."

I take the mesh from Warner's hand, touch it to my lips just as he did. Drop it into my fist.

I take a deep breath. And say six words.

"I want to destroy The Reestablishment."

My voice is so loud, so powerfully projected over the crowd, that for a moment it surprises me. The soldiers are staring at me in horror. Shock. Disbelief. Astonishment. They're starting to whisper.

"I want to lead you into battle," I say to them. "I want to fight back—"

No one is listening to me anymore.

Their perfectly organized lines have been abandoned. They're now converging together in one mass, speaking and shouting and trying to deliberate among themselves. Trying to understand what's happening.

I can't believe I lost their attention so quickly.

"Don't hesitate," Warner says to me. "You must react. *Now.*"

I was hoping to save this for later.

Right now, we're only about fifteen feet off the ground, but Warner told me there are four more levels, if I want to go all the way up. The highest level houses the speakers designated for this particular area. It has a small maintenance platform that is only ever accessed by technicians.

I'm already climbing my way up.

The soldiers are distracted again, pointing at me as I scale the stairs; still talking loudly with one another. I have no idea if it's possible for news of this situation to have already reached the civilians or the spies who report back to the supreme. I have no time to care right now because I haven't even finished giving my speech, and I've already lost them.

This isn't good.

When I finally reach the top level, I'm about a hundred feet off the ground. I'm careful as I step onto the platform, but I'm more careful not to look down for too long. And when I've finally planted my feet, I look up and around the crowd.

I have their attention again.

I close my fist over the microphonic mesh.

"I only have one question," I say, my words powerful and clear, projecting into the distance. "What has The Reestablishment ever done for you?"

They're actually looking at me now. Listening.

"They have given you nothing but meager wages and promises for a future that will never come. They have divided your families and forced them across what's left of this earth. They have starved your children and destroyed your homes. They lie to you, over and over again, forcing you to take jobs in their army so they might control you. And you have no other choice," I say. "No other options. So you fight in their wars, and you kill your own friends, just so you might feed your families."

Yes, I have their attention now.

"The person you allow to lead this nation is a coward," I say to them. "He is a weak man who's too afraid to show his face to the public. He lives in secrecy, hides from the people who rely on him, and yet he's taught you to fear him," I say. "He's taught you to cower when his name is spoken.

"Maybe you haven't met him yet," I say. "But I have. And I was not impressed."

I can't believe no one has shot me yet. I don't care if they're supposed to be unarmed. Someone probably has a gun. And no one has shot me yet.

"Join a new resistance," I say to them, calling out to the crowd. "We are the majority, and we can stand united. Will you continue to live like this?" I ask them, pointing to the compounds in the distance. "Will you continue to starve? Because they will continue to lie to you!" I say. "Our world is not beyond repair. It's not beyond saving. We can be our own army," I say to them. "We can stand together. Join me," I say, "and I promise things will change."

"How?" I hear someone shout. "How can you promise something like that?"

"I am not intimidated by The Reestablishment," I tell them. "And I have more strength than you might realize. I have the kind of power that the supreme commander cannot stand against."

"We already know what you can do!" someone else yells. "That didn't save you before!"

"No," I say to them, "you don't know what I can do. You have no idea what I can do."

I reach my arms out in front of me, both hands pointed in the direction of the crowd. I try to find a good middle. And then I focus.

Feel your power, Kenji said to me once. *It's a part of you—a part of your body and mind. It will listen to you if you can learn how to control it.*

I plant my feet. Steel myself.

And then I pry the crowd apart.

Slowly.

I focus my energy on recognizing the individual bodies and allow my power to move fluidly, working around the soldiers in a gentle fashion, as opposed to rushing through them and accidentally ripping them apart. My power clings to their forms as my fingers would, finally finding a perfect center that divides the group into two halves. They're already looking at each other from across the courtyard, trying to understand why they can't move against the invisible walls pushing them apart.

But once the energy is set in place, I open my arms, wide.

Pull.

The soldiers are knocked back. Half to the left. Half to the right. Not enough to be injured, but just enough to be startled. I want them to feel the power I'm containing. I want them to know that I'm holding back.

"I can protect you," I say to them, my voice still ringing loud over them. "And I have friends who could do more. Who will stand beside you and fight."

And then, as if on cue, the group of them appear out of thin air, in the very center of the courtyard, in the space I've just cleared.

The soldiers jerk back, stunned, shifting farther into their corners.

Castle reaches up one arm, coaxing a small tree in the distance to uproot itself. He uses both hands to pull it out of the ground, and once he does, the tree careens out of control, flying through the air, branches rattling in the wind. Castle pulls it back, yanking on it with nothing more than his mind.

He tosses it higher in the air, just over their heads, and Brendan raises his arms.

Claps his hands, hard.

A bolt of electricity hits the tree at the base and travels up the trunk so quickly, and with such extreme power, it practically disintegrates; the only remaining pieces rain to the ground.

I was not expecting that; they weren't even supposed to be helping me today. But they've just created the perfect introduction for me.

Now. Right now.

All the soldiers are watching. The courtyard has been

cleared. I find Kenji's eyes down below and check for confirmation.

He nods.

I jump.

A hundred feet in the air, eyes closed, legs straight, arms out. And I feel more power rushing through my being than ever before. I harness it. Project it.

And land so hard on the ground that it shatters beneath me.

I'm crouched, knees bent, one hand outstretched in front of me. The courtyard is shaking so badly that for a second I'm not sure I haven't caused another earthquake.

When I finally stand up and look around, I can see the soldiers much more clearly. Their faces, their worries. They're looking at me in awe, eyes wide with wonder and a touch of fear.

"You will not be alone," I say to them, spinning to see their faces. "You don't need to be afraid anymore. We want to take back our world. We want to save the lives of our family members, our friends. We want your children to have a chance at a better future. And we want to fight. We want to *win*." I lock eyes with them. "And we are asking for your help."

There's absolute silence.

And then, absolute chaos.

Cheers. Screams and shouts. Stomping feet.

I feel the mesh square tugged out of my hand. It flies up into the air and into Warner's hand.

He addresses his men.

"Congratulations, gentlemen," he says. "Send word to your families. Your friends. Tomorrow, everything will change. The supreme will be here in a matter of days," he says. "Prepare for war."

And then, all at once.

Kenji makes us disappear.

SIXTY-ONE

We're running through the courtyard and right through base, and as soon as we're out of sight, Kenji pulls back the invisibility. He darts ahead of the group, leading us toward the training room, winding and twisting and darting through the storage facility and up the shooting range until we're all toppling into the room at once.

James has been waiting for us.

He stands up, eyes wide. "How'd it go?"

Kenji runs forward and flips James into his arms. "How do you *think* it went?"

"Um. Good?" James is laughing.

Castle claps me on the back. I turn to face him. He's beaming at me, eyes shining, prouder than I've ever seen him. "Well done, Ms. Ferrars," he says quietly. "Well done."

Brendan and Winston rush over, grinning from ear to ear.

"That was so freaking cool," Winston says. "It was like we were celebrities or something."

Lily, Ian, and Alia join the group. I thank them all for their help, for their show of support at the last minute.

"Do you really think it'll work?" I'm asking. "Do you think it's enough?"

"It's certainly a start," Castle says. "We'll need to move quickly now. I imagine the news has already spread, but the other sectors will surely stand down until the supreme arrives." Castle looks at me. "I hope you understand that this will be a fight against the entire country."

"Not if the other sectors join us, too," I say.

"Such confidence," Castle says. He's staring at me like I'm a strange, alien being. One he doesn't know how to understand or identify. "You surprise me, Ms. Ferrars."

The elevator pings open.

Warner.

He walks right up to me. "The base has been secured," he says. "We are on lockdown until my father arrives. No one will enter or exit the premises."

"So what do we do now?" Ian asks.

"We wait," Warner says. He looks around at us. "If he does not already know, he will within the next five minutes. The supreme will know that some members of your group are still alive. That Juliette is still alive. He will know that I have defied him and stood against him publicly. And he will be very, very angry," Warner says. "This much I can absolutely guarantee."

"So we go to war," Brendan says.

"Yes." Warner is calm, so calm. "We fight. Soon."

"And the soldiers?" I ask him. "Are they really on board?"

He holds my eyes for just a moment too long. "Yes," he says. "I can feel the depth of their passion. Their sudden respect for you. There are many among them who are still afraid, and others still who are rigid in their skepticism, but you were right, love. They might fear, but they do not want to be soldiers. Not like this. Not for The Reestablishment. They are ready to join us."

"And the civilians?" I ask, amazed.

"They will follow."

"Are you sure?"

"I can be sure of nothing," he says quietly. "But I have never, in all my time in this sector, felt the kind of hope in my men that I felt today. It was so powerful, so all-consuming, I can still feel it from here. It's practically vibrating in my blood."

I can hardly breathe.

"Juliette, love," he says to me, still holding my eyes. "You have just started a war."

SIXTY-TWO

Warner pulls me to the side. Away from everyone else.

We're standing in a corner of the training room, and his hands are gripped around my shoulders. He's looking at me like I've just pulled the moon out of my pocket.

"I have to go," he says urgently. "There are many things that must be set in motion now, and I have to reconvene with Delalieu. I will handle every aspect of the military details, love. I will see to it that you have everything you need, and that my men are equipped in every possible way."

I'm nodding, trying to thank him.

But he's still looking at me, searching my eyes like he's found something he can't bear to walk away from. His hands move to my face; his thumb brushes my cheek. His voice is so tender when he speaks.

"You will go on to greatness," he whispers. "I have never deserved you."

My heart.

He leans in, kisses my forehead, so gently.

And then he leaves.

I'm still watching the elevator doors close when I catch a glimpse of Adam out of the corner of my eye. He walks up to me.

"Hey," he says. He looks nervous, uncomfortable.

"Hi."

He's nodding, staring at his feet. "So," he says. Blows out a breath. He's still not looking at me. "Nice show."

I'm not really sure what to say. So I say nothing.

Adam sighs. "You really have changed," he whispers. "Haven't you?"

"Yes. I have."

He nods, just once. Laughs a strange laugh. And walks away.

SIXTY-THREE

We're all sitting around again.

Talking. Discussing. Thinking and planning. James is snoring soundly in the corner.

We're all caught somewhere between being excited and being terrified, and yet, somehow, we're mostly excited. This is, after all, what everyone at Omega Point had always been planning; they'd joined Castle hoping it would one day come to this.

A chance to defeat The Reestablishment.

They've all been training for this. Even Adam, who somehow convinced himself to stand with us, has been a soldier. Kenji, a soldier. All of them in peak physical condition. They are all fighters; even Alia, whose quiet shell contains so much. I couldn't have asked for a more solid group of individuals.

"So when do you think he'll be here?" Ian is asking. "Tomorrow?"

"Maybe," Kenji says. "But I don't think it'll take him more than two days."

"I thought he was on a ship? In the middle of the ocean?" Lily asks. "How is he supposed to get here in two days?"

"I don't think it's the kind of ship you're thinking of,"

Castle says to her. "I imagine he is on an army vessel; one equipped with a landing strip. If he calls for a jet, they will deliver him to us."

"Wow." Brendan leans back, rests on his hands. "This is really happening, then? *The supreme commander of The Reestablishment*. Winston and I never saw him, not once, even though his men were holding us captive." He shakes his head. Glances at me. "What does he look like?"

"He's extremely handsome," I say.

Lily laughs out loud.

"I'm serious," I say to her. "It's almost sick how beautiful he is."

"Really?" Winston is staring at me, eyes wide.

Kenji nods. "Very pretty guy."

Lily is gawking.

"And you said his name is Anderson?" Alia asks.

I nod.

"That's strange," Lily says. "I always thought Warner's last name was *Warner*, not Anderson." She thinks for a second. "So his name is Warner Anderson?"

"No," I say to her. "You're right. Warner is his last name—but not his dad's. He took his mom's last name," I say. "He didn't want to be associated with his father."

Adam snorts.

We all look at him.

"So what's Warner's first name?" Ian asks. "Do you know?"

I nod.

"And?" Winston asks. "You're not going to tell us?"

"Ask him yourself," I say. "If he wants to tell you, I'm sure he will."

"Yeah, that's not going to happen," Winston says. "I'm not asking that guy personal questions."

I try not to laugh.

"So—do you know Anderson's first name?" Ian asks. "Or is that a secret, too? I mean this whole thing is really weird, right? That they'd be so secretive about their names?"

"Oh," I say, caught off guard. "I'm not sure. There's a lot of power in a name, I guess. And no," I say, shaking my head. "I don't actually know Anderson's first name. I never asked."

"You're not missing anything," Adam says, irritated. "It's a stupid name." He's staring at his shoes. "His name is Paris."

"How did you know that?"

I spin around and find Warner standing just outside the open elevator. It's still pinging softly, only just now signaling his arrival. The doors close behind him. He's staring at Adam in shock.

Adam blinks fast at Warner and then at us, unsure what to do.

"How did you know that?" Warner demands again. He walks right through our group and grabs Adam by the shirt, moving so quickly Adam has no time to react.

He pins him against the wall.

I've never heard Warner raise his voice like this before.

Never seen him so angry. "Who do you answer to, soldier?" he shouts. "Who is your commander?"

"I don't know what you're talking about!" Adam yells back. He tries breaking away and Warner grabs him with both fists, shoving him harder against the wall.

I'm beginning to panic.

"How long have you been working for him?" Warner shouts again. "How long have you been infiltrating my base—"

I jump to my feet. Kenji is close behind.

"Warner," I say, "please, he's not a spy—"

"There's no way he could know something like that," Warner says to me, still looking at Adam. "Not unless he is a member of the Supreme Guard, where even then it would be questionable. A foot soldier would never have that kind of information—"

"I'm not a Supreme Soldier," Adam tries to say, "I swear—"

"Liar," Warner barks, shoving him harder against the wall. Adam's shirt is starting to tear. "Why were you sent here? What is your mission? Has he sent you to kill me?"

"Warner," I call again, pleading this time, running forward until I'm in his line of vision. "Please—he's not working for the supreme, I promise—"

"How can you know?" Warner finally glances at me, just for a second. "I'm telling you," he says, "it's impossible for him to know this—"

"He's your *brother*," I finally choke out. "Please. He's your brother. You have the same father."

Warner goes rigid.

He turns to me.

"What?" he breathes.

"It's true," I tell him, feeling so heartbroken as I do. "And I know you can tell I'm not lying." I shake my head. "He's your brother. Your father was leading a double life. He abandoned Adam and James a long time ago. After Adam's mom died."

Warner drops Adam to the floor.

"No," Warner says. He's not even blinking. Just staring. Hands shaking.

I turn to look at Adam, eyes tight with emotion. "Tell him," I say, desperate now. "Tell him the truth."

Adam says nothing.

"Dammit, Adam, *tell* him!"

"You knew, all this time?" Warner asks, turning to face me. "You knew this and yet you said nothing?"

"I wanted to—I really, really wanted to, but I didn't think it was my place—"

"No," he says, cutting me off. He's shaking his head. "No, this doesn't make any sense. How—how is that even possible?" He looks up, looks around. "That doesn't—"

He stops.

Looks at Adam.

"Tell me the truth," he says. He walks up to Adam again, looking like he might shake him. "Tell me! I have a right to know!"

And every moment in the world drops dead just then, because they woke up and realized they'd never be as important as this one.

"It's true," Adam says.

Two words to change the world.

Warner steps back, hand caught in his hair. He's rubbing his eyes, his forehead, running his hand down his mouth, his neck. He's breathing so hard. "How?" he finally asks.

And then.

And then.

The truth.

Little by little. It's pulled out of Adam. One word at a time. And the rest of us are looking on, and James is still sleeping, and I go silent as these two brothers have the hardest conversation I've ever had to watch.

SIXTY-FOUR

Warner is sitting in one corner. Adam in another. They've both asked to be left alone.

And they're both staring at James.

James, who's still just a little snoring lump.

Adam looks exhausted, but not defeated. Tired, but not upset. He looks freer. His eyebrows unfurrowed. His fists unclenched. His face is calm in a way I haven't seen it in what feels like a long time.

He looks *relieved*.

As if he'd been carrying this great burden he thought might kill him. As if he'd thought sharing this truth with Warner might somehow inspire a lifelong war between him and his brand-new biological sibling.

But Warner wasn't angry at all. He wasn't even upset.

He was just shocked beyond belief.

One father, I think. Three brothers. Two who nearly killed each other, all because of the world they were bred in. Because of the many words, the many lies they were fed.

Words are like seeds, I think, planted into our hearts at a tender age.

They take root in us as we grow, settling deep into our souls. The good words plant well. They flourish and find homes in our hearts. They build trunks around our spines, steadying us when we're feeling most flimsy; planting our feet firmly when we're feeling most unsure. But the bad words grow poorly. Our trunks infest and spoil until we are hollow and housing the interests of others and not our own. We are forced to eat the fruit those words have borne, held hostage by the branches growing arms around our necks, suffocating us to death, one word at a time.

I don't know how Adam and Warner are going to break the news to James. Maybe they won't tell him until he's older and able to deal with the ramifications of knowing his heritage. I don't know what it'll do to James to learn that his father is actually a mass murderer and a despicable human being who's destroyed every life he's ever touched.

No.

Maybe it's better James doesn't know, not just yet.

Maybe it's enough for now that Warner knows at all.

I can't help but find it both painful and beautiful that Warner lost a mother and gained two brothers in the same week. And though I understand that he's asked to be left alone, I can't stop myself from walking over to him. I won't say a word, I promise myself. But I just want to be close to him right now.

So I sit down beside him, and lean my head against the wall. Just breathing.

"You should've told me," he whispers.

I hesitate before answering. "You have no idea how many times I wanted to."

"You should've told me."

"I'm so sorry," I say, dropping my head. My voice. "I'm really sorry."

Silence.

More silence.

Then.

A whisper.

"I have two brothers."

I lift my head. Look at him.

"I have two brothers," he says again, his voice so soft. "And I almost killed one of them."

His eyes are focused on a point far, far from here, pinched together in pain and confusion, and something that looks like regret.

"I suppose I should've known," he says to me. "He can touch you. He lives in the same sector. And his eyes have always been oddly familiar to me. I realize now that they're shaped just like my father's."

He sighs.

"This is so unbearably inconvenient," he says. "I was prepared to hate him for the rest of my life."

I startle, surprised. "You mean . . . you don't hate him anymore?"

Warner drops his head. His voice is so low I can hardly hear it. "How can I hate his anger," he says, "when I know so well where it comes from?"

I'm staring at him. Stunned.

"I can well imagine the extent of his relationship with my father," Warner says, shaking his head. "And that he has managed to survive it at all, and with more humanity than I did?" A pause. "No," he says. "I cannot hate him. And I would be lying if I said I didn't admire him."

I think I might cry.

The minutes pass between us, silent and still, stopping only to hear us breathe.

"Come on," I finally whisper, reaching for his hand. "Let's go to bed."

Warner nods, gets to his feet, but then he stops. Confused. So tortured. He looks at Adam. Adam looks back.

They stare at each other for a long time.

"Please excuse me," Warner says.

And I watch, astonished, as he crosses the room. Adam is on his feet in an instant, defensive, uncertain. But as Warner approaches, Adam seems to thaw.

The two are now face-to-face, and Warner is speaking.

Adam's jaw tenses. He looks at the floor.

He nods.

Warner is still speaking.

Adam swallows, hard. He nods again.

Then he looks up.

The two of them acknowledge each other for a long moment. And then Warner places one hand on Adam's shoulder.

I must be dreaming.

The two exchange a few more words before Warner pivots on one foot, and walks away.

SIXTY-FIVE

"What did you say to him?" I ask as soon as the elevator doors close.

Warner takes a deep breath. He says nothing.

"You're not going to tell me?"

"I'd rather not," he says quietly.

I take his hand. Squeeze.

The elevator doors open.

"Will this be weird for you?" Warner asks. He looks surprised by his own question, as though he can't believe he's even asking it.

"Will what be weird?"

"That Kent and I are . . . brothers."

"No," I say to him. "I've known for a while now. It doesn't change anything for me."

"That's good," he says quietly.

I'm nodding, confused.

We've moved into the bedroom. We're sitting on the bed now.

"You wouldn't mind, then?" Warner asks.

I'm still confused.

"If he and I," Warner says, "spent some time together?"

"What?" I ask, unable to hide my disbelief. "No," I say

quickly. “No, of course not—I think that would be amazing.”

Warner’s eyes are on the wall.

“So . . . you want to spend time with him?” I’m trying so hard to give Warner space, and I don’t want to pry, but I just can’t help myself.

“I would like to know my own brother, yes.”

“And James?” I ask.

Warner laughs a little. “Yes. And James.”

“So you’re . . . happy about this?”

He doesn’t answer right away. “I am not unhappy.”

I climb into his lap. Cup his face in my hands, tilting his chin up so I can see his eyes. I’m smiling a stupid smile. “I think that’s so wonderful,” I tell him.

“Do you?” He grins. “How interesting.”

I nod. Over and over again. And I kiss him once, very softly.

Warner closes his eyes. Smiles slightly, his cheek dimpled on one side. He looks thoughtful now. “How strange this has all become.”

I feel like I might die of happiness.

Warner picks me up off his lap, lays me back on the bed. Crawls over me, on top of me. “And why are you so thrilled?” he asks, trying not to laugh. “You’re practically buoyant.”

“I want you to be happy,” I tell him, my eyes searching his. “I want you to have a family. I want you to be surrounded by people who care about you,” I say. “You deserve that.”

“I have you,” he says, resting his forehead against mine. His eyes shut.

"You should have more than me."

"No," he whispers. He shakes his head. His nose grazes mine.

"Yes."

"What about you? And your parents?" he asks me. "Do you ever want to find them?"

"No," I say quietly. "They were never parents to me. Besides, I have my friends."

"And me," he says.

"You are my friend," I tell him.

"But not your best friend. Kenji is your best friend."

I try so hard not to laugh at the jealousy in his voice. "Yes, but you're my *favorite* friend."

Warner leans in, bypasses my lips. "Good," he whispers, kissing my neck. "Now flip over," he says. "On your stomach."

I stare at him.

"Please," he says. Smiles.

I do. Very slowly.

"What are you doing?" I whisper, turning to look at him.

He gentles my body back down.

"I want you to know," he says, pulling on the zipper holding this suit together, "how much I value your friendship." The seam is coming apart and my skin is now open to the elements; I bite back a shiver.

The zipper stops at the base of my spine.

"But I'd like you to reconsider my title," Warner says. He drops a soft kiss in the middle of my back. Runs his hands up my skin and pushes the sleeves off my shoulders, leaving kisses against my shoulder blades, the back of my neck. "Because my friendship," he whispers, "comes with so many more benefits than Kenji could ever offer."

I can't breathe. Can't.

"Don't you think?" Warner asks.

"Yes," I say too quickly. "Yes."

And then I'm spinning, lost in sensations, and wondering how soon we'll be losing these moments, and wondering how long it'll be before we'll have them again.

I don't know where we're going, he and I, but I know I want to get there. We are hours and minutes reaching for the same second, holding hands as we spin forward into new days and the promise of something better.

But though we'll know forward and we've known backward, we will never know the present. This moment and the next one and even the one that would've been right now are gone, already passed, and all we're left with are these tired bodies, the only proof that we've lived through time and survived it.

It'll be worth it, though, in the end.

Fighting for a lifetime of this.

SIXTY-SIX

It took one day.

"I want one." I'm staring at the gun wall in the training room. "Which one is the best one?"

Delalieu arrived just this morning to deliver the news. The supreme has arrived. He's been transported from the ocean by jet, but he's now staying on one of Sector 45's army ships, stationed at the dock.

His guard is close behind. And his armies will be following soon.

Sometimes I'm not so sure we're not going to die.

"You don't need a gun," Warner says to me, surprised. "You can certainly have one, but I don't think you need one."

"I want two."

"All right," he laughs. But he's the only one.

Everyone else is frozen in the moments before fear takes over. We're all cautiously optimistic, but concerned nonetheless. Warner has already assembled his troops, and the civilians have already been notified; if they want to join us, a station has been set up to provide weapons and ammunition. All they have to do is present their RR cards to prove they are residents of Sector 45, and they will be granted amnesty. Shelters and relief centers have been created in the soldiers' barracks to stow away any remaining men, women, and children who cannot, or will not, join the battle. They will be allowed to take refuge here, and wait out the bloodshed.

These extra efforts were all coordinated by Warner.

"What if he just bombs everyone again?" Ian asks, breaking the silence. "Just like he did with Omega Point?"

"He won't," Warner says to him. "He's too arrogant, and this war has become personal. He'll want to toy with us. He'll want to draw this out as long as possible. He is a man who has always been fascinated by the idea of torture. This is going to be fun for him."

"Yeah, that's making me feel real good," Kenji says. "Thanks for the pep talk."

"Anytime," Warner says.

Kenji almost laughs. Almost.

"So he's staying in another ship?" Winston asks. "Here?"

"This is my understanding, yes," Warner says. "Normally he would stay on base, but as we are currently the enemy, it's become a bit of a problem. Apparently he's also granted sector clearance to soldiers across the country in order to have them join him. He has his own elite guard, as well as the soldiers who maintain the capital, but he's also collecting men from around the nation. It's all for show," Warner says. "We are not so vast in number that he'd need that many men. He just wants to terrify us."

"Well, it's working," Ian says.

"And you're sure," I ask Warner, "that he won't be on

the battlefield? You're positive?" This is the part of the plan that's the most important. The most critical.

Warner nods.

Anderson never fights in his own wars. He never shows his face. And we're relying on his cowardice to be our biggest advantage. Because while he might be able to anticipate an attempt on his life, we're hoping he won't be able to anticipate invisible attackers.

Warner has to oversee the troops. Castle, Brendan, Winston, Lily, Alia, and Adam will be supporting him. James will be staying behind on base.

But me and Kenji are going to the source.

And right now, we're ready to go. We're suited up, armed, and highly caffeinated.

I hear the sound of a gun being reloaded.

Spin around.

Warner is looking at me.

It's time to go.

SIXTY-SEVEN

Kenji grabs my arm.

Everyone else is going up and out of Warner's room, but Kenji and I will head out the back way, alerting no one to our presence. We want everyone, even the soldiers, to think we are in the midst of battle. We don't want to show up only to disappear; we don't want anyone to notice we're missing.

So we stand back and watch as our friends load into the elevator to go up to the main floor. James is still waving as the doors close and leave him behind.

My heart stops for a second.

Kenji kisses James good-bye. It's an obnoxious, noisy kiss, right on top of his head. "Watch my back, okay?" he says to James. "If anyone comes in here, I want you to kick the shit out of them."

"Okay," James says. He's laughing to pretend he's not crying.

"I'm serious," Kenji says. "Just start whaling on them. Like just go batshit." He makes a weird fighting motion with his hands. "Get super crazy," he says. "Beat the crazy with crazy—"

"No one is going to come in here, James," I say, shooting

a sharp look at Kenji. "You won't have to worry about defending yourself. You're going to be perfectly safe. And then we'll come back."

"Really?" he asks, turning his eyes on me. "All of you?"

Smart kid.

"Yes," I lie. "All of us are going to come back."

"Okay," he whispers. He bites down on his trembling lip. "Good luck."

"No tears necessary," Kenji says to him, wrapping him up in a ferocious hug. "We'll be back soon."

James nods.

Kenji breaks away.

And then we head out the door in the gun wall.

The first part, I think, is going to be the hardest. Our trek to the port will be made entirely on foot, because we can't risk stealing vehicles. Even if Kenji could make the tank invisible, we'd have to abandon it in its visible form, and an extra, unexpected tank stationed at the port would be too much of a giveaway.

Anderson must have his place completely guarded.

Kenji and I don't speak as we move. When Delalieu told us the supreme would be stationed at the port, Kenji immediately knew where it was. So did Warner and Adam and Castle and just about everyone except for me. "I spent some time on one of those ships," Kenji said. "Just for a bit. For bad behavior." He smiled. "I know my way around."

So I'm holding on to his arm and he's leading the way.

There's never been a colder day, I think. Never been more ice in the air.

This ship looks like a small city; it's so enormous I can't even see the end of it. We scan the perimeter, attempting to gauge exactly how difficult it'll be to infiltrate the premises.

Extremely difficult.

Nearly impossible.

These are Kenji's exact words.

Sort of.

"*Shit,*" he says. "This is ridiculous. I have never seen this level of security before. This is backed *up*," he says.

And he's right. There are soldiers everywhere. On land. At the entrance. On deck. And they're all so heavily armed it makes me feel stupid with my two handguns and the simple holster swung around my shoulders.

"So what do we do?"

He's quiet a moment. "Can you swim?"

"What? No."

"Shit."

"We can't just jump in the ocean, Kenji—"

"Well it's not like we can *fly*."

"Maybe we can fight them?"

"Are you out of your goddamn mind? You think we can take on two hundred soldiers? I know I am an extremely attractive man, J, but I am not Bruce Lee."

"Who's Bruce Lee?"

"*Who's Bruce Lee?*" Kenji asks, horrified. "Oh my God. We

can't even be friends anymore."

"Why? Was he a friend of yours?"

"You know what," he says, "just stop. Just—I can't even talk to you right now."

"Then how are we supposed to get inside?"

"Shit if I know. How are we supposed to get all those guys off the ship?"

"Oh," I gasp. "Oh my God. Kenji—" I grab his invisible arm.

"Yeah, that's my leg, and you're cutting it a little too close there, princess."

"Kenji, I can *shove* them off," I say, ignoring him. "I can just push them into the water. Will that work?"

Silence.

"Well?" I ask.

"Your hand is still on my leg."

"Oh." I jerk back. "So? What do you think? Will it work?"

"*Obviously,*" Kenji says, exasperated. "Do it now, please. And hurry."

So I do.

I stand back and pull all my energy up and into my arms.

Power, harnessed.

Arms, positioned.

Energy, projected.

I move my arm through the air like I might be clearing off a table.

And all the soldiers topple into the water.

It looks almost comical from here. Like they were a

bunch of toys I was pushing off my desk. And now they're bouncing in the water, trying to figure out what's just happened.

"Let's go," Kenji says suddenly, grabbing my arm. We're darting forward and down the hundred-foot pier. "They're not stupid," he says. "Someone is going to sound the alarm and they're going to seal the doors soon. We've probably got a minute before it all goes on lockdown."

So we're bolting.

We're racing across the pier and clambering up, onto the deck, and Kenji pulls on my arm to tell me where to go. We're becoming so much more aware of each other's bodies now. I can almost feel his presence beside me, even though I can't see him.

"Down here," he shouts, and I look down, spotting what looks like a narrow, circular opening with a ladder affixed to the inside. "I'm going in," he says. "Start climbing down in five seconds!"

I can hear the alarms already going off, sirens wailing in the distance. The ship is steady against the dock, but the water in the distance goes on forever, disappearing into the edge of the earth.

My five seconds are up.

I'm climbing after him.

SIXTY-EIGHT

I have no idea where Kenji is.

It's cramped and claustrophobic down here and I can already hear a rush of footsteps coming toward me, shouts and cries echoing down the hall; they must know something has happened above deck. I'm trying really hard not to panic, but I'm no longer sure what the next step should be.

I never anticipated doing this alone.

I keep whispering Kenji's name and hoping for a response, but there's nothing. I can't believe I've already lost him. At least I'm still invisible, which means he can't be more than fifty feet away, but the soldiers are too close for me to take any chances right now. I can't do anything that would draw attention to my presence—or Kenji's.

So I have to force myself to stay calm.

The problem is I have no idea where I am. No idea what I'm looking at. I've never even been on a *boat* before, much less an army ship of this magnitude.

But I have to try and understand my surroundings.

I'm standing in the middle of what looks like a very long hallway; wooden panels run across the floors, the walls, and even the low ceiling above my head. There are little nooks every few feet, where the wall seems to be scooped out.

They're for doors, I realize.

I wonder where they lead. Where I'll have to go.

Boots are thundering closer now.

My heart starts racing and I try to shove myself against the wall, but these hallways are too narrow; even though they can't see me, there's no way I'd be able to slip past them. I can see a group approaching now, can hear them barking orders at one another. At any moment they're going to slam right into me.

I shift backward as fast as I can and run, keeping my weight on my toes to minimize sound as much as possible. I skid to a stop. Hit the wall behind me. More soldiers are bolting down the halls now, clearly alerted to something, and for a second I feel my heart fail. I'm so worried about Kenji.

But as long as I'm invisible, Kenji must be close, I think. He must be alive.

I cling to this hope as the soldiers approach.

I look to my left. Look to my right. They're closing in on me without even realizing it. I have no idea where they're headed—maybe they're going back up, outside—but I have to make a move, fast, and I don't want to alert them to my presence. Not yet. It's too soon to try to take them out. I know Alia promised I could sustain a bullet wound as long as my power is on, but my last experience with being shot in the chest has left me traumatized enough to want to avoid that option as much as possible.

So I do the only thing I can think of.

I jump into one of the doorways and plant my hands against the inside of the frame, holding myself in place, my back pressed against the door. *Please please please,* I think, *please don't let there be someone in this room.* All anyone has to do is open the door and I'll be dead.

The soldiers are getting closer.

I stop breathing as they pass.

One of their elbows grazes my arm.

My heart is pounding, so hard. As soon as they're gone I dart out of the doorway and bolt, running down halls that only lead into more halls. This place is like a maze. I have no idea where I am, no idea what's happening.

Not a single clue where I'll find Anderson.

And the soldiers won't stop coming. They're everywhere, all at once and then not at all, and I'm turning down corners and spinning in different directions and trying my best to outrun them. But then I notice my hands.

I'm no longer invisible.

I bite back a scream.

I jump into another doorway, hoping to press myself out of sight, but now I'm both nervous and horrified, because not only do I not know what's happened to Kenji, but I don't know what's going to happen to me, either. This was such a stupid idea. I am such a stupid person. I don't know what I was thinking.

That I ever thought I could do this.

Boots.

Stomping toward me. I steel myself and suck up my fear

and try to be as prepared as possible. There's no way they won't notice me now. I haul my energy up and into myself, feel my bones thrumming with the rush of it and the thrill of power raging through me. If I can maintain this state for as long as I'm down here, I should be able to protect myself. I know how to fight now. I can disarm a man, steal away his weapon. I've learned to do so much.

But I'm still fairly terrified, and I've never needed to use the bathroom as much as I do right now.

Think, I keep telling myself. *Think. What can you do? Where can you go? Where would Anderson be hiding? Deeper? Lower?*

Where would the largest room on this ship be? Certainly not on the top level. I have to drop down.

But how?

The soldiers are getting closer.

I wonder what these rooms contain, what this doorway leads to. If it's just a room, then it's a dead end. But if it's an entrance to a larger space, then I might have a chance. But if there's someone in here, I'll definitely be in trouble. I don't know if I should take the risk.

A shout.

A cry.

A gunshot.

They've seen me.

SIXTY-NINE

I slam my elbow into the door behind me, shattering the wood into splinters that fly everywhere. I turn around and punch my way through the rest of it, kicking the door down with a sudden burst of adrenaline, and as soon as I see that this room is just a small bunker and a dead end, I do the only thing I can think of.

I jump.

And land.

And go right through the floor.

I fall into a tumble and manage to catch myself in time. The soldiers are jumping down after me, shouting and screaming. Boots chase me as I yank open the door and dart down the hall. Alarms are going off everywhere, sounds so loud and so obnoxious I can hardly hear myself think. I feel like I'm running through a haze, the sirens flashing red lights that circle the halls, screeching and blaring and signaling an intruder.

I'm on my own now.

I'm darting around more corners, spinning around bends in this floor plan and trying to get a feel for the difference between this level and the one just above it. There doesn't seem to be any. They look exactly the same, and the soldiers are just as aggressive.

They're shooting freely now, the earsplitting sound of gunshots colliding with the blare of the sirens. I'm not even sure I haven't gone deaf yet.

I can't believe they keep managing to *miss* me.

It seems impossible, statistically speaking, that so many soldiers at such close range wouldn't be able to find a target on my body. That can't be right.

I slam through the floor again.

Land on my feet this time.

I'm crouched, looking around, and for the first time, I see that this level is different. The hallways are wider, the doors set farther apart. I wish Kenji were here. I wish I had any idea what this means, what the difference is between the levels. I wish I knew where to go, where to start looking.

I kick open a door.

Nothing.

I run forward, kick down another one.

Nothing.

I keep running. I'm starting to see the inner workings of the ship. Machines, pipes, steel beams, huge tanks, puffs of steam. I must be headed in the wrong direction.

But I have no idea how many floors this ship has, and I have no idea if I can keep moving down.

I'm still being shot at, and I'm staying only just a step ahead. I'm slipping around tight bends and pulling myself against the wall, turning into dark corners and hoping they won't see me.

Where is Kenji? I keep asking myself. *Where is he?*

I need to be on the other side of this ship. I don't want boiler rooms and water tanks. This can't be right. Everything is different about this side of the ship. Even the doors look different. They're made of steel, not wood.

I kick open a few, just to be sure.

A radio control room, abandoned.

A meeting room, abandoned.

No. I want real rooms. Big offices and living quarters. Anderson wouldn't be here. He wouldn't be found by the gas pipes and the whirring engines.

I tiptoe out of my newest hiding spot, peek my head out.

Shouts. Cries.

More gunshots.

I pull back. Take a deep breath. Harness all my energy, all at once, and decide I have no choice but to test Alia's theory.

I jump out and charge down the hall.

Running, racing like I never have before. Bullets are flying past my head and pelting my body, hitting my face, my back, my arms, and I force myself to keep running, force myself to keep breathing, not feeling pain, not feeling terror, but holding on to my energy like a lifeline and not letting anything stop me. I'm trampling over soldiers, knocking them out with my elbows, not hesitating long enough to do more than shove them out of my way.

Three of them come flying at me, trying to tackle me to the ground, and I shove them all back. One runs forward again and I punch him directly in the face, feeling his nose break against my metal knuckles. Another tries to grab my arm from behind and I catch his hand, breaking his fingers in my grip only to catch his forearm, pull him close, and shove him through a wall. I spin around to face the rest of them and they're all staring at me, panic and terror mixing in their eyes.

"Fight me," I say to them, blood and urgency and a crazy kind of adrenaline rushing through me. "I dare you."

Five of them lift their guns in my direction, point them at my face.

Shoot.

Over and over and over again, unloading round after round. My instinct is to protect myself from the bullets, but I focus instead on the men, on their bodies and their angry, twisted faces. I have to close my eyes for a second, because I can't see through the barrage of metal being crushed against my body. And when I'm ready, I bring my fist close to my chest, feeling the power rise up inside of me, and I throw it forward, all at once, knocking seventy-five soldiers down like they're made of matchsticks.

I take a moment to breathe.

My chest is heaving, my heart racing, and I look around, feeling the stillness within the madness, blinking hard against the flashing red lights of the alarm, and find that the soldiers do not stir. They're still alive, I can tell, but they're unconscious. And I allow myself one instant to look down.

I'm surrounded.

Bullets. Hundreds of bullets. A puddle of bullets. All around my feet. Dropping off my suit.

My face.

I taste something cold and hard in my mouth and spit it into my hand. It looks like a broken, mangled piece of metal. Like it was too flimsy to stand against me.

Smart little bullet, I think.

And then I run.

SEVENTY

The halls are still now. The footsteps, fewer.

I've already tossed two hundred soldiers into the ocean.

Knocked down about a hundred more.

I have no idea how many more soldiers Anderson has left guarding this ship. But I'm going to find out.

I'm breathing hard as I make my way through this maze. It's a sad truth that while I've learned to fight and I've learned to project, I still have no idea how to run.

For someone with so much power, I'm terribly out of shape.

I kick down the first door I see.

Another.

Then another.

I'm going to rip apart every inch of this ship until I find Anderson. I will tear it down with my own two hands if I need to. Because he has Sonya and Sara. And he might have Kenji.

And first, I need to make them safe.

And second, I need him dead.

Another door splinters open.

I kick the next one down with my foot.

They're all empty.

I see a set of swinging double doors at the end of the hall and I shove through them, hoping for something, anything, any sign of life.

It's a kitchen.

Knives and stoves and food and tables. Rows and rows and rows of canned goods. I make a mental note to come back for this. It seems a shame to let all this food go to waste.

I bolt back out the doors.

And jump. Hard. Stomping through the deck and hoping there's another floor to this ship.

Hoping.

I land badly on the toes of my feet, slightly off-balance and toppling backward. I catch myself just in time.

Look around.

This, I think. This is right. This is totally different.

The halls are huge down here; windows to the outside cut into the walls. The floor is made of wood again, long, thin panels that are brightly glossed and polished. It looks nice down here. Fancy. Clean. The sirens feel muted on this level, like a distant threat that means little anymore, and I realize I must be close.

Footsteps, rushing toward me.

I spin around.

There's a soldier charging in my direction, and this time, I don't hide. I run toward him, tucking my head in as I do, and my right shoulder slams into his chest so hard he goes flying across the hall.

Someone tries to shoot me from behind.

I spin around and walk right up to him, swatting the bullets from my face like they might be flies. And then I grab his shoulders, pull him close, and knee him in the groin. He doubles over, gasping and groaning and curling into himself on the floor. I bend down, rip the gun out of his hand, and clutch a fistful of his shirt. Pick him up with one hand. Slam him into the wall. Press the gun to his forehead.

I'm tired of waiting.

"Where is he?" I demand.

He won't answer me.

"*Where?*" I shout.

"I d-don't know," he finally says, his voice shaking, his body twitching, trembling in my grip.

And for some reason, I believe him. I try to read his eyes for something, and get nothing but terror. I drop him to the floor. Crush his gun in my hand. Toss it into his lap.

I kick open another door.

I'm getting so frustrated, so angry now, and so blindly terrified for Kenji's well-being that I'm shaking with rage. I don't even know who to look for first.

Sonya.

Sara.

Kenji.

Anderson.

I stand in front of another door, defeated. The soldiers have stopped coming. The sirens are still blaring, but from a distance now. And suddenly I'm wondering if this was all just a waste of time. If maybe Anderson isn't even on this ship. If maybe we're not even on the *right* ship.

And for some reason, I don't kick down the door this time.

For some reason, I decide to try the handle first.

It's unlocked.

SEVENTY-ONE

There's a huge bed in here with a large window and a beautiful view of the ocean. It's lovely, actually, how wide and expansive everything is. Lovelier still are its occupants.

Sonya and Sara are staring at me.

They're perfect. Alive.

Just as beautiful as they've ever been.

I rush over to them, so relieved I nearly burst into tears.

"Are you okay?" I ask, gasping, unable to control myself. "Are you all right?"

They throw themselves into my arms, looking like they've been through hell and back, tortured from the inside, and all I want to do is carry them out of this ship and take them home.

But as soon as the initial hyperventilations are out of the way, Sonya says something that stops my heart.

"Kenji was looking for you," she says. "He was just here, not too long ago, and he asked us if we'd seen you—"

"He said you got split up," Sara says.

"And that he didn't know what happened to you," Sonya says.

"We were so worried you were dead," they say together.

"No," I tell them, feeling crazy now. "No, no, I'm not

dead. But I have to go. Stay here," I'm saying to them. "Don't move. Don't go anywhere. I'll be right back, I promise," I say. "I just have to go find Kenji—I have to find Anderson—"

"He's two doors over," Sara says, eyes wide.

"The one all the way at the end of the hall," Sonya says.

"It's the one with the blue door," they tell me.

"Wait!" Sonya stops me as I turn to go.

"Be careful," Sara says. "We've heard some things—"

"About a weapon he's brought with him," Sonya says.

"What kind of weapon?" I ask, heart slowing.

"We don't know," they say together.

"But it made him very happy," Sara whispers.

"Yes, very happy," Sonya adds.

I clench my fists.

"Thank you," I say to them. "Thank you—I'll see you soon," I'm saying. "Very soon—" And I'm backing out, backing away, rushing down the hall and I hear them shouting for me to be safe, and good luck, just behind me.

But I don't need luck anymore. I need these two fists and this spine of steel. I waste no time at all getting to the blue room. I'm not afraid anymore.

I don't hesitate. I won't hesitate. Never again.

I kick it down.

"JULIETTE—NO—"

SEVENTY-TWO

Kenji's voice hits me like a fist to the throat.

I don't even have time to blink before I'm thrown against the wall.

My back, I think. Something is wrong with my back. The pain is so excruciating that I can't help but wonder if it's broken. I'm dizzy and I feel slow; my head is spinning and there's a strange ringing in my ears.

I clamber to my feet.

I'm hit, again, so hard. And I don't even know where the pain is coming from. I can't blink fast enough, can't steady my head long enough to shake the confusion.

Everything is tilting sideways.

I'm trying so hard to shake it off.

I'm stronger than this. Better than this. I'm supposed to be indestructible.

Up, again.

Slowly.

Something hits me so hard I fly across the room, slamming into the wall. I slide down to the floor. I'm bent over now, holding my hands to my head, trying to blink, trying to understand what's happening.

I don't understand what could possibly be hitting me.

This hard.

Nothing should be able to hit me this hard. Not over and over again.

It feels like someone is calling my name, but I can't seem to hear it. Everything is so muffled, so slippery and off-balance, like it's there, just out of reach, and I can't seem to find it. Feel it.

I need a new plan.

I don't stand up again. I stay on my knees, crawling forward, and this time, when the hit comes, I try to beat it back. I'm trying so hard to push my energy forward, but all the hits to my head have made me unsteady. I'm clinging to my energy with a manic desperation, and though I don't manage to move forward, I'm also not thrown back.

I try to lift my head.

Slowly.

There's nothing in front of me. No machine. No strange element that might be able to create these powerful impacts. I blink hard against the ringing in my ears, trying frantically to clear my vision.

Something hits me again.

The intensity threatens to beat me back but I dig my fingers into the ground until they go through the wood and I'm clinging to the floor.

I would scream, if I could. If I had any energy left.

I lift my head again. Try again to see.

And this time, two figures come into focus.

One is Anderson.

The other is someone I don't recognize.

He's a stocky blond with closely cropped hair and flinty eyes. He looks vaguely familiar to me. And he's standing beside Anderson with a cocky smile on his face, his hands held out in front of him.

He claps.

Just once.

I'm ripped from the floor and thrown back against the wall.

Sound waves.

These are *pressure waves,* I realize.

Anderson has found himself a toy.

I shake my head and try to clear it again, but the hits are coming faster now. Harder. More intense. I have to close my eyes against the pressure of the hits and try to crawl, desperately, breaking through the floorboards to get a grip on something.

Another hit.

Hard to the head.

It's like he's causing an explosion every time his hands clap together, and what's killing me isn't the explosion. It isn't direct impact. It's the pressure released from a bomb.

Over and over and over again.

I know the only reason I'm able to survive this is because I'm too strong.

But *Kenji,* I think.

Kenji must be somewhere in this room. He was the one who called my name, who tried to warn me. He must be here, somewhere, and if I can hardly survive this right now, I don't know how he could be doing any better.

He must be doing worse.

Much worse.

That fear is enough for me. I'm fortified with a new kind of strength, a desperate, animal intensity that overpowers me and forces me upright. I manage to stand in the face of each impact, each blow as it rattles my head and rings in my ears.

And I walk.

One step at a time, I walk.

I hear a gunshot. Three. Five more. And realize they're all aimed in my direction. Bullets breaking off my body.

The blond is moving. Backing up. Trying to get away from me. He's increasing the frequency of his hits, hoping to throw me off course, but I've come too far to lose this fight. I'm not even thinking now, barely even lucid, focused solely on reaching him and silencing him forever. I have no idea if he's managed to kill Kenji yet. I have no idea if I'm about to die. I have no idea how much longer I can withstand this.

But I have to try.

One more step, I tell myself.

Move your leg. Now your foot. Bend at the knee.

You're almost there, I tell myself.

Think of Kenji. Think of James. Think of the promises you made to that ten-year-old boy, I tell myself. Bring Kenji home. Bring yourself home.

There he is. Right in front of you.

I reach forward as if through a cloud, and clench my fist around his neck.

Squeeze.

Squeeze until the sound waves stop.

I hear something crack.

The blond falls to the floor.

And I collapse.

SEVENTY-THREE

Anderson is standing over me now, pointing a gun at my face.

He shoots.

Again.

Once more.

I close my eyes and pull deep, deep within myself for my last dregs of strength, because somehow, some instinct inside of my body is still screaming at me to stay alive. I remember Sonya and Sara telling me once that our energies could be depleted. That we could overexert ourselves. That they were trying to make medicines to help with that sort of thing.

I wish I had that kind of medicine right now.

I blink up at Anderson, his form blurring at the edges. He's standing just behind my head, the toes of his shiny boots touching the top of my skull. I can't hear much but the echoes in my bones, can't see anything other than the bullets raining down around me. He's still shooting. Still unloading his gun into my body, waiting for the moment when he knows I won't be able to hold on any longer.

I'm dying, I think. I must be. I thought I knew what it

felt like to die, but I must've been wrong. Because this is a whole different kind of dying. A whole different kind of pain.

But I suppose, if I have to die, I may as well do one more thing before I go.

I reach up. Grab Anderson's ankles. Clench my fists.

And crush his bones in my hands.

His screams pierce the haze of my mind, long enough to bring the world back into focus. I'm blinking fast, looking around and able to see clearly for the first time. Kenji is slumped in the corner. Blond boy is on the floor.

Anderson has been disconnected from his feet.

My thoughts are sharper all of a sudden, like I'm in control again. I don't know if this is what hope does to a person, if it really has the power to bring someone back to life, but seeing Anderson writhing on the floor does something to me. It makes me think I still have a chance.

He's screaming so much, scrambling back and dragging himself across the floor with his arms. He's dropped his gun, clearly too pained and too petrified to reach for it any longer, and I can see the agony in his eyes. The weakness. The terror. He's only now understanding the horror of what's about to happen to him. How it had to happen to him. That he would be brought to nothing by a silly little girl who was too much of a coward, he said, to defend herself.

And it's then that I realize he's trying to say something

to me. He's trying to talk. Maybe he's pleading. Maybe he's crying. Maybe he's begging for mercy. But I'm not listening anymore.

I have absolutely nothing to say.

I reach back, pull the gun out of my holster.

And shoot him in the forehead.

SEVENTY-FOUR

Twice.

Once for Adam.

Once for Warner.

SEVENTY-FIVE

I tuck the gun back into its holster. Walk over to Kenji's limp, still-breathing form, and throw him over my shoulder.

I kick down the door.

Walk directly back down the hall.

Kick my way through the entry to Sonya and Sara's room, and drop Kenji on the bed.

"Fix him," I say, hardly breathing now. "Please fix him."

I drop to my knees.

Sonya and Sara are on in an instant. They don't speak. They don't cry. They don't scream. They don't fall apart. They immediately get to work and I don't think I have ever loved them more than I do in this moment. They lay him out flat on the bed, Sara standing on one side of him, Sonya on the other, and they hold their hands to his head, first. Then his heart.

Then they alternate, taking turns forcing life back into different parts of his body until Kenji is stirring, his eyes flickering but not opening, his head whipping back and forth.

I'm beginning to worry, but I'm too afraid, and too tired to move, not even an inch.

Finally, finally, they step back.

Kenji's eyes still aren't open.

"Did it work?" I ask, terrified to hear the answer.

Sonya and Sara nod. "He's asleep," they say.

"Will he get better? Fully?" I ask, desperate now.

"We hope," Sonya says.

"But he'll be asleep for a few days," Sara says.

"The damage was very deep," they say together. "What happened?"

"Pressure waves," I tell them, my words a whisper. "He shouldn't have been able to survive at all."

Sonya and Sara are staring at me, still waiting.

I force myself to my feet. "Anderson is dead."

"You killed him," they whisper. It's not a question.

I nod.

They're staring at me, slack-jawed and stunned.

"Let's go," I say. "This war is over. We have to tell the others."

"But how will we get out?" Sara asks.

"There are soldiers everywhere," Sonya says.

"Not anymore," I tell them, too tired to explain, but so grateful for their help. For their existence. For the fact that they're still alive. I offer them a small smile before walking over to the bed, and haul Kenji's body up and over my shoulders. His chest is curved over my back, one of his arms thrown over my left shoulder, the other hanging in front of me. My right arm is wrapped around both his legs.

I hoist him higher up on my shoulders.

"Ready?" I say, looking at the two of them.

They nod.

I lead them out the door and down the halls, forgetting for a moment that I have no idea how to actually exit this ship. But the halls are lifeless. Everyone is either injured, unconscious, or gone. We sidestep fallen bodies, shift arms and legs out of the way. We're all that's left.

Me, carrying Kenji.

Sonya and Sara close behind.

I finally find a ladder. Climb up. Sonya and Sara hold Kenji's weight between them and I reach down to haul him up. We have to do this three more times, until we're finally on the top deck, where I toss him up over my shoulders for the final time.

And then we walk, silently, across the abandoned ship, down the pier, and back onto dry land. This time, I don't care about stealing tanks. I don't care about being seen. I don't care about anything but finding my friends. And ending this war.

There's an army tank abandoned on the side of the road. I test the door.

Unlocked.

The girls clamber in and they help me haul Kenji onto their laps. I close the door shut behind them. Climb into the driver's side. I press my thumb to the scanner to start the engine; so grateful Warner had us programmed to gain access to the system.

It's only then that I remember I still have no idea how to drive.

It's probably a good thing I'm driving a tank.

I don't pay attention to stop signs or streets. I drive the tank right off the road and straight back into the heart of the sector, in the general direction I know we came from. I'm too heavy on the gas, and too heavy on the brakes, but my mind is in a place where nothing else matters anymore.

I had a goal. Step one has been accomplished.

And now I will see it through to the end.

I drop Sonya and Sara off at the barracks and help them carry Kenji out. Here, they'll be safe. Here, they can rest. But it's not my turn to stop yet.

I head directly up and through the military base, up the elevator to where I remember we got off for the assembly. I slam through door after door, heading straight outside and into the courtyard, where I climb until I reach the top. One hundred feet in the air.

Where it all began.

There's a technician stand here, a maintenance system for the speakers that run throughout the sector. I remember this. I remember all of this now, even though my brain is numb and my hands are still shaking, and blood that does not belong to me is dripping down my face and onto my neck.

But this was the plan.

I have to finish the plan.

I punch the pass code into the keypad and wait to hear the click. The technician box snaps open. I scan the different fuses and buttons, and flip the switch that reads ALL

SPEAKERS, and take a deep breath. Hit the intercom key.

"Attention, Sector 45," I say, the words rough and loud and mottled in my ear. "The supreme commander of The Reestablishment is dead. The capital has surrendered. The war is over." I'm shaking so hard now, my finger slipping on the button as I try to hold it down. "I repeat, the supreme commander of The Reestablishment is dead. The capital has surrendered. The war is over."

Finish it, I tell myself.

Finish it now.

"I am Juliette Ferrars, and I will lead this nation. I challenge anyone who would stand against me."

SEVENTY-SIX

I take a step forward and my legs tremble, threaten to bend and break beneath me, but I push myself to keep moving. I push myself to get through the door, to get down the elevator, and to get out, onto the battlefield.

It doesn't take long to get there.

There are hundreds of bodies in huddled, bloody masses on the ground, but there are hundreds more still standing; more alive than I could've hoped for. The news has spread more quickly than I thought it would. It's almost as if they've known for a little while now that the battle was over. The surviving soldiers from Anderson's ship are standing alongside our own, some still soaking wet, frozen to the bone in this icy weather. They must've found their way ashore and shared the news of our assault, of Anderson's imminent demise. Everyone is looking around, staring at each other in shock, staring at their own hands or up into the sky. Others still are checking the mass of bodies for friends and family members, relief and fear apparent on their faces. Their worn bodies do not want to go on like this.

The doors to the barracks have burst open and the remaining civilians flood the grounds, running out to reunite with loved ones, and for a moment the scene is both so terribly bleak, and so terribly beautiful, that I don't know whether to cry out in pain or joy.

I don't cry at all.

I walk forward, forcing my limbs to move, begging my bones to stay steady, to carry me through the end of this day, and into the rest of my life.

I want to see my friends. I need to know they're okay. I need visual confirmation that they're okay.

But as soon as I walk into the crowd, the soldiers of Sector 45 lose control.

The bloodied and beaten on our battlefield are shouting and cheering despite the stain of death they stand in, saluting me as I pass. And as I look around I realize that they are *my* soldiers now. They trusted me, fought with me and alongside me, and now I will trust them. I will fight for them. This is the first of many battles to come. There will be many more days like this.

I'm covered in blood, my suit ripped and riddled with splintered wood and broken bits of metal. My hands are trembling so hard I don't even recognize them anymore.

And yet I feel so calm.

So unbelievably calm.

Like the depth of what just happened hasn't managed to hit me yet.

It's impossible not to brush against outstretched hands and arms as I cross the battlefield, and it's strange to me, somehow, strange that I don't flinch, strange that I don't hide my hands, strange that I'm not worried I'll injure them.

They can touch me if they like, and maybe it'll hurt, but my skin won't kill anyone anymore.

Because I'll never let it get that far.

Because I now know how to control it.

SEVENTY-SEVEN

The compounds are such bleak, barren places, I think, as I pass through them. These should be the first to go. Our homes should be rebuilt. Restored.

We need to start again.

I climb up the side of one of the little compound homes. Climb its second story, too. I reach up, clinging to the roof, and pull myself over. I kick the solar panels off, onto the ground, and plant myself on top, right in the middle, as I look out over the crowd.

Searching for familiar faces.

Hoping they'll see me and come forward.

Hoping.

I stand on the roof of this home for what feels like days, months, years, and I see nothing but faces of soldiers and their families. None of my friends.

I feel myself sway, dizziness threatening to overtake me, my pulse racing fast and hard. I'm ready to give up. I've stood here long enough for people to point, for my face to be recognized, for word to spread that I'm standing here, waiting for something. Someone. Anyone.

I'm just about to dive back into the crowd to search for their fallen bodies when hope seizes my heart.

One by one, they emerge, from all corners of the field,

from deep inside the barracks, from across the compounds. Bloodied and bruised. Adam, Alia, Castle, Ian, Lily, Brendan, and Winston each make their way toward me only to turn and wait for the others to arrive. Winston is sobbing.

Sonya and Sara are dragging Kenji out of the barracks, small steps hauling him forward. I see that his eyes have opened now, just a little. Stubborn, stubborn Kenji. Of course he's awake when he should be asleep.

James comes running toward them.

He crashes into Adam, clinging to his legs, and Adam hauls his little brother up, into his arms, smiling like I've never seen him smile before. Castle nods at me, beaming. Lily blows me a kiss. Ian makes some strange finger-gun motion and Brendan waves. Alia has never looked more jubilant.

And I'm looking out over them, my smile steady, held there by nothing but sheer force of will. I'm still staring, waiting for my last friend to show up. Waiting for him to find us.

But he isn't here.

I'm scanning the thousands of people scattered around this icy, icy ground and I don't see him, not anywhere, and the terror of this moment kicks me in the gut until I'm out of breath and out of hope, blinking fast and trying to hold myself together.

The metal roof under my feet is shaking.

I turn toward the sound, heart pounding, and see a hand reach over the top.

SEVENTY-EIGHT

He pulls himself up onto the roof and walks over to me, so steadily. Calm, like there's nothing in the world we'd planned to do today but to stand here, together, looking out over a field of dead bodies and happy children.

"Aaron," I whisper.

He pulls me into his arms.

And I fall.

Every bone, every muscle, every nerve in my body comes undone at his touch and I cling to him, holding on for dear life.

"You know," he whispers, his lips at my ear, "the whole world will be coming for us now."

I lean back. Look into his eyes.

"I can't wait to watch them try."

~~Her touch is lethal.~~
Her touch is power.

DISCOVER THE *NEW YORK TIMES* BESTSELLING
SHATTER ME: SERIES ONE.

STORYTIDE
[I]mprint of HarperCollins*Publishers*

epicreads.com

NEW YORK TIMES BESTSELLING AUTHOR OF THE SHATTER ME SERIES
TAHEREH MAFI
THIS WOVEN KINGDOM

THESE INFINITE THREADS
#1 INTERNATIONAL BESTSELLING AUTHOR OF THE SHATTER ME SERIES
TAHEREH MAFI

THE HEART-WRENCHING THIRD BOOK IN THE WOVEN KINGDOM SERIES
ALL THIS TWISTED GLORY
#1 INTERNATIONAL BESTSELLING AUTHOR OF THE SHATTER ME SERIES
TAHEREH MAFI

THE MESMERIZING FOURTH BOOK IN THE WOVEN KINGDOM SERIES
EVERY SPIRAL OF FATE
TAHEREH MAFI